A Chr
u
a
Cran___..y
Kiss
at the Cosy Kettle

BOOKS BY LIZ EELES

THE COSY KETTLE SERIES
New Starts and Cherry Tarts at the Cosy Kettle
A Summer Escape and Strawberry Cake at the Cosy Kettle

THE SALT BAY SERIES
Annie's Holiday by the Sea
Annie's Christmas by the Sea
Annie's Summer by the Sea

A Christmas Wish and a Cranberry Kiss at the Cosy Kettle

LIZ EELES

Bookouture

Published by Bookouture in 2019

An imprint of Storyfire Ltd.
Carmelite House
50 Victoria Embankment
London EC4Y 0DZ

www.bookouture.com

ISBN: 978-1-78681-673-3
eBook ISBN: 978-1-78681-672-6

For Freddie, with love

Chapter One

I stand back, with my hands on my hips, and gaze around me. The Cosy Kettle is looking fabulously festive, if a tad over-blinged. The plastic angel with hair like golden candyfloss is maybe a bit OTT with her flashing neon halo.

Millicent obviously thinks so. She's staring at the angel with her mouth open as its halo blinks on and off, at the top of the tree. She folds her arms across her ample bosom and frowns.

'Where on earth did that monstrosity come from, Becca? Oh, don't tell me. Stanley!'

I nod. 'He brought it along specially because it was a favourite of his wife's. He said Christmas wasn't Christmas until Edna came out of her box.'

'Edna?'

'That's what they called the angel,' I say, hoping that Millicent isn't about to cause a non-festive fuss. 'She looks like Stanley's Auntie Edna, apparently.'

'Only if she wafted round in a cheap nightie, never brushed her hair and flashed at all and sundry.'

Is Millicent making a joke? I giggle but stop when she glares at me, although I've learned since I started working at The Cosy Kettle that Millicent's bark is worse than her bite. She lives in an amazing house in the posh village next to Honeyford and puts on airs and graces, but I reckon she's quite lonely really. Why else would she spend so much of her time in here, a small café in the back of a little Cotswolds bookshop?

'What about everything else?' I ask, tilting my head at the decorations I came in early to put up. Shining strands of red and silver tinsel are looped across the walls, sparkly gold stars are hanging from the ceiling, and I've draped pink fairy lights along the shelves. A tall, slightly listing fir tree in the corner is dripping with red baubles and glass snowmen, and a plastic reindeer with a light-up nose is standing on the counter, near the till.

Millicent sniffs. 'It's rather more…' – she hesitates – '*showy* than I'd choose. Live by the old adage "less is more", and you can't go wrong, in my book. Personally, I can't bear an overly colourful Christmas.'

She'd hate my parents' house, then. Dad decks the outside of the building with enough lights to drain the National Grid, and inside, it's a riot of rainbow colours and tatty papier-mâché decorations that Jasmine and I made at school.

Thinking of Mum and Dad makes me feel guilty because I haven't visited them for a while. Mum rang yesterday to let me know that Jasmine had called in, and there was a hint of reproach in her voice along with the unspoken question: *How come you and Jasmine are so different?*

Jasmine and I are sisters – twins, actually, but no one would guess it. Jasmine, older than me by a few minutes, is the family's golden girl. She's poised and confident and only has hissy fits in private – usually in front of me. Whereas I'm a bit of a disaster: shy, scared of just about everything, and prone to occasional panic attacks in public. It doesn't seem fair, really, that my sister sucked out all my good genes in the womb, like a tiny foetal vampire, and claimed them for herself.

I glance at my reflection in the glistening chrome coffee machine and sigh. We even look different. Jasmine's long blonde hair tumbles around her perfect heart-shaped face. She's all ephemeral, glowing beauty, and drop-dead gorgeous.

My oval face is pale against my hair which is dyed sapphire blue and cut much shorter. My features are regular and my eyes – arguably my best feature – are green and fringed with dark lashes. I'm more *not bad, does the best she can* attractive. Zac, my housemate, did tell me I was pretty, a while back, but I don't think he had his glasses on at the time.

But at least I'm happy here. I look around the glittering café and smile. Serving coffee and cake might not be everyone's idea of a high-flying career but I get pleasure from doing a good job. And I feel safe in this little back room that's been transformed into a welcoming space where people can meet and relax.

I've been happier generally since I moved – or rather, fled – from Birmingham to Honeyford ten months ago. The country town's butter-yellow buildings and the rolling Cotswold Hills beyond are cheerful. They lift my mood and make life seem less likely to end in disaster.

Yes, things have definitely improved since I helped to set up the café and ended up working here full-time when it got busy. And I've got used to the regular customers, who are starting to accept me – people like Millicent and Stanley, who belong to the afternoon book club that's meeting here this afternoon.

Millicent has wandered back to the club members who are huddled together in a corner of the café. Behind them on the wall is a large poster of a fir tree that's so thickly covered in sparkling snow, it looks like it's coated in tiny diamonds. I expect she'll have a go at me about that later on, too.

But she looks content for the moment, sitting with her book club friends, who have become a close-knit gang of five, in spite of all being very different.

As well as Millicent and Stanley, there's knackered new mum, Mary, Stanley's friend Dick – who looks more like Father Christmas every day with his long white beard – and Phyllis.

When I glance at Phyllis, she catches my eye and gives me a wave from her wheelchair. She's become a surrogate gran to me since we met near the river, back in the spring. I was worried her chair was about to roll into the water. Of course; it was a disaster waiting to happen. But she assured me that her chair's brakes were on and she wasn't about to drown.

That would have been that, but sadness was coming off her in such waves, I couldn't just walk away. So we talked and she told me about her husband who'd died and her daughter and grandchildren who'd moved to Australia. And we kept in touch. There's a soothing matter-of-factness about Phyllis that cuts through my brain's overactive alarm system and makes me feel calmer.

A clipped voice suddenly cuts into my thoughts. 'I said I'd like a double espresso, if it's not too much trouble.' When I turn around, there's a short balding man in a suit behind me. He's drumming his stubby fingers on the café counter. 'And could you turn the music down? I might need to take an important work call and it's far too loud.'

'No problem,' I say, scooting behind the counter to turn down the volume on Wham!'s 'Last Christmas' – though it wasn't very loud to begin with. 'Can I get you something to eat as well?'

The man glances at the magnificent cake display laid out in front of him and sniffs, as though there's a bad smell. 'I don't think so. And can you hurry up with the coffee because I have an appointment to keep. I haven't got all day.'

The man's just being an arse and I shouldn't let him get to me. But my hands start shaking as I tamp down the ground coffee beans and choose one of our patterned china cups. Thick treacly liquid starts dribbling from the spout of the coffee machine as the man stares at me.

'There you go,' I say, placing his drink on the counter in front of him. 'I hope you enjoy it.'

'Hmm.' He inspects the espresso, wrinkling his nose. 'How much is that?'

'One pound eighty please.'

When the man hands over a crisp ten-pound note, I ring up the purchase at the till and count out his change. He squints at the money in his hand and frowns.

'You've short-changed me. I gave you twenty pounds.'

'You gave me a ten-pound note.'

'No, I definitely gave you twenty which means that I need more change. I'm hardly going to pay eleven pounds and eighty pence for this, am I?' He nods at his coffee, which is sending wisps of steam towards the tinselly ceiling.

'I'm sure you gave me ten pounds.' I don't sound that sure because my voice has gone all wobbly.

'I know what I gave you and it was a twenty-pound note,' retorts the man, raising his voice.

Members of the book club glance up and stare at us as the man's mobile phone starts ringing. Its shrill tone vibrates across the café.

He pulls the phone from the front pocket of his suit jacket and clicks onto the call. 'Hello, Martin. Would you mind if I called you back in two minutes? Yes, absolutely, I won't be long but I'm being ripped off in a café and need to sort things out.'

Being ripped off? My cheeks start to burn as he ends the call and holds out his hand, palm up, waiting for more change.

'I really don't have time for this,' he says, his voice getting even louder. 'I'm a busy man with places to be so just give me the correct change and we can both get on with our lives.'

I hesitate as Wham! fades to nothing and blood starts pounding in my ears. I'm absolutely certain that the man gave me a ten-pound note. If it was my money, I'd give him change for a twenty, just to make him go away – but it's not. The money belongs to Flora, who owns The Cosy Kettle, and she's trusting me to keep a careful eye on it.

'Is everything all right over here, Becca?'

Phyllis has zoomed up so fast in her wheelchair, the man had to take a swift step backwards to avoid being run over.

'Yes, thank you, Phyllis,' I say, swallowing hard as Stanley wanders over behind her.

'Are you having a bit of a prob, hun?' he asks me, adjusting his low-slung jeans which reveal a glimpse of white underpants. He's wearing a Killers T-shirt and a denim jacket and must have been freezing, walking through Honeyford. But, as he informed me earlier, 'Fashion comes before comfort. That's what I've discovered.'

He's discovered a lot of things since he hit eighty earlier this year, including a death wish according to his granddaughter, Callie. His quest to be his 'true self' before he kicks the bucket is turning poor Callie prematurely grey.

But I think Stanley is brilliant. The way he mangles youth slang is a bit like nails down a blackboard sometimes, and his scrawny buttocks in tight jeans are disconcerting. But I admire his courage and the fact he doesn't care what anyone thinks of him. It's the type of kick-ass attitude to which I can only aspire.

'This girl has short-changed me, though I don't see why that's any of your business,' huffs the man, his fleshy face turning puce. Anger is bristling off him and I soak up his agitation like a sponge. My heart is hammering and my throat has started to tighten, even before I spot Millicent striding over to join us.

She looks the man up and down and barks: '*This girl* is called Becca and we're her friends so it's definitely our business.'

'I'm sure *Becca* can look after herself.'

Before I can agree and try to cool things down, Stanley leaps in. 'That's where you're very wrong, mate. Becca's a bright and caring young woman, but she needs looking after. She's fragile.'

The man pulls back his shoulders. 'Then she really shouldn't be in charge of this tin-pot café and short-changing customers.'

'Tin-pot café? How dare you!' snorts Phyllis, as Mary and Dick join the throng.

Everyone starts arguing with the man while I stand there, like a right lemon, wondering how to defuse the situation. As the arguing continues, the angel's halo blinks on the tree and the man's coffee cools.

'Please stop arguing, everyone, and I'll sort this out,' I say, but no one's listening. The Christmas soundtrack that's been adding festive cheer to the café all morning is completely drowned out by the sound of raised angry voices.

Suddenly, Flora's loud voice cuts across the mayhem. 'What the hell is going on? It sounds like a zoo in here.' She marches across the café and stands with her hands on her hips in front of the throng which has gone quiet. 'Well, Becca?'

I swallow as all eyes turn to me. 'This gentleman…'

'Not much of a gentleman,' mutters Phyllis.

I clear my throat and try again. 'This gentleman ordered a coffee and says that I haven't given him enough change.'

'So why is everyone else getting involved?' asks Flora, brushing dark hair from her face. She looks totally bemused.

'Becca can't look out for herself so we were looking out for her,' declares Stanley, blinking behind his John Lennon specs. 'It's like The Three Musketeers in The Cosy Kettle. One for all and' – he does a swift head count – 'six for one. We never leave one of our own behind. Not in the face of enemy fire.'

'Too much,' murmurs Dick, behind him, shaking his head. 'Always too much.'

Flora places a steadying hand on Stanley's shoulder. 'Coming to Becca's aid is admirable but I'm sure it's not necessary. So perhaps you could all go back to your table and talk about books and I'll sort this out.'

With a fair bit of grumbling, the club members head back to their abandoned coffees and Flora addresses the disgruntled customer, who's still proffering his hand for more change.

'I do apologise for the fuss. Perhaps you could tell me what the problem is?'

'And you are?' asks the man, coldly.

'I'm Flora Morgan and I own this café and Honeyford Bookshop.'

'I see. Then you should know that your employee… Becca, is it? She's only given me change for a ten-pound note when I gave her twenty. And then those people over there joined in and were most abusive. I must say I've never had treatment like this before in a retail establishment.'

'What exactly did you order?'

'A double espresso – which has gone stone cold.' When he pushes the cup across the counter, thick dark coffee slops over the rim and into the saucer.

Flora goes to the till, opens it and pulls out a crisp ten-pound note which she hands to the man.

'Here's your money, sir, and I'm very sorry about what's happened. Becca will make you another double espresso on the house and perhaps you'd like a mince pie or a slice of Christmas cake to go with it? Please take your pick.'

She gestures at the fabulous array of festive confectionery on display – snowmen made of gingerbread, sticky cinnamon and cranberry buns, tiny Christmas puddings in silver fluted cases, and thick chunks of yule log covered in chocolate frosting.

But the man doesn't even look. 'Don't bother. I don't intend to stay in here a moment longer than necessary. And I won't be back.' He strides to the door before stopping and turning round. 'Oh, and perhaps it would be best not to have someone "fragile",' – he puts the last word into ironic air quotes – 'in charge of your café.' With that, he strides out, slamming the door behind him.

As the bang echoes through the café, Flora turns to me with her arms folded and her mouth turned down at the corners. 'What on earth, Becca? You shouldn't have let things get out of hand like that.'

'I'm so s-sorry,' I stutter, feeling awful. 'I'm sure he gave me a ten-pound note, and then everyone piled in when we started discussing it. I realise I should have handled the situation better.'

'Yes, you should have. We can't afford to upset customers.' Flora's face softens. 'But the book club can be rather overwhelming at times.' She sighs and her shoulders drop. 'It's OK, Becca. These things happen. But please don't let anything like that happen again.'

'Of course not. I promise.'

When Flora has disappeared back into the bookshop, I clear away the man's cold coffee and turn up the Christmas soundtrack – though Slade's 'Merry Xmas Everybody' doesn't match my mood.

'You all right, Beccs?' shouts Stanley across the room. 'Did she tear you off a strip? She's a cool dude, that Flora, but she can be a bit in your face at times.'

'I'm fine,' I tell him, collecting up used mugs and plates and sweeping cake crumbs into the bin. But the truth is I'm not fine. I'm gutted that I'm seen as fragile and in need of rescuing – like an abandoned puppy. I'm twenty-five, for goodness' sake, and should be able to stand up for myself.

But even though Stanley's 'fragile' description was harsh – his insistence on *telling it like it is* can be a pain at times – it was the man's follow-up remark that really hit home. Maybe he's right and someone like me doesn't have the personality and the mental resilience needed to run a place like this. Flora believed in me when I didn't believe in myself, but perhaps that was her heart talking rather than her head.

I reach below the counter for my bag and find my purse. I'm convinced that the man did give me a ten-pound note, which means Flora is out of pocket because I messed up and didn't handle things properly. Pulling out a tenner, I place it carefully into the till. I can't really afford it, especially with Christmas presents to buy, but it seems only fair.

Chapter Two

Ten minutes later, I'm too busy to fret about what happened. There's no room for negative feelings when you're making coffee with one hand, serving cake with the other, and advising a small child with a death wish not to clamber up the Christmas tree.

But I start reliving the scene as I'm walking home through Honeyford, and go over what I should have said. By the time I reach the honey-hued arches of the mediaeval market house I've taken charge of the situation. Before walking past the weathered war memorial, I've confidently told the book club to back off. And as I turn off the High Street into Weavers Lane, I've asserted with such conviction that Rude Man is mistaken about his change, he's begging for my forgiveness. There's no messing up, no shouting, and no boss thinking that *her* mistake was in employing me in the first place.

If only we could rewind time and live life with the benefit of hindsight. I'd have done so many things differently. In fact, I'd be a completely different person. I'd certainly have handled the break-up of my relationship with my ex, Charlie, better. He's a big part of the reason I felt I had to run away from Birmingham – though it was during my first months at university there, before I'd ever met Charlie, when things first started to go wrong.

I've always been more 'sensitive' than Jasmine, more likely to worry and be unsettled by life events, and these stirrings of anxiety became a rumble and then a roar when I went to university and moved away from home for the first time.

I managed to keep everything damped down, apart from the occasional panic attack, and, in my third year, started dating postgrad student, Charlie. Heaven knows what handsome, competent Charlie saw in me, though I later realised that he was drawn to women who found life challenging – maybe he liked being the big hero, riding in to rescue them.

But we were happy and, after university, I started working in Birmingham for a large company as a trainee manager. I was fast-tracked for swift promotion and Mum and Dad were so proud of me. But that was when my life started to properly unravel. I became unhappy at work, which was a hotbed of gossip and bitchiness, my panic attacks increased, and then Charlie left me. It turned out I wasn't what he wanted after all – but my friend, Chloë, was.

Everything came to a head one rainy Wednesday, two weeks after Charlie had walked out, when I was hauled over the coals at work for making a minor mistake. Suddenly, my life crumbled, the world went black and I fell into a big hole.

I walked out of my job and spent the next three months hiding under my duvet, until my savings ran out and I ran away from Birmingham and took refuge in Honeyford with my best friend, Zac. Gradually, since then, my life has improved, but I've never completely shaken off the anxiety that dogs me – or my reputation within my family for being emotionally unstable. They're not unkind people. They just don't properly understand.

I sigh, my breath hanging white in the frosty air, and quicken my pace past pale stone cottages whose windows are glowing with amber lamplight.

At least I now get to go home to Zac. The small cottage we share is at the end of the lane and the lights are on so he's already home. It's a welcoming sight after the day I've had.

When I bundle through the front door, he looks up from the sofa as I drop my bag with a clatter onto the flagstones.

'Hi, Beccs. Shut the door quickly 'cos the central heating's on the blink again and I've only just got the fire going. Did you have a good day?'

'Not really. It's been a bit pants, to be honest.' I slip off my coat and head for the flames that are flickering in the grate. Rubbish central heating aside, I love our rented cottage – the small rooms with their thick Cotswold stone walls, the pitted brown beams across the ceilings and the soot-blackened fireplaces. I stretch my hands towards the glowing orange flames. 'How was your day?'

'Better than yours, by the sound of it. My meeting went well and Paul hinted that I might be up for promotion if my project doesn't go tits up.'

'That's brilliant, Zac. You deserve it.'

He really does. Zac works hard as a designer for a growing engineering company on the outskirts of Cheltenham. He's confident and resourceful and just the kind of level-headed, resilient employee that every business needs.

I stand in silence for a moment and watch Zac tapping on his laptop. A question is bubbling up inside me and I suddenly blurt it out: 'Can I ask you something? Do you think I'm fragile?'

Zac closes the lid of his computer and draws his legs up under him on the sofa. He knows this isn't likely to be a two-minute conversation.

'What makes you ask that?' He pushes his fingers through his brown hair, which is flopping about all over the place. He's been nicking my expensive conditioner again.

'Stanley described me as fragile this afternoon and it struck a nerve, I suppose. It made me feel rather inadequate as a café manager.'

The corner of Zac's mouth lifts. 'Would that be eccentric Stanley who prides himself on "saying it like it is" and subsequently upsets people all over the place?'

'Yeah, though he doesn't mean to upset anyone. He's just trying to be his best self at all times.'

'A bit like you then.'

'I guess.'

I throw myself down on the sofa beside him and sigh loudly. Zac smiles because he's heard it all before. Every New Year I vow to be a better, brighter version of myself – and every year it goes brilliantly for, ooh, at least a day. I'm confident and gregarious and a real laugh, until it all becomes too much of a strain and the old self-defeating thoughts creep in through the cracks.

Becca, you're hopeless! Of course you're not good enough! You mess everything up!

Honestly, I'd never speak to anyone else like that. But my inner voice is a hard taskmaster, and now there's 'fragile' to add into the toxic mix of self-flagellation.

'What happened today then?' asks lovely, long-suffering Zac, who insists that he likes living with me despite my flaws. We met a few years ago at university, when he was going out with a friend of mine, and hit it off immediately. He was easy to talk to and he made me laugh and I didn't turn into a tongue-tied mess around him because I didn't fancy him. He was far too nerdy in his round metal-rimmed glasses, baggy sweatshirts and scruffy jeans.

Actually, he looks different today.

'Are they new glasses?' I ask, squinting at him.

'Oh, yeah,' says Zac, pushing them self-consciously up his nose. 'I picked them up this afternoon when I had a meeting in Oxford.'

'They're nice and they suit you.'

They really do. The square horn-rimmed specs frame his eyes and make him look… I don't know, cosmopolitan, intellectual, kind. He always looks kind.

Zac shrugs. 'Just thought I could do with a change. Plus I needed a stronger prescription. My eyes are screwed.' He blinks and grins. 'Come on then, why did Stanley describe you as decrepit?'

'Fragile!' I grin, play-punching him on the leg. 'Basically, I cocked things up at work and now Flora thinks I'm even more hopeless.'

'What, your super-hot boss?' laughs Zac, who's got a bit of an older-woman crush on Flora. I'm not sure he's taking my distress seriously enough. 'What did you do?'

He listens while I outline the situation with Rude Man and laughs when I describe the book club piling in. 'He sounds like a prat, Beccs.'

'So you don't think I'm fragile then?'

Zac grabs my hand and stares into my eyes. 'I see you as many things, but fragile isn't one of them – not the way you bulldoze your way around the house and slam doors without meaning to. I'd describe you as more nervy and self-sabotaging.'

'Lovely!' I snort, pulling my hand away in mock outrage. 'Feel free to mince your words a bit.'

'I don't need to because you can take the truth from me,' says Zac, simply.

He's still staring into my eyes and I suddenly feel uncomfortable. It must be the new glasses and Zac not quite looking like my Zac any more. I swallow and look away.

'Are you thirsty?' he asks, uncurling himself from the sofa and heading for our tiny kitchen. 'I fancy a beer. Do you want one?'

'Thanks. That would be great.'

He ducks with practised ease under the low dark beam over the doorway and looks back. 'Don't worry about that man or what Stanley said. I love you being the fragile, hopeless mess that you are.'

He chuckles as I launch a cushion at his head and disappears along the narrow passageway that links to the kitchen extension. I stretch out on the sofa and stare out of the window at the full moon that's risen over Honeyford. Silver beams are shining on Memorial Park which lies at the end of our lane. If it wasn't so chilly outside, I'd wander through the park and down to the river that cuts through the town. I can just picture the moon reflecting in the cold, clear water.

Zac is taking ages with my beer and it's lovely and warm in here. I've closed my eyes and am drifting off when I'm jolted awake by the shrill ring of my mobile phone. I fumble for it in my bag and wince when I spot who's calling.

'Hey, Jasmine.'

'Hello, Becca. Are you busy?'

My twin sister sounds cool and distant, as always.

'Not really,' I say, swinging my legs off the sofa and sitting up. I wander over to the fire and give it a prod with the poker. Flames crackle as glowing logs tumble over one another.

'What are you up to tomorrow morning? I'm going to a meeting in Cirencester and was planning to do a quick detour and nip round.'

'I'll be busy at work,' I say, wearily, because Jasmine doesn't really count working in The Cosy Kettle as a proper job. She recently started a new job with a big PR company and loves talking about her high-flying clients. But she tends to change the subject whenever the café comes up.

'I'll come into The Cosy Teapot then and have a drink. Do you sell smoothies?'

'Afraid not,' I say, thrown by the thought of Jasmine stepping foot inside the café that she's turned her nose up at for months now. 'Um, why don't we meet at my place? I can nip out for a bit if I square it with Flora.'

'No, I'll come to the café. I can only spare ten minutes anyway because I have to prepare for a really exciting meeting. It's to hook in a very important client. They're a household name but I can't tell you who. It's all very hush-hush.' She pauses, expecting me to beg her to spill the beans. But there's no point because she enjoys the secrecy. 'Anyway,' she continues, 'it won't take long but there's something we need to discuss.'

'Is everything all right?' I ask, a sudden surge of anxiety gnawing at the pit of my stomach. Jasmine never nips in to see me. Even if she lived in Honeyford – heaven forbid – I doubt she'd ever call in for a chat. It's a shame, really. I'd love a closer relationship with her but we're just too different.

'Everything's fine,' says Jasmine, airily. 'We can talk about things when we see each other. Gotta go. Bye for now.'

Talk about things? That sounds ominous.

'Who was that?' asks Zac, placing a tall glass of lager on the wooden side table next to me. He's such a considerate housemate.

'Just Jasmine, saying she's going to call into The Cosy Kettle tomorrow.'

'That's lovely. The two of you can bond over yule log and mince pies.'

'I'm not sure a mince pie has ever touched my sister's lips,' I laugh. 'She prefers superfood salads, mung beans and quinoa.'

Which is probably why she's a petite size ten and I'm not. Being surrounded by delicious cakes all day doesn't help and my arse has definitely spread a little since I started working in the café. The place always smells heavenly, and there are only so many slices of chocolate gateau, choux buns stuffed with caramel cream, and oaty flapjack a girl can resist.

'Are you going to be OK with her coming into work?' asks Zac, taking a slurp of his drink and wiping condensation from the outside of the glass with his finger.

'I guess so, though we do tend to clash.'

'You're not going to have a wrestling match in the middle of the café, are you? 'Cos if you are, I'll have to call in to watch.'

A vision of me and Jasmine fighting, like when we were kids, pops into my head. In The Cosy Kettle scrap, Millicent is standing by with her lips pursed, Stanley is taking bets on the winner, and tinsel and cake are flying everywhere.

'Nope. Sorry to disappoint you, Zachary, but our meeting will consist of little more than a passive-aggressive chat over a cappuccino. She'll diss my job, I'll feel inadequate and start fantasising about pushing her face into a Victoria sandwich, and then she'll sweep out, back to her golden life.'

'Spoilsport,' mutters Zac.

'How come you're home so early tonight anyway?'

'I took a couple of flexi hours this afternoon and went to the gym on the way home. You should join. They do loads of classes – yoga, Pilates, kick-boxing.'

I nod, though I'm not sure about the idea. Lots of unfamiliar people in new environments make me nervous. And I'd hate to end up working out in front of Logan, Zac's friend from the gym and the man I can't stop thinking about. Sitting and watching Logan work out might be rather nice – he's blond, chunky and handsome in a Greek god kind of way, with muscles to die for under his sensible work shirt. I couldn't help but notice them straining beneath the cotton when Zac introduced me to him in the pub a month ago. But I doubt voyeurism is encouraged at the gym so I'd have to work out too and then I'd just end up hot and sweaty and having a panic attack in the spin class. Logan would think I was a complete idiot.

'Penny for them,' says Zac, sitting next to me and nudging me with his shoulder. 'You're miles away. What are you thinking about now?'

'Christmas!' I lie, hauling myself off the sofa and ferreting about in the large carrier bag I abandoned by the front door. 'Aha!' I pull out a miniature plastic fir tree, only half a metre high, and wave it at Zac. 'What do you reckon?'

'I reckon…' He wrinkles his nose. 'I reckon it's probably the smallest Christmas tree in the world.'

'That's possibly true but size isn't everything, and I do have baubles.'

'Well, in that case…' He laughs as I pull a box of tiny glass spheres from my bag and dump them on the sofa beside him. 'Where did you find them?'

'In the gift shop on the High Street. I was buying a few extra decorations for the café and thought we could tart this place up too, in honour of the festive season.'

I set the tree on the side table and together we start hanging baubles from its vivid green branches. Plastic pine needles dig into our fingers as we suspend globes of blue, red and gold glass that glisten in the firelight.

The tree looks really pretty when we're done, and Zac grins. 'I feel more festive already. All we need now is a jug of eggnog, a massive box of chocolates and my gran making inappropriate comments in the corner and it could be Christmas Day at my house.'

'It sounds like your gran would get on well with Stanley.'

'She'd eat him alive.' Zac gets to his feet and stretches. 'I can't wheel out my gran or eggnog, but there is a very large bar of Dairy Milk in the fridge that could help us celebrate the festive season and prepare ourselves for a flurry of manic present-buying.'

'Sounds good to me. We can have our pudding before our shepherd's pie and peas, which are also in my bag near the door, by the way.'

Zac rescues our tea from the carrier and heads for the kitchen while I settle back on the sofa and wonder how many other people over the centuries have anticipated the run-up to Christmas in this cosy Cotswolds cottage. Were they excited, or did they feel a bit miserable like me? I so *want* to feel festive. I want to look forward to Christmas and to the new year that stretches beyond it, full of hope and possibilities. That's how a normal person would feel; a normal un-fragile person whose insides aren't often a tangle of shyness and anxiety. I bet that's how Jasmine feels.

'Happy early Christmas!' says Zac, ducking under the low beam and chucking the chocolate bar into my lap. 'Eat, drink and be merry!'

I break off a chunk and breathe in the rich smell of chocolate before popping it into my mouth. It starts melting on my tongue as I stare at our plastic Christmas tree and will myself to be merry. I mean, what's not to be merry about? I'm in a beautiful part of the world, working in a job I love, my family cares about me – even if they do think I'm a screw-up – and I'm living with my best friend.

When I give Zac a smile, he plonks down beside me, grabs my legs and swings them up and over his knees. 'What do you reckon? One episode of *Stranger Things* before we start cooking? I really like that stunted tree, by the way. It's dead cheerful.'

He points the remote at the TV with one hand and snatches the chocolate bar with the other, while I marvel at his ability to relax and live life in the moment without letting worries and fears blunt his happiness.

Chapter Three

Christmas songs are wafting through The Cosy Kettle, the decorations are glinting in the cool winter sunlight streaming through the windows, and the rich, sweet aromas of coffee beans and cake are heavy in the air.

The café is at its best, but every time someone comes in I jump, in case it's Jasmine. It's ridiculous to be nervous about seeing my own sister, but she'll probably find some reason to run the café down. And I feel oddly protective about The Cosy Kettle which kind of saved me, really.

Fortunately, we're mega busy today and I'm distracted by customers all morning. They struggle in, rosy-cheeked, with armfuls of parcels, desperate to take a break from their Christmas shopping.

We're also visited by our regulars, or 'the lost and lonely' as Flora calls them, not unkindly. They include Gladys, who is in her seventies and whose husband died a few months ago, forty-something Janine, who's out of work, and Paul, who's coping with long-term illness. They're very different people but they all need company and conversation, which I'm happy to provide, along with extra-large slices of cake.

I'm so rushed off my feet, I don't realise that Logan Fairweather has come into The Cosy Kettle until he's standing right in front of me. I don't clock that the man who makes my knees wobble and the power of coherent speech desert me is only a foot away until he says: 'Those buns look tasty.'

When I look at him, he winks and – damn my stupid flammable cheeks – I start to blush. Heat leaches out of me. I could save the planet with the renewable energy radiating from my face. I dip my head and wish I had longer hair to cover my embarrassment.

Logan's full mouth twitches as he studies the array of confectionery on offer and points at a large custard creation, topped with glazed cranberries.

'I think I fancy a tart instead. And a large cappuccino with lots of foam. Thanks, um…?' He raises his eyebrows at me.

'Becca,' I say, slightly miffed that this is the third time he's asked my name. You'd think he'd remember me, if only for the tragic blushing that ensues every time he's around.

Zac very definitely told him my name the first time we met in the local pub. He noticed me staring at Logan, who was propping up the bar looking magnificent in distressed Levi's, and rolled his eyes – he doesn't approve of my taste in men. But he introduced us anyway because that's the kind of good friend he is.

Logan was confident and funny and occasionally flirty after we joined him at the bar. He and Zac discussed weights and cross-trainers and some bloke who hogs the running machine while I stood there, fairly mute with a face like a furnace. But I did say that I worked at The Cosy Kettle, and Logan has been in a couple of times since, asking my name every time.

He works for a business that sells printers and his dad is some bigwig in the Honeyford Heritage Trust. That's all I know about Logan Fairweather, even though I've googled him. Obviously. His Instagram account has lots of pics of him out with his friends, many of whom seem to be female. He exudes confidence and happiness and uncomplicated non-weirdness, which I always find compelling.

Logan takes the custard tart and coffee from me and smiles. 'Thank you, Becca.'

I beam because he remembered my name – even though I only reminded him of it thirty seconds ago. Even a goldfish would be hard put to forget it in that space of time.

'Here,' he says, proffering a fiver. 'Keep the change.' Which is kind, even though the bill comes to four pounds eighty. I drop twenty pence into the charity box on the top of the counter and watch Logan snake his way between tables to a seat near the Christmas tree.

Uh-oh. Jasmine has just appeared in the café doorway, backlit by light from the bookshop, like a real-life Christmas angel. She stands there for a moment, inspecting the café, before sashaying towards me. I'm not sure if she does it deliberately but her narrow hips swing as she moves, like she's on a catwalk. I tried walking like that once, but Zac had hysterics and suggested an urgent hip replacement.

'Hiya, Beccs,' says Jasmine when she gets to the counter. Her thick musky perfume tickles my nose. 'I absolutely love the apron. Very "country kitchen".'

I run my hand self-consciously down the pretty floral apron I'm wearing over my usual 'uniform' of black jeans and dark sweatshirt. The apron's a bit twee but it's cheerful and adds to the cosy country feel of the café.

'Hi, Jazz. You found me then. Would you like a drink?'

'Yeah, a latte would be good.' She inspects the cakes on offer and wrinkles her perfect button nose. 'Do you have any salads?'

'Afraid not. It's cakes and pastries only. They're freshly made by a local bakery and taste delicious.'

'I'm sure they do but carb-loading before my important meeting is a no-no. I'll pick up something healthy later.' She stresses *healthy* as she looks around the café and frowns. 'There's nowhere to sit. I didn't realise this place would be so popular, seeing as it's so hidden away.'

'We're usually busy at this time of day and we had to take out a couple of chairs to make room for the Christmas tree. But we can sit in the garden with our coats on. If you head out there, I can join you in a minute once Flora comes in. She said she'd take over for a while about now.'

On cue, Flora appears in the café doorway and wanders over. She smiles at me and pulls her dark shoulder-length hair into a neat ponytail.

'Why don't you take a break, Becca?' She glances at Jasmine, who's waiting for me at the end of the counter. 'You can have a chat with your friend, then.'

'Jasmine's not my friend, she's my sister.'

'Oh.'

And there it is. The barely concealed astonishment that always flits across people's faces whenever I introduce Jasmine as my sibling.

'Didn't you say that you and your sister are twins?' asks Flora, taking in Jasmine's general goldenness.

'We're non-identical twins,' I answer, although it's patently obvious.

'Different eggs, different genes and different temperaments,' laughs Jasmine, flicking her long hair over her shoulder. 'We used to fight like cat and dog when we were kids.'

'I can't imagine Becca fighting anyone.' Flora grins at me. 'She's extremely quiet and well-behaved.'

'I can imagine. Beccs wouldn't say boo to a goose. You must be her boss.'

'Yep, that's right. Flora owns the bookshop and café,' I say, making myself a tall hot chocolate and shoving in a huge scoop of fresh cream.

Jasmine might not be into carbs right now but I'm going to need a few to get me through the next ten minutes. It's not that I don't care about Jasmine – she's my sister and I love her. But we're so unalike – me, shy and quiet; her, confident and loud – we tend to rub each other up the wrong way. And I can't shake the feeling of being second best that's dogged me since childhood.

'Well, it's lovely to meet you,' says Jasmine, flashing Flora her best toothy smile. 'I've just called in to say hello before a meeting in Oxford. I work for a PR company.'

'Ah, you're alike in your promotion skills then,' says Flora, slipping on the spare apron that's behind the counter. 'Becca runs The Cosy Kettle's social media accounts and does a fabulous job.'

'I'm sure she does. I deal with rather larger accounts but it must be great posting cute pictures of coffee and cake all day.'

Is Jasmine being sarcastic or am I being over-sensitive? Sometimes it's hard to tell. Flora doesn't appear to take umbrage so I say nothing, grab my coat from under the counter and lead Jasmine through the back door and into the small courtyard garden.

Pale watery sunlight is falling on the flagstone patio and across the two filigree metal tables and chairs.

'Bloody hell, Beccs, it's chilly out here,' says Jasmine, sinking onto a chair and wincing as the cold of the metal seeps through her smart black trousers. She buries her face in the collar of the steel-grey puffa jacket she's wearing.

'We can go back inside and nab a table as soon as someone moves.'

I cup my hands around my hot chocolate, glad that I remembered to switch on the garden lights this morning. Even dimmed by weak sunlight, the strands of multi-coloured fairy lights, pinned to the old Cotswold stone walls, make the space more cheerful and welcoming.

'So I finally get to see where you work,' says Jasmine, before taking a sip of her latte. 'Mmm, nice coffee. The café's cosy, and very festive. And I didn't realise you had tables outside.'

She stares across the tiny garden which I helped to create from an overgrown weed patch. In the summer, the garden is a riot of colour. But right now it's all brown earth, save for a splash of red berries on the firethorn shrubs edging the gate to the alleyway. I hope Jasmine will make a return visit when spring arrives, and see the garden coming back to life.

As she settles into her chair, it suddenly hits me that I *am* pleased to see Jasmine. We do clash – always have – but she's my sister and we have lots of shared memories: ganging up on Mum and Dad, family holidays in Devon, fan-girling over Justin Timberlake.

'How's your new job going?' I ask.

'Oh, you know. Busy, invigorating, exciting. I've only been in the role for a few weeks but my boss is already giving me lots of extra responsibility. She says she's grooming me for bigger and better things.'

'That's great, Jazz. You must be made up about it.'

'I am. You know how ambitious I am and keen to get on.'

'Well, you've worked hard and deserve success. I'm really pleased for you.' I drum my fingers against the thick china of my hot chocolate mug. 'I've got ambitions for The Cosy Kettle, too.'

'Really?' Jasmine glances through the window at the people chatting and laughing in the café, with their heads bent close together. 'I don't think of you as the ambitious type, Becca. Not since…'

She tails off and takes a big slurp of coffee.

'Not since I went bananas in Birmingham, gave up my job and moved in with Zac?'

'That's not how I'd have put it.'

'That's how Mum and Dad put it. In their eyes, I failed to hold on to my boyfriend or my career and had a rather embarrassing breakdown.'

'Hmm. Is that why you're avoiding them?'

'I'm not avoiding them.'

'You haven't been home for at least six weeks,' she says, leaning over to push away the ginger cat that's been 'adopted' by café customers. He usually gets plenty of strokes and belly rubs but Jasmine doesn't want ginger cat hairs on her trousers. Not before her very important meeting.

'I went home for Mum's birthday.'

'Which was ages ago. It's not fair to leave all the visits to me, and anyway…' She pauses. 'Things are a bit odd at home so you should definitely visit.'

'What, more odd than usual?'

'Yeah, way more odd. Mum's not herself at all. The last time I was there, she was crying in the kitchen.'

'What, Mum? Was she peeling onions or something?'

When Jasmine shakes her head, I frown because Mum never cries. She's the most long-suffering person I know. She's had to be, putting up with Dad, who's a walking sexist stereotype. He's fine with his wife working and bringing in a wage, but he still expects her to be in the kitchen and putting a meal on the table the minute he gets home.

'So was she proper crying?' I ask, slightly panicked. 'You know – sobbing, can't breathe, snot everywhere, kind of thing?'

'No,' says Jasmine, looking puzzled. She obviously doesn't cry like that. 'Her eyes were leaking a bit when she thought I wasn't looking and she kept sniffing. She wasn't distraught or anything, but it was alarming because she's usually so cheerful.'

'You don't think she's ill, do you?'

Catastrophic thoughts of Mum with some terrible illness are tumbling around my head and tightening my chest. I can't imagine life without her.

Jasmine frowns. 'I don't think so. She's just kind of… different. Oh, I don't know. You need to see for yourself this weekend. Mum's organising one of her big Sunday lunches and she's going to invite you.'

'*This* Sunday?'

'Yes, this Sunday. You'd better be there, and you'd better stay over at Christmas too – I'm staying, so you've got to as well. It's about time you stopped hiding away in tiny, picture-perfect Honeyford.'

'I'm not hiding away. I'm working hard to build up The Cosy Kettle.'

'I'm sure, but it's just…' Jasmine trails off and studies the dregs of her latte.

'Just what?'

She looks up and stares at me with her clear blue gaze. 'It's just a shame that you're wasting what potential you've got.'

'I'm not wasting anything. I'm happy here.'

'What, working in a café at the back of a little local bookshop?'

'Yes. I'm not like you, Jazz.' *However much our parents would like me to be.* I spoon up a huge mound of cream from the top of my hot chocolate and shove it into my mouth.

Jasmine shifts uncomfortably on her chair and glances at her watch. 'Right, I've gotta go because I need time to prepare before the meeting starts.' She gets to her feet, brushing imaginary dirt from her trousers. 'Just think about what I said about coming home, Becca, and make sure you're there on Sunday. You can't opt out of life completely because you're a bit…' *Don't say it. Please don't say it!* She wrinkles her nose. 'Fragile.'

Urgh. I gather up our cups and follow Jasmine back into the café. A wall of warmth hits us as we step inside and I close the door behind us. The Christmas tree lights are twinkling in the corner and a sweet smell of cinnamon and caramelised sugar is hanging in the air. I'm so proud of The Cosy Kettle and how I've helped to build it up, but is Jasmine right that I'm wasting my potential? I rather fear that she's over-estimating my potential, to be honest, judging by yesterday's confrontation with the rude customer. I didn't exactly handle that with professional aplomb.

Logan lifts his head from his mobile phone and catches my eye.

'Hey, Becca,' he calls out, as I get closer. A little buzz of pleasure shudders through me that he can still recall my name.

'Is everything all right?' I ask, stopping by his table. I'm still shivering with cold but my heart feels warm that Logan wants to chat to me. I definitely have a huge crush on the local heartthrob and maybe, just maybe, he might see something in me too?

'Everything's good, I just wondered…' He breaks off and stares at Jasmine, who's stopped and is walking back towards us. 'I just wondered… who's your friend? I haven't seen her around Honeyford before.'

Of course. Logan only wants to talk to me because he's interested in Jasmine. People usually are. My warm heart begins to cool.

'This is Jasmine,' I say, as she arrives back at the table and gives Logan a wide, pearly-white smile. 'She's my sister.'

And there's that flicker of astonishment again, ricocheting across Logan's square-jawed, handsome face.

'No way!' he splutters. 'I'd never have guessed it in a million years. The two of you are sisters?'

'Twin sisters, actually,' purrs Jasmine, stretching her beautifully manicured hand towards him.

'Now you're just teasing me.'

'Not at all. We're non-identical twins. I'm the older one.'

'You don't look it,' says Logan, wrapping his fingers around hers and squeezing her hand rather than shaking it. 'I'm very pleased to meet you, Jasmine. I'm Logan. Do you live in Honeyford?'

'No, I have a flat on the outskirts of Oxford. I'm just passing through and thought I'd pop in to see how Becca's doing.'

'Then you'll have to pop in again soon,' says Logan, as my heart sinks into my boots. 'Honeyford has an awful lot to offer.'

'Maybe I will then,' replies Jasmine with the flirty toss of the head she's been perfecting from the age of eighteen. I've tried it with people I fancy but it was wholly unsuccessful. I looked like I was doing some sort of strange twitch. It doesn't help that I've got short hair that doesn't ripple down my back in a golden wave.

'Excellent,' says Logan, not taking his big blue eyes from her face. 'I look forward to seeing you again.'

When I walk Jasmine out of the café, she whispers to me: 'Who was *that*?'

'Logan? Zac knows him from the gym. He lives just outside Honeyford and works for a company that sells printers.'

'He is totally hot.'

'Do you think so? I hadn't noticed.'

'Oh, please. Your face looks like a tomato.'

'That's just 'cos we've come in from the cold and it's warm in here.' I blow air up into my fringe to cool my face and resist the urge to throttle Jasmine, who has to be the most annoying twin ever.

'You're hopeless, Becca.' She shakes her head. 'I want you to be happy but you live in your own shy little world. How long is it since you last went on a date?'

'Not long,' I mumble.

'Not since that idiot Charlie decided he'd rather be with Chloë and ditched you, I bet.' *Gee, Sis, feel free to sugar-coat it.* 'What about that Zac bloke you live with? Is there anything going on with him?'

'What, with Zac? Definitely not. We're just good friends.'

'Hmm. Well, I don't know how he puts up with you being so stressy about everything, Beccs. I know you can't help it but you've got to admit that you are a bit weird. Anyway, I'll see you on Sunday.'

Without waiting for a reply, Jasmine air-kisses me on both cheeks before tapping across the bookshop flagstones on her stiletto heels.

Logan brushes past me as she gets to the front door of the bookshop, and he stands in the doorway watching her as she clip-clops down the High Street towards her company car. His thick blond hair is ruffling in the cold breeze and I have an urge to push my fingers through it. He'd probably have me arrested for assault.

With a sigh, I turn on my heel and head back into The Cosy Kettle, feeling unsettled, as I often do after spending time with my sister.

Chapter Four

By early afternoon, the sun is blotted out by thick black clouds and thunder is rumbling around the hills that surround Honeyford. The garden is empty and bright flashes are lighting up the sky, warning of the storm to come. But inside The Cosy Kettle it's warm and fabulously festive.

'You've done a grand job in here, Becca.' I jump as Flora's voice sounds in my ear. 'You're putting me to shame. I've only managed to string up a few baubles in the shop so far.'

She waves at Vernon, who runs the town's butcher's store. He always turns up about this time for a Belgian bun and flat white coffee.

'Is everything all right?' I ask. One thing about being a nervous person is that I pick up on anxious vibes from others. Zac says it's a superpower though, quite honestly, I'd prefer the ability to make myself invisible.

Flora frowns. 'Not really. The school just rang to say that Caleb's not well and someone needs to pick him up, but Daniel's in London on a training course.'

Caleb's only ten and Flora has become a surrogate mum to him since she started going out with Daniel, his dad.

'What about his gran?'

Flora shakes her head. 'Luna's at home with the same bug. She's been under the weather for a few days.'

'Then you must go and collect the child,' booms Millicent, who's nipped in for a quick decaf and has been earwigging shamelessly. She rolls up the sleeves of her sensible beige blouse. 'Becca can run the shop while I keep an eye on the café. I mean, how hard can it be?'

Quite hard, actually, when everyone wants serving at the same time and I'm trying to guesstimate the number of cakes we'll need tomorrow. But it's relatively quiet at the moment, now a storm's brewing and people aren't venturing out to the shops.

'That would be wonderful, if the two of you don't mind,' says Flora, already texting the school to let them know she's on her way.

'Of course we don't mind. Millicent and I will be fine, and Caleb needs you.'

'I should be back within the hour.'

'Great.'

I plaster on a smile as familiar naggings of anxiety about being left in charge start edging in. Yesterday Flora had to come to my rescue, for goodness' sake, when I cocked things up in the café.

Flora gives me a sideways look. She knows me pretty well after all these months. 'I'll probably be much less than an hour, actually. I'll take Caleb home to Starlight Cottage, get him settled and head straight back. Luna can keep an eye on him, as she's at home anyway. Are you quite sure that's OK?'

'Absolutely. You go and sort out Caleb.'

I mean, what else can I say? Flora's my boss, and, although she's quite sensitive to my anxieties, she's not the nervous type herself. Even breaking up with her cheating husband a few months ago didn't throw her – not really. And she's totally reinvented herself since into a confident and successful small business owner with a whole new family. She's living with widower Daniel and his mum, Luna, at the moment but is looking around for her own place. I think she's amazing, and always feel a little bit in awe whenever she's around.

Flora rushes off with a wave and I head into the bookshop which is even quieter than the café. I breathe in the smell of ink and paper, and relax. This'll be fine. I love being surrounded by the books which are crammed into the shelves and standing in piles on the flagstones. They provide me with hours of reading pleasure but require nothing in return.

That's why I came into the bookshop when I was having a panic attack, eight months ago. I sought refuge here because books ground me, and it was one of the best moves I ever made. It was the first time I properly met Flora and Callie, who was working in the shop then, and a moment when my life changed for the better.

'I'm helping myself to a free cranberry cupcake, by the way,' calls Millicent, poking her head around the café door. 'In lieu of payment for helping you out.'

'Of course. You can help yourself to a coffee too, if you'd like.'

'Oh, I am, don't you worry.'

As she disappears back into The Cosy Kettle, I leaf through a stand of Honeyford postcards that Flora has placed near the till, choose one and smooth its glossy surface with my thumb. It's a photo of the old stone toll bridge spanning the narrow, shallow river that winds its way through the town. Two ducks are lazily floating towards the stone arch and patches of sunlight are twinkling on the crystal-clear water.

It was taken on a much warmer day than today. Outside in the High Street, shoppers are hurrying past in thick coats with collars turned up against the chill and, as I watch, fat raindrops start to splatter and burst on the pavement.

Not long to go until Christmas and I haven't bought a single present yet. My parents are easy: toiletries and books for Mum and a jumper for Dad. But Jasmine is more tricky – she has expensive tastes for someone brought up in a modest house like ours. And I need to get something special for Zac. He's been such a support since I moved in with him.

I'm pondering on what to buy a geeky twenty-seven-year-old with an appalling taste in music when the shop door tings and a middle-aged man in a well-cut suit rushes in. He brushes glistening raindrops from his steel-grey hair before striding forward.

'You're not Flora,' he declares, frowning slightly at my bright blue hair. He puts down his bulging briefcase, extends his hand towards me and waits.

'I'm afraid Flora's had to nip out,' I say, holding out my hand and receiving a brisk handshake in return.

'That's a shame. I'm Jonathan Frank, CEO of Frank Commodities, and she knew I was coming in this afternoon. Who are you?'

'I'm Becca,' I say, feeling my breathing change from long and deep to short and shallow. There's a familiar prickle of pins and needles in my fingertips as my ridiculous hair-trigger nervous system goes into overdrive.

'You work here, do you?' asks Mr Frank, staring at my sweatshirt which I suddenly realise is smudged with icing sugar from this morning's cake delivery. There's also glitter from the café's decorations scattered across my fingers, and now across his, thanks to our handshake.

'I work in the café here, The Cosy Kettle. I'm the manager.'

'Are you, indeed?'

Mr Frank's mouth lifts in the corner as though he can't quite believe it.

'Can I help you while Flora's out?' I ask, as a bright flash lights the darkness outside and a loud clap of thunder echoes overhead.

'I had a discussion with Flora about hiring the shop and café for an event I'm running in the new year and I need to know if that's going to be possible.'

When I look at him blankly, he sighs. 'Flora and I spoke on the phone and I said I'd call in this afternoon to finalise the deal.'

I glance at my watch. Flora's been gone forty-five minutes.

'She shouldn't be too long,' I tell him, but he only sighs again.

'That's a problem because I need to know right now. There's another option which I'll lose if I don't book it straight away. I also need to get to another appointment, as long as I don't drown in the process.' He glances outside and winces at the rain that's started falling in torrents.

'I can give Flora a call.'

'Please do that.'

He starts clicking his tongue against the roof of his mouth while I call Flora's number on my mobile, but there's no ringing tone. Starlight Cottage is just outside Honeyford and often a black hole when it comes to a phone signal. The storm won't be helping either. Rain is running in rivulets down the shop window.

'I'm afraid I can't reach her at the moment. Can I get her to call you when she gets back?'

Mr Frank shakes his head. 'I'm afraid not. I need a decision now, so what do you say?'

He stares at me, with an eyebrow raised. But I can't possibly make a decision without checking first. I've heard nothing about this event and I've no idea what Flora has in mind. What if I say yes and she says no and, in the meantime, Mr Frank loses out on the other venue? He'd be furious and it wouldn't be good publicity for The Cosy Kettle. Someone gung-ho would say 'yes' and damn the consequences but I've never been gung-ho in my life. I'm always too worried about doing the wrong thing.

Jasmine reckons it's fear that makes me indecisive but, to be honest, it's my vivid imagination. This enables me to picture all the things that could possibly go wrong – and, believe me, there are a lot of them. I envy people who swan around totally oblivious to the dreadful things that could happen at any moment. It must be wonderful.

Mr Frank is still staring at me so I pull back my shoulders, inwardly berating myself for being such a wuss. 'It will probably be fine, but I really do need to double-check with Flora before I can give you a definite yes,' I tell him.

'Really?' He sniffs. 'Well, maybe it's for the best if I go with the other venue anyway.'

'She honestly won't be long. She'll be back any minute.'

'Sadly, I don't have time to wait.' Mr Frank takes a small silver case from his inside pocket and pulls out a creamy-white business card. 'Please be good enough to tell Flora that I called in.'

'Don't you want to wait until the rain goes off?'

'I don't have the luxury of time but I do at least have an umbrella.' He pulls a fat black umbrella with a curved wooden handle from his briefcase and strides towards the door. I'm tempted to go all gung-ho for the first time ever and call him back, but he's already disappeared into the storm. After the door bangs behind him, I sit behind the till, gnawing at a torn nail on my thumb, and replaying our conversation in my head. Have I done the right thing?

Less than ten minutes after Mr Frank has left, Flora rushes in. She drapes her dripping coat over the leather armchair in the corner, ignoring the puddles that start pooling on the flagstones, and heads for the kitchen to put her drenched umbrella in the sink.

A minute later she's back, pushing her hands through her dark hair. Her sleek shoulder-length bob has gone slightly frizzy in the damp.

'Honestly,' she puffs, 'it was like a monsoon out there when I parked near the war memorial, but the sky lightened up and it stopped raining the moment I got to the shop door. Typical!'

'It was quite a storm. How's Caleb doing?'

'Poor boy. He's feeling pretty sorry for himself but I've wrapped him up in a duvet on the sofa and he's watching telly, so he'll be fine. Has everything been OK here?'

'It's been really quiet, except for Mr Frank coming in.'

'Mr...?' Flora wrinkles her nose and then bangs the heel of her hand against her damp forehead. 'Oh no, I forgot he was coming in to finalise the event he's holding. Did I tell you about it? He wants to take over the shop and Cosy Kettle for a whole afternoon, for a business event. I know it's a new direction we haven't tried before, but it'll be good for income and great exposure for the café – it might even get us some new customers to tide us over the quieter new year period, until the tourists come back.'

A wave of heat washes over me and my stomach starts churning. I should have said yes. Of course I should have.

I take a deep breath. 'He wanted a decision straight away and I couldn't get hold of you on the phone so he left. He said he might book a different venue instead.'

'Oh, I certainly hope not.' Flora frowns. 'We could do with the money and the kudos. I'd better ring him.'

Flora walks to the back of the shop to make her call while I keep busy, serving a customer who's just come in. She returns as the customer goes out of the shop with his purchase, and shakes her head.

'Unbelievable. He's gone with the other venue already and he won't change his mind.' She sighs. 'I wish you'd said that we'd do it, Becca. You're in charge of the café now so you could have agreed to go ahead with it.'

Disappointment sparks in her eyes and I feel awful, because I've let her down... for the second time this week. Flora put her trust in me and I've screwed things up.

'I'm so sorry. I didn't feel that I had the authority and I was worried I'd make the wrong decision. I was trying to do the best for the business but...'

When I trail off, Flora shakes her head and gives a strained smile. 'Never mind. It wasn't fair to leave you in charge, and I hadn't discussed the event with you so you weren't to know.' She closes her eyes as though she can't bear to look at me.

'I really am sorry. I didn't think...'

'No, you didn't.' Flora opens her eyes and pats my hand. 'Look, don't worry about it, Becca. It's not the end of the world. Why don't you go and check out what Millicent's doing in the café.'

Crikey, I'd forgotten Millicent. But there's no need to worry. She's sitting at the café counter, inspecting her nails and looking bored when I rush back in.

'Flora's back, is she? I bet she got soaked in that storm. I've never seen rain like it. It must be all that global warming.' She peers at my face. 'What's the matter with you? You look like you're about to burst into tears.'

'No, I'm fine,' I gulp, grabbing a cinnamon whirl and shoving it into my mouth. The sticky sweetness hits the spot and instantly calms me down – no wonder my arse is spreading if I'm plugging my competence gap with calories.

Millicent narrows her eyes. 'Hmm, if you say so. Right, if you no longer need my unpaid labour, I'd better be off because my personal trainer is arriving in an hour.'

'How long have you had a personal trainer?' Millicent has the same physique as my gran – stout from chest to hips with no discernible waist. And I haven't noticed any change in the months I've known her.

'Oh, ages,' says Millicent, airily. 'I've hired a young woman who comes to the house and tries to make me do squats in the sitting room. She's not always successful.'

I bet she isn't.

After Millicent has bustled off, I serve cappuccinos and slices of ginger cake to a damp young couple who've wandered in. I make myself a mocha with an obscene amount of caramel syrup – more comfort calories – and drop some coins into the till, seeing as I'm eating and drinking the stock. Then I sit at the counter, surrounded by tinsel.

The fairy lights are twinkling, the copper kettles that give the café its name are gleaming, and Bing is dreaming of a white Christmas on the radio, but I've never felt less festive. I've really let Flora and The Cosy Kettle down this afternoon – by being me, basically. Shy, worried Becca who makes wrong decisions by not making decisions at all. High-flyer Jasmine would never have let such a business opportunity pass her by, I tell myself, sipping at my coffee. Jasmine grabs life by the horns, without shyness or fear holding her back.

I start mentally listing all the things I'm afraid of... spiders, big crowds, speaking in front of people I don't know, speaking in front of people I do know... but give up when my list gets depressingly long.

What a day! Jasmine's visit, Logan's total lack of interest in me and then my corporate cock-up to wind things up nicely. Would it be over the top to choose another cake from the mouth-watering display in front of me? Or am I merely feeding my despair?

Oh, get over yourself, Rebecca, a little voice whispers in my ear and I have to smile, because it sounds exactly like Zac. But I pick up a massive slice of Christmas cake anyway, peel off a thick slab of white icing and marzipan and shove it into my mouth.

Chapter Five

Zac is sitting on a low wall, bundled up in a green parka and striped woolly hat, and doesn't see me as I get closer. All hint of the earlier thunderstorm has disappeared, and the temperature has dropped as the clouds cleared. Zac is gazing into space, staring at the pinpricks of stars that are scattered across the inky sky. The market house arches are dark shapes behind him. He looks still and calm and rather lovely, actually. Like a still-life painting.

I fasten the toggles on my black duffel coat and hurry up to him. Just the sight of kind, caring Zac makes me feel more cheerful.

'Hey. I got your text. What's with all this coming to walk me home business, when it's only a ten-minute stroll through the Badlands of Honeyford?'

Zac looks up at me and smiles. 'I fancied some fresh air and thought you might like some company seeing as yesterday and today were a bit rubbish.'

'How do you know that today wasn't great?'

'I guessed because I knew that Jasmine was calling in. How was she?'

I shrug. 'All right, really. Just a bit… supercilious.'

'Good word. Well done,' murmurs Zac, with a wink.

'Yeah, and I know the word *patronising* as well.'

Zac sniggers as I shoulder-barge him off the wall. He stands up and brushes tiny stones from his jeans. 'I met Stanley in the street on the way here and he was full of how he came to your rescue yesterday when that customer got – and I'm quoting Stanley directly here – "well arsey". Then he called me "mate" a lot and wandered off with his jeans falling down.'

'He's trying to perfect the low-slung jeans look but it's not working too well. People keep pulling them up for him. He gets very cross.'

Zac throws back his head and laughs. 'Stanley is a total legend. Anyway, can we walk home as we talk, before my feet turn into blocks of ice? I've already lost the feeling in my toes.'

'Sounds good to me. You are crazy coming out again when you could be slobbing in front of the fire.'

'I needed a walk.'

'That sounds ominous. Are you OK?' I ask, linking my arm through Zac's as we wander past the town's Christmas tree that went up a couple of days ago. It has a slight slant, probably thanks to the thunderstorm, but it's very pretty. Ice-blue lights are scattered through the branches and a large golden star is wobbling on the top.

'Yeah, things are just a bit hectic at work.'

'Nothing yet from Kirsty?' Zac shrugs his shoulders at the mention of the woman in his accounts department who he's fancied for weeks. 'Maybe you need to be more direct?'

'Nah, I don't think she's interested.'

'Then she must be an idiot. You're a brilliant catch – kind, strong, good-looking.'

'Almost as good-looking as the lovely Logan Fairweather who you crossed paths with at work today.'

'How do you know he came into the café?'

'My spy, Stanley, spotted him going into the bookshop and, as Logan obviously only reads comics, I guessed he must be thirsty.'

He groans when I give him a thump in the side. 'You're being very physical this evening.'

'You'd better watch it, or I'll bring out my best karate moves.'

'My lips are sealed,' he says, drawing a gloved finger across his cold lips.

'Logan, who I'm sure reads all kinds of high-brow literature, did come into the café, actually.'

'I expect you were happy to see him on your home turf.' He gives me a sideways glance. 'Though I'm not sure your heart can take it.'

'What do you mean?'

'I know you well enough to sense when you really like someone, Becca.'

'Did the furnace face give it away?'

'Every time.' He pauses. 'I thought you might mention your growing attraction to Mr Fairweather, but you've haven't.'

'Nah, no point, really. Nothing's going to happen.'

'Why not? You're a very lovely person.'

'Cheers.' I link my arm through Zac's as I wonder why I didn't tell him that Logan makes my heart miss a beat, seeing as he already knows loads about my disastrous love life.

'So how did it go with Logan?'

'Not brilliantly, seeing as he made it abundantly clear that he has the hots for my sister.'

'Ah.' Zac comes to an abrupt halt and turns to look at me. 'Are you sure?'

'Absolutely. He was practically salivating as she did her flicky head thing.'

'Flicky head thing?'

When I give him a demonstration, he wrinkles his nose. 'Yeah, that would probably do it. Sorry, Beccs. Just remember that you're far too good for him anyway so it's his loss. He is an eejit and you are magnificent.'

I grin. It feels good to be hanging out with someone who doesn't see me as terminally fragile or throwing away her potential.

'I am definitely magnificent, but do you think I'm weird?' I ask, my mouth watering when we pass Amy's old-fashioned sweet shop. Fairy lights are scattered around the glass jars of striped humbugs and chocolate limes in the window.

'Why do you ask?'

'Nothing really. It's just something that Jasmine said.'

Zac pulls my arm tighter against his side. 'Honestly? You're totally off-the-scale weird but that's OK. I like weird. Weird is good.'

We stop for a moment in front of the weathered war memorial and I scan down the list of names chiselled into the stone. There are so many for such a small town – young men in the prime of life, many of them teenagers. I expect some of them were weird, and I bet they were scared when they swapped this beautiful, peaceful town for the horrors of the trenches. But they had a war to fight and didn't have the luxury of being nervy and self-sabotaging for no good reason at all.

'We're so lucky to live here, aren't we, Zac,' I say, looking at the dark hills rising above Honeyford's solid stone buildings.

'Very lucky.' He reaches out and traces one of the names with his fingers. 'Come on, let's get home.'

'We *could* go home.'

'Or what? You don't sound too keen.'

'I just fancied walking on a bit further after being cooped up in the café all day. What do you reckon? We won't go too far.'

'It's a bit chilly.'

'Walking will keep us warm and when we get home, I'll light the fire and make you one of my alcoholic hot chocolates. I also have leftovers from work in my bag.'

'Mince pies?' Zac narrows his eyes. He's addicted to them and can eat several in one sitting.

'I have two mince pies and a thick slice of apple cake. Flora took the eclairs for Caleb.'

When Zac hesitates, I add quietly: 'The mince pies are iced.'

'*Iced* mince pies? I can't work out whether that's an abomination or the best thing ever.' He thinks for a moment. 'Nah, best thing ever. Come on then. Where do you want to walk?'

'Let's go into the Memorial Park. It'll be really pretty in the moonlight.'

'Pretty, freezing and wet,' grumbles Zac, but he follows me towards the park's high Cotswold-stone wall.

I'm expecting the park to be empty but, when we slip through the wrought-iron gates, the full moon is casting silver beams across the grass and gardens, and two other couples are walking ahead of us.

'So what else is going on at work then?' asks Zac, hooking his arm through mine.

'Why? What have you heard?'

'Nothing, but you seem a little off and now you're being defensive. So tell me.'

I hesitate because I've deliberately not mentioned my indecision over Mr Frank. After yesterday's 'wrong change' incident, it feels like a mess-up too far. And I don't want to disappoint Zac like I've disappointed my parents over the years. Not when he's the only person in the whole wide world who thinks I'm magnificent.

'Come on. It can't be that bad,' says Zac, kicking at the gravel path as we walk on. 'Did you push Jasmine head-first into your confectionery counter?'

'I did not, because that would have been a terrible waste of fudge cake.' I pause, still reluctant to put today's cock-up into words. Maybe it's all too much for Flora and I've screwed up the career that I happen to love, even if Jasmine doesn't much rate it.

'You'll tell me in the end so you might as well do it now.'

We walk on for a while, our feet crunching on the gravel and our breath hanging white in the air.

'OK,' I blurt out. 'The Cosy Kettle and the bookshop lost out on some business today because of me. That's it and I don't want to talk about it.'

'Are you quite sure you don't want to talk about it?'

'Absolutely sure.'

'Even though it's eating you up, and talking about it will give me a perfect opportunity to be bossy and tell you what to do?'

'I can't tell you because you'll think I'm an idiot.'

'I think you're an idiot already, so what is there to lose?'

Which is a very good point. So I outline the situation with Mr Frank, as we carry on walking, past the pond coated in a thin layer of shimmering ice.

When I've finished the sorry tale, Zac pulls my arm tight against him. 'It's a shame but it was a tricky decision to make on the spot, especially if Flora hadn't mentioned anything to you about it.'

'I guess, but I could have just said yes and worked things out later. I could have and should have, but I basically bottled it. I'm a serial bottler.'

'You basically did the best you could with the information you had,' insists Zac.

'I didn't have any information.'

'Exactly, and it doesn't really matter 'cos no one died. So stop beating yourself up. OK?'

How does he do it? Zac's talent for cutting through angst with clear-headed reason never ceases to amaze me. He's just so… normal. Merely being with him makes me feel better. But on this occasion he's wrong because it does matter. It matters to Flora and to The Cosy Kettle. And it matters to me.

He gives me a sideways glance when I don't reply. 'Have you seen the well? I stumbled across it a few days ago when I went for a run.'

When I shake my head, he dips into the trees and leads me along a narrow path I've never noticed before. It's darker in here, even though the branches are bare of leaves and the moon is shining brightly overhead. When I stumble slightly on the path, Zac grabs my hand and holds it until we emerge into a clearing.

The trees around the edges are in shadow but the clearing itself is glowing in the moonlight. The frosted tips of the wet grass are a carpet of white and, in the centre, there's an old tumble-down well. Moss has grown in the cracks between the stones and an ancient metal pump handle is dark with rust but the rim of the well and the wooden boards across it are coated in frost and sparkling with reflected moonbeams.

'Oh, this is gorgeous! The well looks like it's been dipped in diamonds.' I run my fingers across the ice-cold stone and gaze up at the tiny gable roof above the well opening. It's in the shape of an upside-down V, and covered in frosted stone tiles. 'How long do you think this has been here?'

'I'm not sure. Ages, I suppose. There was probably a house around here once but now only the well is left behind.'

'Like an oversight.'

'Maybe.' Zac shrugs his broad shoulders and grins.

'What? Why are you smiling?'

'I'm just thinking that maybe it was left here on purpose because…' He leans in closer and opens his eyes wide. 'It's a wishing well.'

'Yeah, right.'

'Yeah, really. A magical wishing well that makes people's heartfelt wishes comes true.'

'That would be useful, right now.'

I turn away as hot tears start trickling down my face and brush them away, impatiently. Zac has started knocking on the boards across the well opening, to see how sturdy they are, and hasn't noticed me blubbing, thank goodness. He'd only ask why I'm crying, and my answer would totally kill the magical vibe of this special place: *Well, Zac, let's see. I'm rubbish at standing up for myself, my decision-making is pants, I turn into a human fireball every time I speak to the man I have a hopeless crush on, my parents are disappointed in me, and my sister, who reckons I'm wasting my potential, might be right seeing as she's much better at life than I am.*

Plus, I've turned into a right miserable cow recently, I decide, shoving my hands into my jacket pockets. Poor Zac. My fingers close around a freezing cold coin which glints when I pull it into the light.

'What's that?' asks Zac, wandering over. 'A coin for the wishing well?'

'Hardly. It's only ten pence,' I say, sniffing back more tears.

'That's enough, I reckon, to make a wish. There's a crack in the wood you can drop the coin through.'

'I'll feel daft.'

'It's almost Christmas and a magical time of year. Woo!' He waves his hands around my head in what he presumably thinks is a mystical kind of way. 'You must have a wish burning in your soul, so go for it. I'll give you a bit of personal space.' He backs off, sits on a fallen log at the edge of the clearing and starts scrolling through his mobile phone. 'Go on. I'm not watching.'

Feeling a bit of a prat, I run my hands over the frosted boards across the well and find a split in the wood. Then I carefully manoeuvre the coin through the gap and hold it between the tips of my fingers.

'And don't wish for world peace or a lottery win for your Cosy Kettle regulars. I know what you're like,' calls Zac. 'This is your Christmas wish and it has to be for you only. Right, I'm honestly not looking, so carry on.' He goes back to studying Twitter, his face glowing in reflected light from the phone screen.

I wish… I wish… A dozen different possibilities swirl around my head and coalesce into one huge and impossible wish.

I wish I could become a different person – a new, improved, better Becca.

As I drop the coin, my attention is caught by movement on the opposite side of the clearing and when I look up, breath catches in my throat. There, standing beneath the trees, is a stag. Moonlight is dappled across the animal's dark back and shadowing its antlers as it stares straight at me, its breath rising in wisps of white. It's the most proud and beautiful creature I've ever seen.

There's a faint splash as the coin hits the water below and the spell is broken. The animal starts and is swallowed up by the dark trees.

'Did you see it?' I call to Zac, who glances up from his phone.

'See what?'

'A stag, in the clearing over there.'

'A stag? Have you been adding whisky to your macchiatos?'

'No, honestly. I saw a stag over there, underneath the trees.'

'Are you sure? It might have been a fox or something.'

'Only if foxes have antlers. It was definitely a stag and it was absolutely magical.' I shiver because, all of a sudden, the prospect of my wish coming true doesn't seem quite so fantastical.

'Aw, I've never seen a deer in the wild and I was too busy looking at Instagram to see this one. Typical,' moans Zac, patting the space next to him. 'Why don't you come and park your arse on this freezing cold log and tell me what you wished for?'

I settle down beside him, our arms pushing tightly together for warmth.

'Don't laugh but my wish was to improve myself and become a different, better person.'

'Oh dear. I thought you'd wish for some mega-expensive Christmas present, but instead it's New Year's Eve all over again. You're always trying to change something about yourself and it never lasts.'

'No one keeps New Year's resolutions. It's the law. But this is different and bigger, Zac. I've dabbled with tweaking my personality here and there in the past because I wanted to. But the events of yesterday and today have shown me that I *need* to change, big-time. I need a comprehensive overhaul. There is no alternative.'

'Well, there is. You could stay just the way you are,' says Zac, who's being no help whatsoever.

He doesn't seem to grasp the gut-wrenching importance of my wish. This is about the whole of the rest of my life. Do I want to carry on as shy, fragile, self-sabotaging Becca who works in a café and will probably die alone, or as confident, assertive Becca who could end up running a multi-national corporation with a couple of toyboys on speed dial, or even Logan Fairweather in my contacts book? My Christmas wish simply *has* to come true.

When Zac stays silent, I give him a nudge. 'Aren't you going to have a go and make a wish, then?'

'Nah, I have everything I could possibly want right here.'

'What? Frozen feet, a numb bum and a neurotic best friend? You're living the dream, Zac.'

I expect him to laugh but he stares up at the sky as a cloud passes across the moon and the glow from the frosted grass dims. Above us, a carpet of stars stretches across the blackness.

'So what's your dream, Becca?' he asks, quietly. 'Why do you want to change so much?'

'I want to be different for my sake, but I also need to change ASAP for the sake of The Cosy Kettle.'

'I thought you were doing a good job in the café?'

'Not good enough. Flora missed out on that booking today because I was too nervous to make a decision. And yesterday I didn't cope assertively enough with the rude customer and she ended up out of pocket. Well, *I* did really 'cos I made up the money.' Zac shakes his head beside me. 'But that's not the point. The point is that being shy and indecisive isn't only damaging me, it's damaging The Cosy Kettle too. I need to change, Zac. And this feels like the time to do it.'

'How exactly are you going to bring about this transformation? I hate to break it to you, Beccs, but wishing wells aren't renowned for positive, evidence-based outcomes. If you want your wish to come true, you'll probably have to make it happen yourself. I was only doing all that woo-woo stuff to wind you up.'

'I know, but this place honestly seems pretty magical to me.' A vision of the stag, proud and still, watching me as my coin dropped into the well, swims into my mind. 'But I'll sort out some proper goals to aim for – a sub-set of smaller wishes. Practical things I can work towards and change so I'll be transformed, preferably by Christmas.'

Zac shifts beside me. '*This* Christmas?'

'Yes, this Christmas because I have to stay at my parents' and I need a whole new personality to cope with that.'

'They can't be that awful.'

'They're not awful at all They're just...' How can I explain the sense of disappointment that radiates from my parents whenever they talk to me about my life? 'You should meet them, really. Why don't you come to lunch with me on Sunday? Mum won't mind. She'll be delighted that I'm bringing a friend home. They worry that my lack of success in life puts people off me.'

'Well, they might have a point.'

Zac does laugh, this time, when I pinch him on the arm, though I doubt he felt it through his thick parka.

'So will you come home with me on Sunday?'

'Of course. There's nothing I like better at weekends than being involved in passive-aggressive family dynamics.'

'You're such a good friend, Zac.' I rest my head on his shoulder and we sit for a while, watching shooting stars streak across the dark sky. Zac informs me they're a meteor shower passing through the Earth's atmosphere but, as they score the sky above the frosted well, they seem like a heavenly sign that my life is about to change for the better. And, whatever it takes, I will make my Christmas wish come true.

Chapter Six

I still feel buoyed up next morning when I wake and stretch out, starfish-style, across my double bed. My dreams were filled with wishing wells and shooting stars, and I have a vague memory of Stanley prancing around the clearing invoking the spirit of Christmas. Which is just the kind of thing he'd do, so it's probably best to keep schtum about the wishing well. But even though the magical feeling from last night has worn off, I feel more optimistic and cheerful than I have done for a while.

Zac is working from home today and is only just getting up as I set off for work. But we've arranged to meet in the pub at lunchtime for a drink, which is why I bump into him outside the Pheasant and Fox, four hours later.

'Hey, you. That's good timing,' he says, holding open the door of the old coaching inn so I can go in first. 'How was your morning?' he shouts, as we're hit by a blast of warm air and loud conversation.

'Manic. How was yours?' I ask, making my way to the bar which is twinkling with fairy lights.

'Wonderfully peaceful and I got loads done. This working from home thing is great, especially as I'm only ever twenty seconds away from the chocolate digestives in the fridge.'

'I hope you've left me some.'

Zac narrows his eyes. 'There weren't that many left to begin with. But I'll buy you a drink to make up for it.'

Five minutes later, we're sitting in a corner, surrounded by gleaming horse brasses on the stone walls and within spitting distance of a roaring log fire.

'Crikey,' says Zac, pulling off his hat and pushing his hands through his tawny-brown hair. 'It's like a sauna in here.' He takes off his glasses that have steamed up and wipes them on the bottom of his grey V-neck jumper.

'You'll scratch them if you do that. Mum's glasses are criss-crossed with scratches because she wipes them with whatever comes to hand.'

'They're fine.' Zac pulls his jumper over his head, puts his glasses back on and blinks at me from behind the frames.

'Wow, you've got real guns these days,' I say, nodding at his muscly arms.

He self-consciously tugs at the short sleeves of his T-shirt and smiles. 'All the work at the gym isn't a complete waste of time, then. You could always come along.'

'I could but I've already told you that me and Lycra don't mix. Plus I don't like sweating, or weights, or exercise.'

Zac grins while I marvel at how relaxed I feel in his company, when the romantic stakes aren't high. With him, I can be laid-back and funny and confident, but put me within ten paces of Logan Fairweather and I morph into a mute nervous wreck. However, not for much longer.

'Have you got a pen?' I ask, ferreting about in my handbag.

'Not on my person, no.' Zac takes a huge gulp of his orange juice and lemonade. 'Why do you need one?'

'What you said last night about my Christmas wish was true. I need to make it happen rather than expect it to just happen by magic. Anyway, I'm not sure I'd get much magic for ten pence.'

'I forgot that was all you dropped into the water, you cheapskate.'

My fingers close around a ballpoint pen and I pull it from my bag, triumphantly.

'Result! Now all I need is something to write on.'

There's nothing in my bag to make notes on except a Boots receipt and a leaflet for the local deli that's so glossy my pen slides off without making a mark.

'What about this?' Zac pushes a beer mat across the table. It's perfect when I turn it over. 'So what exactly are you doing?'

'I'm writing a list of mini wishes that, when I make them happen, will help to make my main Christmas wish come true.'

'Of course you are.' Zac grins and sits back in his chair with his arms folded. He watches closely as I write *Christmas Wish Action Plan* at the top of the beer mat and start sucking the end of my pen. 'So what do you want to change?'

'Everything.' When Zac raises his eyebrows at me, I scrunch up my nose. 'OK, not everything, but lots. I want to become a better version of myself, without all the fear and the angst and the screwing things up. And this is what I need to do to make my wish come true.'

I narrow my eyes and think hard before scrawling down a list:

1) *Be more assertive and confident, particularly as regards café*
2) *Impress Flora with business acumen*
3) *Make parents proud of me*
4) *Conquer fear of public speaking*
5) *Secure date with Logan*

Number five is a stretch but, what the hell, I'm aiming high. With Logan in mind, I think of a final one to add to the list:

6) Make myself look more like Jasmine

'Can I see your mini wish list?' asks Zac, leaning across the table.

I scoop the beer mat into my lap. 'You'll only take the mick.'

'Of course I will. That's what I do. But let's have a look anyway.'

Against my better judgement, I hand it over and he scans down the numbered points.

'Conquer fear of public speaking? That's a bit left field. You don't do any public speaking.'

'My point exactly. I don't do it because I'd probably hyperventilate to the point of unconsciousness. But it's the kind of thing I need to be better at if I'm going to be a good manager of The Cosy Kettle, or chief executive of Microsoft.' I wave my hand when Zac raises an eyebrow. 'Whatever. Who knows when I might need to make a speech at an event?'

'What event?'

'It doesn't matter what event. I just need to be able to do it.'

'O-K,' says Zac, slowly. 'I can see that being a bit more assertive generally might be good but a lot of these wishes depend on what other people think of you, Becca – like your parents and Flora. Is that a good idea?' He frowns. 'And I see that Logan gets his very own wish.'

'Why do I get the feeling that you don't approve?'

'I don't *not* approve. I like him well enough. I just don't know if he's right for you. And why do you want to look like your sister?'

'You've obviously never met her.'

'No, but that's not the point.'

'The point is I don't want to look exactly like Jasmine. I just want to look a bit more… polished.'

'Polished?' snorts Zac. 'What, like a table?'

'Yes, Zac. Exactly like a table.' I roll my eyes. 'Look at me, though. I still dress like I'm at university but now I'm the manager of a café and I ought to look like it. So people like that rude customer take me more seriously.'

Zac winces as 'Driving Home for Christmas' starts blasting out of the jukebox and leans across the table towards me. 'OK, but how are you going to bring about this ambitious transformation?'

Good question, seeing as any moves towards amending my personality and appearance have failed miserably in the past. But things have changed. I'm working again, this time in a job that I love, I'm keen to start dating again after last year's messy break-up with Charlie and, more to the point, I don't want to spend the next quarter of a century chucking obstacles in my own way. I want to be relaxed and happy and accepted by the people I love.

'I'm going to achieve this by working my way through the mini wish list and ticking off every single one,' I tell him. 'It's do that or spend the rest of my life like I am now.'

'Would that really be so awful?'

'Yes, it would! I don't want to spend my life being fragile and shy and anxious.'

'Or Logan-less,' murmurs Zac so quietly I'm not sure that's what he said at all.

'So will you help me with some encouragement rather than teasing me mercilessly? This means a lot to me, Zac.'

Zac puts down his drink and breathes out slowly. 'Then it means a lot to me, too.'

He reaches across the table to give me a high five, and when he smiles, the skin around his eyes crinkles as though he smiles a lot. Which he does.

'What would I do without you, Zac?'

Fear suddenly clutches my heart at the thought of ever being without him: steady, strong Zac who smiles his way through life.

'You'd drive another housemate mad with your out-of-tune singing and woeful cookery skills,' says Zac, pulling his hand away.

'Harsh. I haven't set the smoke alarm off for at least a week.'

'A week of relative peace. Bliss.' Zac downs the last of his pint and frowns at Chris Rea, who's still belting out of the jukebox. 'I'd better head for home because I've got a conference call before two o'clock. What's happening with tea tonight?'

'I thought I'd cook spag bol to celebrate the start of my new braver life, if you're up for that? Then you can put your feet up and mash mince pies into your face while I slosh an obscene amount of whisky into our hot chocolates.'

Zac grins. 'Don't let anyone ever tell you that you're not perfect just the way you are.'

He starts weaving his way through the pub towards the door while I put the scrawled-on beer mat into my handbag. Then I follow him, out into the frosty air.

Deciding on your mini wishes while sitting in a cosy pub with your best mate is easy-peasy. Anything seems possible when Christmas songs are playing, a log fire is burning and a peaceful evening with your feet up stretches ahead of you.

Achieving your goal of being more assertive in The Cosy Kettle is another thing entirely when you're rushed off your feet by a post-lunchtime surge of customers – and are currently being harangued by the afternoon book club. It's not an official book club day – meetings to discuss the latest novel under review are now held once a week – but members seem to be in the café all the time at the moment.

'You took ages,' moans Millicent, destabilising the tray I'm carrying when she grabs her latte and plonks it on the table in front of her.

'Yeah, none of us are getting any younger. We could have croaked by the time you got over here,' grumbles Stanley.

'Leave the poor girl alone.' Phyllis gives me a thumbs-up from her wheelchair. 'Can't you see she's busy?'

'Urgh.' Dick has taken a sip of his espresso and screws his face into a grimace. 'There's sugar in my coffee.'

'You always have sugar in your coffee, Dick. You get me to stir it in at the counter so it's ready to drink.'

'Not any more. Sugar's not good for my teeth.'

'For the three teeth that are still your own,' murmurs Stanley. 'Be a good girl and get Dick another espresso, Beccs.'

When I glance at the queue building up by the till, wish number one comes to mind: *Be more assertive and confident, particularly as regards the café*. Here goes. 'I will in a minute when I've served the people at the counter,' I say, decisively.

'We're regular customers and should come first,' booms Millicent, who's in a right old mood this afternoon. She's already complained that there's no marmalade cake left and claimed that the lemon drizzle slices are dry, although they're not. I had one with my lunch and it was delicious.

'I'll be as quick as I can but I need to serve a few other customers first.'

'Those other customers are strangers who won't ever come here again.'

'They certainly won't unless I serve them. They've been waiting quite a while.'

'Are you saying they're more important than us, your regular clientele?' grumps Millicent as the woman at the head of the queue starts tapping her long fingernails on the counter.

'No, I'm not saying…'

'Only that's how it sounds.'

'I didn't mean it to sound like that but I need to serve some people before the queue gets any longer,' I say, calmly and pretty damn assertively, actually.

'So how long does Dick have to wait for his coffee?'

'I won't be long. Just a few minutes.'

'A few minutes? That's not on when Dick is a regular customer who—'

'Oh, please!' I blurt out. 'Stop wanging on for one minute and I'll be back with Dick's sugar-free espresso before you know it.'

Oh dear. That's the trouble with trying to be assertive when you're basically a wuss. It so easily tips over into being downright rude. The members of the book club are staring at me with their mouths open and I feel my cheeks begin to burn.

'Sorry. So sorry.' I rush over to the queue, and start serving coffee and cake at top speed. Flora wouldn't approve of me being snappy with customers, even when it's the book club gang and they're being annoying. I feel as if I've fallen at the first hurdle.

When I take over a mega-sized sugar-free espresso for Dick a while later, they carry on discussing the thriller they've been reading without even glancing at me. This being a different person business is not going to be easy.

An hour later, the rush has died away and the only people left in the café are me and the book club. I wander over and make a big deal of wiping the table next to them free of crumbs.

'Sorry about earlier,' I say, quietly. 'I didn't mean to be rude, Millicent.'

'Hmm,' she snorts, putting her nose in the air. 'I was only giving my opinion and I most definitely do not "wang on", whatever that means.'

'No, you don't and I'm sorry.'

'So what's going on, Becca?' asks Phyllis, closing her fingers around my arm. Her thin wedding band glints gold next to her arthritis-swollen knuckles.

'Nothing's going on. Not really.'

'Have you fallen out with that good-looking young man of yours?'

'Which young man?' I ask in a bit of a panic, hoping the book club haven't cottoned on to my Logan crush.

'The tall man with curly brown hair and a lovely smile.'

'Oh, you mean Zac.' *Phew.* 'No, we haven't fallen out, and he's not my young man. He's just a friend.'

'But you live together.'

'Platonically, Phyllis. We're good friends from university.'

What is it with people assuming that Zac and I are a couple? Just because we share a house, it doesn't mean that we're sharing a bed. That would be weird.

'So what's the matter with you today? You're definitely not yourself.'

'I wish.'

'What does that mean?'

'It means… oh, it doesn't matter. Honestly, just ignore me.' I shove my cloth into the pocket of my apron.

'Come on, Becca. What does it mean?' asks Mary, pushing cake crumbs into her baby son Callum's mouth. He starts gumming them and dribbling. 'Is it something we can help with?'

'Not unless you're skilled in personality transplants.'

'You're talking in riddles,' says Stanley. 'So what's your actual prob, hun?'

I sigh and perch on the edge of the table. 'It's not a problem. Not really. I'm just trying to… adjust the sort of person I am and be a bit… better.'

'Is this because of that plonker who disrespected you on Tuesday?' asks Stanley.

'Kind of. Not entirely. It's a culmination of lots of things really which have led me to want to be a bit… better at being me.'

'Ah, you're trying to reinvent yourself. I used to do that all the time but then I had Callum and I've been too knackered ever since to even try.' Mary stifles a yawn. 'Everyone's tried to do it.'

Millicent doesn't look convinced. 'Do what? Be a different person? Some of us are very happy with ourselves just the way we are, thank you very much.'

'Lucky you,' I say, piling the club's empty cups and saucers onto a tray.

'You don't need to change, Becca,' insists Phyllis. Which is lovely, but then she spoils it by adding: 'The world isn't only for confident and successful people. Sensitive, panicky people who find life difficult also have a place.'

'But that's just it. I'm fed up with finding life difficult and I want to change.'

'So have you got a plan?' asks Mary, who seems particularly au fait with the concept of self-transformation.

'I have a—' I swallow. 'A kind of wish list plan. Yes.'

'And a deadline?'

'Christmas.'

'*This* Christmas?' Mary pushes out her bottom lip. 'Ambitious.'

'You definitely need our help if you're on a festive deadline,' pipes up Stanley. 'The afternoon book club relish a challenge, and our support can be like our present to you. Rest assured, Becca, we will make your Christmas wishes come true.'

'Honestly, Stanley, just a card would be lovely. Everything's being taken care of so there's no need to get involved.'

But Stanley is already rubbing his hands together in glee. 'Don't be silly. We'd love to be involved 'cos you're part of The Cosy Kettle gang. You're in the hood, girl. You're fam.'

Millicent sighs. 'Good grief, Stanley. Don't you ever talk in normal sentences any more?'

'Just keeping up with the yoof, Millie.'

'So what do you want to change about yourself, Becca?' asks Dick, running his hand over his long white beard. 'You seem like a lovely young girl to me.'

'Thank you, Dick. That's very kind.'

I put my hand in my apron pocket and run my fingers along the beer mat that I'm carrying around like a talisman. There's no way I'm showing them the list – not when *Secure date with Logan* is number five. It's awkward enough already when he comes into the café.

'I'd just like to be a bit more assertive,' I tell them.

'Is that what you were attempting to do when you accused me of "wanging on"?' sniffs Millicent. 'If so, you could certainly do with some practice in that area. But is that it? You just want to be more assertive?'

'That, and more confident generally, in life and in the café. Just a bit different in how I dress and behave. Nothing major.'

Though it is quite major, actually. Last night, next to the wishing well with Zac in the moonlight, anything seemed possible. *Your dearest wish is a complete personality and body overhaul? No problem.* However, in the cold light of day, it all seems rather more radical and unobtainable. But it *will* happen. It has to.

'Well, I can tell you for nothing to lose the head-to-toe black,' says Millicent, running her eyes over me. 'It's a harsh colour that does nothing for your pale complexion. It drains you, and the baggy stuff you wear looks like a sack. That rather short, severe hairstyle you had was awful, too. I'm so glad you're growing it out, but it's a shame you haven't ditched the dye. Why on earth do you want blue hair? Honestly, young people today!'

Millicent, it seems, has no difficulty in being assertive.

'Give the girl a break,' says Phyllis, grabbing my other arm. 'She's got such a pretty face and a kind and gentle personality. All that's needed are a few minor changes.'

'Then we need to work out a plan,' declares Stanley. 'I have experience of becoming your best self and the Cosy Kettle Afternoon Book Club likes to get its teeth stuck into something.' I give a wobbly smile, not sure that I want this lot sticking their teeth into me. But Stanley's on a roll.

'Right.' He consults the calendar on his mobile phone. 'I'll draw up a meeting schedule' – *meeting schedule?* – 'and we'll have an action plan in place by the beginning of next week. Don't worry, Becca. Your personality is in safe hands.'

'OK. Thank you,' I say, very unassertively, before carrying the empty cups past the Christmas tree to the counter. My quest to make my wish come true just became a whole lot more complicated.

But looking on the bright side, at least I can't back out now. It's rather like telling everyone you're on a diet so people will shout if you stuff your face with biscuits. Stanley and his gang will help to keep me on track when the going gets tough, and it's kind of them to care. So it's a good thing, really. Good for my Christmas wish, and good for me.

Chapter Seven

Zac takes his eyes off the road and snorts. 'You've got the afternoon book club on the case? That is unreal! I mean, what could possibly go wrong?'

'Do you think it's going to be disastrous, then?'

'Not disastrous, but definitely interesting.' He laughs and turns left into my parents' housing estate. 'How do you feel about it?'

'Nervous, though I guess it'll be fine as long as Stanley doesn't go overboard on his action plan.'

'He's drawn up an action plan?' When Zac snorts again, his battered Renault Clio swerves slightly and lightly clips the kerb.

'Hey, watch where you're going. If we don't turn up in one piece, my mum will kill you.'

'Is she fierce?'

'Not usually, but she turns into a tigress when she's protecting her cubs, me and Jasmine. The only time I ever saw her stand up to authority was when I got a detention for reading a book in class. I'd finished my work so it was either read or sit there doing nothing for ten minutes. Mum told the teacher he was a plonker drunk on power, then spent sleepless nights worrying about it.'

'Like mother, like daughter,' murmurs Zac, turning into my parents' road of suburban, featureless semis. 'Which house is theirs?'

'The one right at the end with the green door.' I twist towards him in my seat. 'Are you sure about coming with me to see them? You didn't have to.'

'I know, but I figured it was about time I met your family.' He makes it sound like we've just got engaged or something. 'Anyway, we're here now. Whoah!'

He pulls up outside my childhood home and peers through the windscreen. Dad has turned on the Christmas lights early, in honour of our visit, and they're shining at us through the gloom of a grey winter's day. Though 'shining' isn't really the right word for them – 'glaring', maybe. Or 'blinding'.

Dad always goes overboard with the external decorations and he's outdone himself this year. A huge plastic Father Christmas is waving at people from the garden. There's a family of reindeer on the roof with bright red noses, and the walls of the house are hidden behind hanging strands of flashing multi-coloured lights. Millicent would have a fit.

Zac gets out of the car and stretches his long legs. 'I get the feeling your family are quite keen on Christmas.'

'My parents always make a bit of a fuss. Whatever you do, don't criticise Dad's display or he'll go off on one and that'll be it for the afternoon.'

'I wouldn't dream of it. They're great, don't you think? Maybe we should do something similar outside our place.'

'Can you imagine the reaction of the Honeyford Heritage Trust if we besmirched their historic town with such a garish display?'

'Alan would probably self-combust if we installed Rudolf on the roof.' We both grin at the thought of Alan's reaction. He heads the voluntary Trust and likes to think that nothing happens in Honeyford without his say-so.

'Right. I'm going in.' Zac opens the gate and heads for the front door.

'Happy holidays!' says a tinny voice as he passes the Santa on the lawn. Dad has installed an actual talking Father Christmas in the garden! My anxiety levels shoot up as I wonder whether inviting Zac to meet my family was a good idea. It seemed sensible and mutually beneficial at the time – he provides me with moral support and, in return, enjoys one of Mum's legendary roast dinners. It's a win-win situation. But maybe he'll think my family are totally over the top and odd.

Oh well, too late now.

Before I can fit my key into the lock, the front door is wrenched open and a huge dalmatian bowls past me and starts savaging Santa, shaking him from side to side.

'Bad dog! Leave him alone or you'll get electrocuted,' shouts my dad, standing on the doorstep with his hands on his hips. 'Bloody stupid animal,' he mutters. 'Hello, Beccs, long time no see. Go on through while I sort the mutt out.'

'Hi, Dad. Can't you keep that dog under control? He frightened the life out of me.' I steal a glance at Zac, who's watching the destruction of Santa with his mouth open. This is probably not the best introduction to my family. Taking his arm, I lead him past Dad into the hallway and hang up his coat.

'That's an enormous dog.' Zac peers out of the hall window, into the front garden. 'I had no idea your parents had a dog like that. You've never mentioned him.'

'That's 'cos he's not ours. Dad looks after him for Sid, down the road, when Sid's visiting his daughter or on holiday. Though it's always Mum who ends up taking him for walks. Follow me.'

I lead Zac through the hall and into the kitchen at the back of the house, where I know I'll find Mum because the smell of roasting meat is wafting through the house. And there she is, at the sink, peeling carrots. Everything around her is neat and tidy, even though she's in the throes of cooking for five adults.

'Becca!' she says, her face breaking into a huge grin. She wipes her hands on her apron before giving me a hug. She smells of lavender soap, as always, but she feels less cuddly than usual, as though she's lost weight since I was last here. I give her an extra, anxious squeeze.

She releases me and smiles at Zac. 'And you've brought your young man with you. How lovely.'

'This is Zac, who's the good friend I live with.'

'Well, it's about time you brought him around. We've heard enough about him.'

'All good stuff, honestly,' I tell Zac, who says hello and offers to help with the carrots. When Mum refuses, he wanders past me and stares at her paintings that are propped up drying in the utility room.

I don't know where Mum finds the time to paint, and she didn't for ages when Jasmine and I were growing up. But I'm glad she seems to have got her art mojo back recently. Dad thinks it's a waste of time because her art doesn't bring in any money, but she always seems more relaxed and happier with a paintbrush in her hand.

She spots Zac peering at the pictures and winces. 'Ignore my dabblings, Zac. They're not terribly good but they keep me out of mischief.'

'They're more than dabblings.' He walks closer to Mum's watercolour of the nearby canal. In the centre of the picture is a decaying houseboat whose blue paint is flaking into the murky brown water. 'This is really good,' he says. 'It's very atmospheric. You're very talented.'

Mum's cheeks flush pink at the compliment.

'Do you think so? That's lovely of you to say so but Peter wouldn't agree. He reckons my pictures are ugly because I like painting things that are old or broken down. But I find them more fascinating than pretty-pretty landscapes.'

'Dad's not an art critic, Mum, and Zac's right – your paintings are really good and you should have more confidence in yourself.' I pause for a moment to savour the irony of me telling someone else to be more confident. 'Talking of Dad, how long has he said you'll have the dog this time?'

'Until Sid returns from skiing in Andorra with his new wife.'

'Has Sid got married again?' When Zac looks puzzled, I mouth at him, 'Number four.'

Mum sighs. 'What can I say? That man is addicted to love and romance… and divorce,' she adds in an undertone. 'Anyway, while he's off honeymooning once more, we get to look after Tiny.' She rolls her eyes at Zac. 'Sid likes to think he has a sense of humour. But believe me, it's not funny when you're yelling "Tiny" at a massive dalmatian in the park and everyone thinks you're off your head.'

Did I imagine it or did she give me The Look when she said 'off your head'? I'm never going to live down the months I spent hiding under my duvet in Birmingham, withdrawing from life.

Mum scoops up the scraped carrots and drops them into a pan of bubbling water. 'Why don't you take Zac into the sitting room and get him a drink before lunch? Jasmine will be down in a minute. She's upstairs at the moment with another box of her stuff that she wants to store here. Honestly, I feel like I'm living in a storage facility sometimes.'

'Why don't we give you a hand, Mum? You look tired.'

Usually Mum's skin is glowing and her thick brown hair is pulled into a bun. But today her hair is hanging loose to her shoulders and looks as though it's hardly been brushed. And her blue eyes look less bright than usual, as though a light has gone out. Jasmine's right. There's something up with Mum.

'I wouldn't hear of it because it's your job to look after our guest.' She starts shooing me and Zac towards the door with a tea towel. 'Everything's organised in here and I'm fine.'

Zac follows me back into the hall, ducking under paper chains looped across the ceiling, and steps into the sitting room. A fire is burning in the grate and a few fat flakes of snow are drifting down outside the double-glazed doors that open out into the back garden.

The garden has been spared my parents' enthusiasm for all things Christmas. But inside, it's a different story. Every available surface is draped with tinsel or covered with festive ornaments – from a china Santa and his elves to a miniature crib surrounded by wooden animals. The walls are festooned with Christmas cards fastened to long strands of scarlet ribbon with tiny clothes pegs.

'What's this?' asks Zac, picking up a tubular mass of red crepe paper with blobs of cotton wool randomly applied to it.

'That's Father Christmas, made by me from an empty toilet roll, circa the year 2000.'

'It's a shame you haven't inherited your mother's artistic talents,' he snorts, which is rather uncalled for, seeing as I was only six at the time. He picks up a glitter-encrusted piece of card and waves it at me. 'And what's this masterpiece?'

'Honestly, Zac. Don't you know anything? That is obviously an advent calendar made by Jasmine from an old cornflakes box.'

'Of course it is. So do your mum and dad bring this stuff out every year?'

'Yep, every single year.'

'Aw, I think it's sweet.'

'It is quite sweet, though it's like our family Christmases have been frozen in time and Jasmine and I are still kids. I'll be kicking off about eating broccoli before you know it.'

Zac grins as he carefully places Jasmine's masterpiece back on the coffee table.

'What about your parents, Zac? Do they go overboard at Christmas too?'

'A bit, though they don't have the same level of expertise, or vintage artwork.' He nods at the snowman I made at school twenty years ago out of two ping-pong balls. Its eyes, drawn on with felt-tip pen, have smudged so it looks like its mascara has run. 'It's quite over the top, but it's cheerful in here, isn't it? More cheerful than our place.'

He's got a point. The plastic mini-tree remains the only nod to Christmas in our cottage. But I'm getting a lovely full-on festive fix in The Cosy Kettle which twinkles all day with fairy lights and tinsel.

'Your mum and dad seem nice,' says Zac, wiping purple glitter from his hands.

'They are, though Dad can be a bit overbearing at times. And I'm worried about Mum because there's something wrong with her. Jasmine mentioned it when she came into The Cosy Kettle.'

'Did I hear my name?' Jasmine pokes her head around the door and smiles. 'Hi, Becca. You managed to drag yourself out of Honeyford then. And who's this?'

'This is my friend Zac. He's come for lunch.'

'So you're the elusive Zac.' Jasmine walks into the room, all blonde and glowing, and holds out her hand. 'How lovely to finally meet after I've heard such a lot about you. I'm Jasmine, Becca's sister.'

Here it comes... I brace myself for the look of astonishment on Zac's face. Even people who are expecting to meet my sister and know that we're related can't hide their surprise. But there's not a flicker of emotion on Zac's face.

'It's lovely to meet you too,' he says, shaking her hand.

'Likewise. I think Becca's been hiding you away,' she giggles.

Oh. My. God. Did Jasmine just give Zac her legendary head flick? There was definitely some head-shaking and tumbling hair going on. An unfamiliar feeling of possessiveness bubbles up inside me as Jasmine gazes around the sitting room.

'Good grief. I can't believe Mum's still getting this old crap out of the loft every Christmas.'

'I know. What did you think of the front garden?'

'Dad's excelled himself this year.'

'Did Santa wish you a happy Christmas?'

'Yeah, I almost had a heart attack. It must seem like a madhouse to you, Zac.'

'Not at all. It's just very... festive.'

'It's that all right.' Jasmine gives Zac a sideways glance. 'Has Becca offered you a drink?'

'Not yet.'

'Becca, you're failing in your job as host.' Jasmine crosses to the old-fashioned drinks cabinet and starts rooting around. 'What can I get you? Whisky, gin or... yep, I thought as much... advocaat. Mum always gets a bottle in at this time of year though no one likes it. This is probably left over from last year, to be honest.'

'Zac's driving,' I pipe up.

'What are you, his mother? Zac, what's your drink of choice?'

Zac sinks into one of Mum's squashy armchairs and clears his throat.
'I wouldn't mind something soft, actually.'

'Orange juice? There's probably some in the fridge.'

'That would be lovely, thank you.'

'You're very welcome.'

As Jasmine sashays out of the room, I perch on the arm of Zac's
chair.

'What do you think of Jasmine, then?'

He looks up at me and narrows his eyes. 'What do you mean?'

'Just what I said. What do you think of Jazz?'

'She seems nice.'

'Nice?'

'Yeah, very nice.'

'Very nice.'

Zac frowns. 'Are you going to repeat everything I say? You're being
a bit odd.'

'I am not,' I tell him. Though I definitely am.

I'm not sure why I'm behaving strangely but my head feels out of
sync. It's being at home that does it. All this harking back to a past
before life got tricky messes with my mind.

The clock ticks loudly on the mantelpiece as a strained silence
stretches between me and Zac.

'Here you go, Zac,' trills Jasmine, bursting back into the room
with a glass of orange juice in her hand. She places it on the side
table next to his chair. 'Zac, that's a good strong name. Is it short
for Zachariah?'

She is most definitely flirting.

'It's Zachary, actually, but no one ever calls me that except my mother, when I've done something wrong.'

'Tell me about it. The only place I'm ever called Rebecca is in this house.'

'Because that's your name,' says Dad, huffing into the room. He's completely bald, and has been for as long as I can remember, but thick tufts of grey hair are poking out near the buttons of his pale blue polo shirt. 'So this is your young man at last. It's about time we met him.'

'This is Zac, the friend I share a house with.'

'So not your boyfriend, then?' says Dad, upping the embarrassment a notch.

'Nope, Zac is definitely a non-boyfriend.'

'It's good to meet you, sir,' says Zac, standing up and shaking hands with Dad.

'Sir?' Dad smiles. 'I like this one, Becca. He's so much better than the last one you brought home. Charlie, was it? He was a bit of an idiot. It's just as well he ditched you.'

Zac raises his eyebrows at me in sympathy. He knows all about good-looking Charlie, who broke my heart. Jasmine flirted with him too, if I remember rightly.

'Lunch is ready,' says Mum, sticking her head around the door, looking harassed and hot. 'Come and sit down quickly or the food will get cold.'

'Thank you, my sweet,' says Dad, walking over to kiss her. But she moves before his lips can land on her cheek. Jasmine opens her eyes wide at me and hangs back as we head for the dining room.

'Told you,' she whispers, coming in close. 'There's definitely something weird going on. You're the super-sensitive one so find out what it is. I'll create a diversion.'

I'm so busy wondering what Jasmine's diversion might entail, I'm sitting at the dining table before I fully take in my surroundings. Wow! I was worried I might have over-blinged The Cosy Kettle with our Christmas decorations. But the café, and my parents' sitting room next door, are bastions of understatement compared to this room, which is a riot of colour.

Dozens of paper streamers are looped across the ceiling, the walls are dripping with fairy lights and Christmas paintings done by me and Jasmine decades ago. No surface remains un-festived.

But the tree in the corner is undecorated. Jasmine and I glance at each other again. An undecorated tree is an anathema to Mum; a wrong in the universe that needs to be righted immediately with swathes of tinsel and festive tat. But the branches of the tree are bare.

'I put up all the other decorations in the house so I left the tree for your father to decorate, but he hasn't got around to it yet,' says Mum, pulling her mouth into a tight line. 'He'd have to put all the decorations above dog height anyway or Tiny will try to eat them.'

'I've been busy, Pauline, as you well know. And I promised that we'd look after the dog until Sid got back so that's that. Anyway, don't make a fuss when we've got a guest here. Zac, you'd better serve yourself first before the gannets get going.' Dad takes a seat at the head of the table and pushes a serving dish piled high with crunchy roast potatoes towards my housemate.

We all get stuck in because Mum's a great cook. She's had lots of practice after cooking for us for years. And even Jasmine takes a break from her latest diet to polish off Mum's roast dinners.

'I've got news,' says Jasmine, taking a second helping of succulent roast lamb, sprinkled with rosemary. 'I won the new account with Chellingfords and my boss is super-pleased with me.'

'Oh, clever girl, Jasmine, that's wonderful,' says Mum, frowning at Dad as he heaps an obscene amount of potatoes onto his plate. 'We've always had every faith in you so I'm not surprised.'

'We're very proud of you,' says Dad, spooning a potato onto Jasmine's plate. 'Here, have the last potato to celebrate.'

He's never given me the last potato. But then I've never won a new account with Chellingfords. Urgh, I'm being jealous and ridiculous, and Jasmine has worked hard for her success.

'That's great, Jazz. Well done,' I say, as Zac reaches for the gravy in the porcelain gravy boat covered in painted sprigs of holly that comes out every Christmas. 'How much work will the new account be?'

'Loads because it's pretty high profile, and there might be some foreign travel involved over the next few months.'

'Fabulous! Where to?'

'Oh, you know,' Jasmine waves a hand, airily. 'Paris, Madrid, Hamburg, Milan – Chellingfords have offices all over Europe.'

'How wonderful,' says Mum, pushing the leftover food on her plate into a pile. She hasn't eaten much. 'That means you'll literally be my high-flying, globe-trotting daughter.'

With mini wish number three in mind, I was going to tell Mum and Dad about how I've blinged up The Cosy Kettle. I thought that might make them proud of me. But it all seems rather pathetic compared to Jasmine's jet-setting achievements, especially bearing in mind my two recent mess-ups, which I definitely wasn't going to mention. I shovel in a forkful of carrots and decide to stay quiet.

Jasmine stops dripping mint sauce over her meal and glances at me. 'Did I tell you I went into the café where Becca works? It's really cute, and her boss said she's doing a good job as supervisor.'

'Manager,' I murmur.

'Becca's doing a brilliant job,' says Zac, giving me a smile. He really is a lovely non-boyfriend.

'Tell me, Zac. How long have you two been living together?' asks Jasmine, using a piece of potato to mop up the gravy on her plate.

'About ten months, isn't it, Beccs? You moved in last spring.'

Jasmine gives a ladylike snort. 'Ten months? You deserve a medal, Zac, for putting up with such a messy housemate. Sharing a room with her when we were little was a nightmare. She drops everything on the floor.'

Dad laughs beside her and my heart sinks. He and Jasmine get on well and I often feel rather excluded when the two of them get together. Maybe it's because Jazz is like Dad in many ways, whereas I'm more like Mum.

'Actually,' I say, in the spirit of assertiveness. 'That was years ago and I'm not so untidy any more. And we get on really well, don't we, Zac.'

'We do. Becca's the tidiest and in fact the best woman I've ever lived with.' He nudges my leg under the table and thankfully doesn't mention that I'm the only woman he's ever lived with. His housemates at university were all huge smelly blokes who left half-eaten takeaways on the sofa and rarely changed their socks. Compared to them, I'm a total dream.

Talk turns to Christmas plans after that and before long the lunch has been demolished and we're groaning after eating too much. Once the plates have been piled into the kitchen, Jasmine suggests that Dad take Zac out into the back garden to show him his shed. Zac looks vaguely panicked as Dad takes his arm and leads him away, with Tiny following.

Jasmine and I both offer to help Mum sort out the kitchen, but Jasmine soon grabs her jacket and wanders off into the garden too.

This might be the 'diversion' she mentioned, so I'd have time alone with Mum, but I can see her laughing with Zac and flicking her head from the kitchen window, as I rinse off the dirty plates.

I'm just about to ask Mum outright what's bothering her when she speaks first.

'Zac seems like a nice sensitive young man.'

'He is,' I say, scraping crispy slivers of roast potato off the baking tray and into my mouth. 'We muddle along nicely together.'

'And Jasmine's doing so well in her new job.' Mum takes a folded tea towel from a drawer and shakes it out.

'Yes, she is. Her new contract sounds very exciting.'

'It must be stressful for her, though, being so high-powered.'

'Probably, but she seems to enjoy it.'

'She's always been ambitious and high-achieving. Even as a child, we could tell she was destined for great things.'

'Yep, that sounds like Jasmine,' I say, scraping the last bits from the baking tray into the bin and finding room for it in the dishwasher. I brace myself, knowing what's coming next.

'And what about you, Becca? What's going to become of you?' Mum's big blue eyes are full of concern. 'Your dad and I do worry and so want you to be happy.'

'You don't need to worry because I'm absolutely fine. Honestly.'

'Are you sure? We thought you were fine in Birmingham. You were doing so well in your job and we were so proud and now... well... you're working in a café in a tiny little town and not using your degree at all.'

'But I'm working hard, I love where I live, and I'm happier, Mum. That counts for something, doesn't it?'

'Of course.' Mum pats my shoulder but hanging in the air between us is the tang of disappointment, and my parents' incomprehension about what happened after university.

'Also,' I say, remembering my Christmas wish, 'my life is about to improve. I'm sure of it.'

Mum is still staring at me, biting her lip, though I'm not sure she's seeing me at all. I take the tea towel from her, lead her to a kitchen chair and gently push her onto the seat. 'OK. What's going on with you, Mum? You don't seem yourself at the moment.'

'I'm fine, just like you.'

'Really? Jasmine said she saw you crying.'

A deep crease appears between Mum's eyebrows. 'Did she? It's unfortunate she saw that, and she shouldn't have told you.'

'Of course she should have told me. I'm your daughter too.'

'I know that but I don't want to worry you both.'

'Worry us both about what? I'm definitely worried now.'

'It's nothing. Just me being silly.'

'Tell me.' I take the seat opposite her and reach across the table for her hand.

'I'm just finding work stressful at the moment.'

'Can't you change jobs?'

'What, at my time of life? It's not so easy to switch jobs when you get to my age. I've worked in the admin department at Shelleys for ages and that's where I'll stay.'

'But isn't there anything you can do to make your life a bit more…' I look around the kitchen where Mum spends most of her life when she's not working. 'I don't know… fun?'

'I'd love to. Actually, there's a…' She pauses.

'A what?'

'You'll think I'm being silly.'

'I honestly won't. Just tell me.'

Mum takes a deep breath to steady herself. 'There's an art course at the local university that's open to mature students and I'd love to do it. The course is part-time and I've got some money left to me by your gran that would cover the cost.'

'Then do it. You've got real artistic talent, Mum. Have you applied for the course?'

'I applied last week, on a whim. But it's pointless. I won't get in and, even if I did, it's two full days per week so it's out of the question.'

'Can't you go part-time at work?'

'They'd probably go for it because they're trying to cut costs at the moment. But your dad isn't keen. He said it was a pipe dream when I told him about the course, and pipe dreams don't pay the bills. He'd go mad if he knew I'd even applied.'

'But it's your dream, Mum.'

'And a daft one, so that's that.' She stands up and plasters a no-nonsense smile onto her face. 'Pass me those dirty dishes, Becca, and I'll find room for them. Tell me how things are going in your little café.'

Little café? I sigh quietly. 'It's good, thanks, Mum. Everything's fine in my little café.'

Zac suddenly bustles in through the back door, swiftly followed by Jasmine and Dad. Jazz is looking flushed and gorgeous with her scarf wrapped around her head.

'It's freezing out there,' she says, giving a tinkly laugh. 'We almost had to huddle together for warmth, didn't we, Zac?'

'It was a bit chilly.' Zac's nose is bright red with the cold. He glances between me and Mum. 'Is everything all right in here? Do you need some help?'

He grabs another tea towel but Mum shoos him away.

'I won't hear of it. You're a guest. I hope you enjoyed your lunch.'

'I did. It was the best roast meal I've had in ages. Thank you so much, Pauline.'

Mum beams while Jazz stands behind her and opens her eyes wide at me. I give a slight nod to let her know that the deed has been done, and a discreet thumbs-up to indicate that Mum doesn't have some terrible illness. But I'm still worried about her and annoyed with Dad for being so negative when all she wants is to do something fun. She needs to stand up for herself – but I know that's easier said than done.

We all retire to the sitting room where Jasmine plonks herself next to Zac on the sofa and starts chatting away about her job. Mum and Dad listen with proud smiles on their faces while I sit quietly in the corner, mentally going through my Christmas wish list. There's a lot to be done – this visit home has only underlined that fact – but what's the alternative? Watch shyly from the sidelines while Jasmine makes a success of her life, until we're both old and wrinkled? Actually I can't imagine my sister with wrinkles – no doubt she'll age beautifully and I'll end up with a face like a road map.

I pull my shoulders back and take a deep breath. Reinventing myself will be hard work but it's worth putting in the effort now. Then I can spend the rest of my life being more confident, more assertive, more content... more like Jasmine. As if she can read my mind, my sister clutches at Zac's arm, throws back her head and laughs.

*

'What did you think of my family, then?' I ask Zac we pull away from the house.

Mum is waving from the front door, surrounded by winking fairy lights.

'They're really nice people,' he says, turning right very slowly at the end of the street. The road surface is getting icy as afternoon turns to evening and the temperature drops even further.

'Nice is such a fudgy kind of word.'

Zac glances at me and grins.

'OK, your Mum is lovely and a bit nervy, just like you, and your dad's a character. He's quite forceful and a bit bossy to your mum but he was very friendly to me. I think he was just relieved that I wasn't Cheating Charlie.'

'Yeah, he and Charlie were equally bossy and almost came to blows once.' I hesitate. 'And what about Jasmine?'

'She was very friendly too.'

'And?'

'And what?'

He curses under his breath at a motorist who pulls out of a junction and cuts in front of us.

'And, did you like her?'

'Of course. She's a bit scary but I liked her very much.'

'What did you like about her?'

'What do you mean?' he asks, keeping his eyes on the road.

'Did you like her… general goldenness?'

When Zac snorts, the car swerves slightly. 'Her what?'

'General goldenness. You must have noticed it.'

'I did indeed notice that her colouring is very different from yours. She doesn't have green eyes and Smurf-blue hair for a start.'

'And?'

Zac signals left as we reach a T-junction before pulling out slowly. 'And… blonde hair really suits her.'

Hmm. Is that bloke code for 'I fancied the pants off her'? And if he does, what of it? She obviously liked him and, if they end up getting married, he'll be a member of our family and therefore a part of my life forever. That would be good, wouldn't it?

I give my head a shake. I think I'm rather getting ahead of myself here. And who knows what Jasmine thinks of Zac? She does tend to flirt with any bloke who's not hideous. And Zac is definitely not hideous.

I steal a glance at him as we drive away from the urban sprawl, back towards the Cotswold Hills, which are dark shapes on the horizon. He's got a gentle face and smashing eyes and his hair is thick and floppy, and his new glasses really do suit him.

But he's not a huge high-flyer, so ambitious Jasmine won't be interested in him.

I settle back in my seat, close my eyes and let the gentle thrum of the engine lull me to sleep.

Chapter Eight

My mobile rings early next morning while I'm rushing round, getting ready for work.

'Hi, Jazz,' I mumble, toothbrush still in my mouth. 'Bit busy at the moment. Can I call you back?'

'No need,' says Jasmine, crisply, down the line. 'I was just ringing up to see how you thought lunch went yesterday.'

'Pretty well, considering,' I say, before rinsing my mouth with water and quietly spitting into the basin.

'You spoke to Mum about her being weird, then.'

'I did a bit, while we were in the kitchen. She wants to do an art course at the local uni but it would mean cutting down her work days and Dad's not keen.'

'Is that all?' Jasmine breathes a sigh of relief. 'Honestly, she had me thinking that she might be ill or something.'

'She's frustrated and sad.'

'Yeah, but she'll soon cheer up. It's Christmas.' Jasmine lowers her voice. 'Your housemate is hot, by the way.'

I hesitate, before wiping smears of toothpaste from the corners of my mouth.

'Do you think so?'

'Absolutely. He's a bit of a nerd but there's something very attractive about him that I can't quite put my finger on.'

'He's kind.'

'Nah, it's not that. I don't know. He's just rather… appealing. He's got a very nice face, and he's tall, and he *did* look good in those jeans.'

'Did he?' I didn't really notice, though it's struck me a few times recently that Zac's getting more good-looking the older he gets. He's kind of growing into his body as all traces of the gangly adolescent disappear.

There's a pause, then Jasmine asks: 'Are you sure there's nothing going on between you?'

'Between me and Zac?' I laugh. 'No, we're just friends.'

'So you wouldn't mind if I asked him to come with me to my work's do just before Christmas? It's a plus-one event, which is a pain 'cos I'm between boyfriends at the moment, and I don't want to rock up on my own like a saddo, when I'm so new to the company. Zac was asking me about PR yesterday so I thought he might like to come along. But I don't want to tread on your toes.'

'Of course you wouldn't be treading on my toes,' I say, feeling slightly sick. 'We're just housemates and good friends.'

'That's cool, then. I know where he works so I'll email him there. I'm feeling very go-for-it now I'm in this new job. Actually, I'm in the office at the moment, working on a new proposal for Claire, my boss. Are you at work, too?'

'Oh, yeah,' I lie, closing the bathroom door so Jasmine won't hear Zac swearing. He must have hit his head on a beam. Again. You'd think he'd have learned to duck after living here for months. 'I had to get in early to…' Oh dear, I haven't thought this through. '… prioritise the confectionery orders and go over my business plan for the Cosy Kettle Christmas… um, extravaganza.'

Does that sound like utter rubbish? Jasmine seems to swallow it.

'Cool. Well, you sound busy so I'd better leave you to it. Have fun.'

She rings off as I hear Zac call up the stairs: 'Bye, Beccs. Knock 'em dead today.'

And then the front door bangs.

I'm not sure how I feel about my sister having the hots for my housemate. I'd convinced myself she was auto-flirting yesterday because she can't help herself. But if she really does like Zac, what if they hit it off and she starts staying over? What if she starts wafting round looking all ethereal in a negligee and I can hear them getting amorous through the wall? How awkward would that be?

I'm so distracted on my walk to work, I hardly notice Dick when he yells hello at me from his sports car. And I stride beneath the yellow stone arches of Honeyford's market house without imagining all the people who have walked there before me over the centuries.

I don't even glance up at the crooked roofs of the buildings in Honeyford High Street, or the rolling hills above the town that are often dusted with white these days as the temperature plummets. But then a thought strikes me and I breathe a sigh of relief. Zac is bound to turn down my sister's invitation. He mentioned that he was a bit scared of Jazz so there's no way he'll go on a kind of date with her. He'll definitely cry off.

Feeling reassured that life isn't about to get super-weird, I say good morning to Flora and start opening up The Cosy Kettle for another busy festive day. Switching on the Christmas tree lights is one of my favourite things and their glow floods into every corner of the café.

It's so busy all morning, I'm run off my feet and hardly notice when Logan and another man come into the café just before lunchtime.

Logan takes a seat beneath the shelf of copper kettles that give the café its name, while his companion comes to the counter and places their orders. He doesn't wait for their coffees, so I take a deep breath and wander over with their cappuccinos and two slices of cranberry cheesecake.

'Thanks, um… Becca,' says Logan. He remembered my name! 'No Jasmine today, then?' And my sister's name, too. Of course.

'Not today,' I tell him, willing myself not to blush, which makes my cheeks redden immediately. 'It's just me today.'

'That's great.'

Logan doesn't look like he thinks it's great. He doesn't look happy at all. He's frowning so hard there's a furrow between his eyebrows, and he's sighing. Manly little sighs that blow the froth on his coffee into tiny peaks.

I take a cloth from my apron pocket and start wiping the next table. I'm not listening in. Not really. But I can't help overhearing when Logan slumps back in his chair and says: 'So, basically, Stu, I'm royally screwed.'

'It'll be all right, mate,' says Stu, forking in a mouthful of rich, creamy cheesecake. 'Your boss will understand,' he mumbles.

'He won't. I was supposed to organise the Christmas party ages ago but never got round to it and now everywhere local is booked up. Colin's VIP French clients have saved the date but they'll be partying in a freezing cold field at this rate. I'm so screwed I even contemplated hiring Honeyford Community Centre but the roof's sprung another leak so it's out of action for the foreseeable. Bloody typical.'

'Can't you just explain to Colin what's happened?'

'If I do, he'll go mad, say I'm disorganised, and *poof!* There go my promotion prospects. I want to impress him, not upset him. It's a nightmare, man.'

He prods his finger into his cheesecake, and pouts. He looks particularly lovely when he pouts – all mean and moody.

Local butcher Vernon has come in for his Belgian bun and a drink, so I head back to the counter to serve him. But I keep an eye on Logan and his friend through curls of steam while Vernon's milk is frothing. Logan is sitting staring into his coffee, his body language screaming defeat.

An idea starts forming in my brain. A mutually beneficial idea which, as well as helping Logan, could be a big step towards making my Christmas wish come true. *Be more assertive and confident, particularly as regards café?* Tick. *Impress Flora with business acumen?* Tick. *Secure date with Logan?* Hmm, I doubt it, but at least I'd get to spend more time with him, and secure more custom for The Cosy Kettle. I might even impress my parents so much they'd look at me like they looked at Jasmine yesterday, when she told them about her achievements at work. But do I have the nerve to carry it through?

'How's the coffee coming along?' calls Vernon, as I stare into space.

'Oops, sorry. I was miles away.'

After I've handed over Vernon's coffee and bun, I sit with my elbows on the counter and my chin in my hands, gazing at Logan. He's still pouting, like a handsome grumpy prince in need of rescuing by a fabulously assertive princess who wants to impress *her* own boss.

I slide off my stool, smooth down my sapphire-blue hair and start walking towards Logan and Stu. This is going to take some chutzpah – which is something I'm not sure I possess – but, whatever. I'm going in.

Both men look up as I get to their table and stand over them. I swallow hard and put my hands on my hips. 'Excuse me for butting in but I overheard what you were saying a while back. I'm sorry. I honestly wasn't listening in.' Aargh, I've started apologising horribly unassertively already. I pause for a moment before continuing. 'What I want to say is, what about holding your party in here?'

'In here?' repeats Stu, his lip curling in the corner.

'Yes, in here. We could host a Christmas party for you in The Cosy Kettle if that would help you out.'

'It's certainly festive in here,' says Logan, looking around him at the lights and the tinsel and the paper garlands. 'But it's not big enough.'

'There's the garden too.'

'What, just before Christmas?' laughs Stu. 'Logan's boss doesn't want his important French guests freezing in a snowy garden in December.'

'Of course not, but we can hire outdoor heaters and transform the garden into a cosy enchanted winter wonderland,' I say, thinking on my feet. 'With hot punch and fairy lights and a Father Christmas and carols.'

'Father Christmas?' Logan gives Stu a look I can't interpret. 'Who would be Father Christmas?'

'I have someone in mind,' I say, crossing my fingers that Dick might be up for it. He looks like Santa already with his long white beard. He might as well milk the resemblance.

'And what about the drinks and canapés?' asks Stu, dabbing at the cheesecake crumbs on his plate before licking his fingers.

'We could provide hot chocolate and gingerbread lattes, as well as the punch, and I can ask our baker to rustle up bite-sized Christmas-themed cakes. Everyone loves miniature stuff. Especially the French.'

I have no idea if John, our local baker, can do bite-size, or if the French are particularly partial to small things, but nothing can hold me back. I feel powerful and in charge and ready to tick a few wishes off my list. Securing a date with Logan is definitely a stretch. But we'll have to work together closely on party arrangements and I can dazzle him with the magnificent makeover of my personality and appearance that's about to happen any time soon. All I need to do is keep Jasmine out of the picture.

'What about the cost?' asks Logan, staring at my face as though seeing me for the very first time.

'We can sort that out,' I say, airily. 'Let me know your budget and I'm sure I can make it work.'

'The party's for thirty-five of our most important clients. Can you cope with that many people?'

'Of course,' I say, trying to push down the anxious feelings that are bubbling up.

We had about thirty people in here during the Honeyford Bake-Off, back in the summer, and that felt pretty cramped.

'It's really important that this party is a success and enjoyed by our guests from France. My company's a major distributer of repair parts for corporate printers and is expanding massively into the French market.'

'Gosh, that's impressive,' I lie, because schmoozing a potential client seems important right now.

'And I also need to make a *very* good impression on my boss.'

'I know the feeling, and it's not a problem. Everything will run like clockwork.'

'Don't you need to check it out with *your* boss first?' asks Stu, pursing his narrow lips.

'No. It'll be fine. I manage the café and the events that are held in here. When it comes to The Cosy Kettle, I'm in charge.'

I say 'events' as though we're a regular party venue, even though all we've ever hosted is the Bake-Off, the book club and a few coffee mornings. But it's weird – I feel like I'm having an out of body experience. A new, improved Becca has taken over and is asserting herself big-time. Logan certainly looks impressed.

'It just might work,' he says, his face shining in reflected light from the Christmas tree. 'Becca, you're an absolute life-saver! This place is cosy and festive and the coffee and cakes are great. Are you OK with us working together on the arrangements?'

'Absolutely, Logan,' I say, as though I'm as confident a business-woman as my twin sister. 'Together, we'll make a great team.'

A wide, pearly-white smile spreads across Logan's lovely face. 'Why don't you take a seat and I'll talk you through what I have in mind.'

'Of course. We can seal the deal.'

I pull up a chair, imagine how Flora would handle it, and start negotiating the terms of the event.

My confidence lasts until Logan and Stu have polished off their coffee and cake. But the minute they disappear out of the café door, new, improved Becca does a runner.

What the hell have I done? Outdoor heaters? Dick dressed up as Santa? Bite-sized Christmas cupcakes? When it all goes tits-up, Logan will blame me. And what on earth will Flora say? It's all very well channelling my boss but I still need her actual permission.

Flora stops rearranging a display of women's fiction bestsellers and stares at me. She's kneeling on the floor, with books piled up either side of her.

'You did what?' she asks, sitting back on her kitten heels.

'I made an executive decision and told Logan Fairweather that we could host his firm's Christmas party in The Cosy Kettle, from seven o'clock on December the twentieth.'

'Is that a Friday?'

'Yes. That was the date he specified and the café's always closed by five on Fridays so that'll work fine. It'll mean catering for up to thirty-five guests.'

'Wow!' Flora lets out a low whistle. 'Is The Cosy Kettle big enough for that many people?'

'I said we could get some outdoor heaters so guests could spill into the garden. And—' I take a deep breath. 'I kind of promised that the garden would be transformed into an enchanted winter wonderland.'

Flora hesitates for a moment, a look of surprise on her face, before bursting into peals of laughter.

'Golly, Becca! You're really coming into your own at last.'

'You don't mind then?'

'Of course not. So close to Christmas isn't ideal and it'll involve a lot of work, but it sounds like a good business decision to me, as long as you ensure that we're making a decent profit.'

'I will, definitely. So are you OK with it?'

Flora nods. 'More than OK. You acted swiftly and instinctively to benefit the business. That's great, Becca. Well done. I'm impressed.'

Yay! I mentally give wish number two, *Impress Flora with business acumen,* a half-tick. I need to pull off the party and make it a great success before that wish gets a full tick.

'Well done about what?' asks Millicent, who's just come into the shop, pushing Phyllis in her wheelchair.

'Becca has just secured a prestigious event to be held in The Cosy Kettle.'

'Is that part of your wish list, Becca?' pipes up Phyllis.

'What wish list?' Flora looks puzzled.

'Nothing,' I tell her, quickly, because she thinks I'm weird enough already. 'Come on, Phyllis. Let me push you through to the café.'

As I'm getting Phyllis and Millicent settled with drinks, Stanley, Dick and Mary also troop in. Mary has Callum strapped to her chest in a sling and he's fast asleep and dribbling.

'What are you lot doing here? It's not book club day.'

'This is our inaugural planning meeting regarding your transformation,' declares Stanley. 'We're gonna make you hip, Beccs. Help you to take control of your life, achieve your potential and become your best self, like I did.'

'We've got lots of ideas,' says Mary, stifling a yawn. Callum is teething and she doesn't get much sleep these days.

'What sort of ideas?' I ask, nervously.

'Ideas like me taking you shopping for some new clothes to suit your brand new personality and lifestyle. I didn't always dress like this,' she says, running a hand down her sloppy green sweatshirt and jeans. 'I used to dress really well for work but then I had a baby and, like many new mums, had to abandon my career hopes and dreams.' She pauses. 'Do I sound bitter?'

'Only a little bit, love,' says Phyllis, soothingly, patting her hand.

'What was it you used to do, Mary, before you had Callum?' asks Dick.

'I ran a city make-up store.'

'Coolio,' says Stanley, high-fiving Mary.

'I can't be arsed to put make-up on these days. But I can give you a makeover, Becca. No problem. You've got cheekbones to die for, and your green eyes are absolutely beautiful. Or they would be if you drew attention to them.'

She leans forward and peers at my face, as though she's studying a painting.

'I know you can't work miracles, but could you make me look a bit more… polished?'

'Polished, sophisticated and gorgeous.'

I grin, liking the sound of that.

'Becca's already taken a step towards her more assertive self by arranging to have a party here, in the café,' butts in Millicent.

'It's going to be a Christmas party for Logan Fairweather's company, and the garden is going to be transformed into a winter wonderland. There's going to be a Father Christmas and I was wondering…'

I trail off and stare at Dick. Is this a good idea?

'What?' asks Dick.

'I was wondering if you might agree to dress up and be Father Christmas on the night?'

'Why me?' asks Dick, running his fingers through his long white beard.

''Cos you look like him, you daft bugger,' says Stanley. 'Like a very tall, elderly Santa.'

'With a sports car,' says Dick, whose ancient green sports car is the love of his life.

'Yep, a Santa on wheels. And I can be an elf.'

'An elf?' I squeak.

'Absolutely.' Stanley pats my hand. 'We're here for you, Becca, to help make this event the best party ever. And I'm willing to dress up as an elf for the occasion. Anything to support you and The Cosy Kettle.' Oh my. I'm not sure Stanley in full elf get-up will enhance the vibe I'm going for, but it's kind of him to offer. 'Anyway, we'll hold our meeting and will report back our findings ASAP.'

There doesn't seem to be much point in arguing so I carry on serving customers in the café, glancing nervously at the book club. They sit in a little huddle for an hour, staring at me occasionally, with Millicent making notes in her Liberty print notebook.

I feel like an animal in a zoo.

Zac is laughing so much, flour has gone up his nose and now he's started sneezing.

'It's not funny,' I tell him, as he sneezes three times in quick succession.

'Oh, I think it is,' says Zac, wiping tears from his eyes. 'The Famous Five had an inaugural committee meeting about turning you into an uber-confident supermodel. That's priceless. You know what inaugural means, don't you? There are going to be more committee meetings. Many more. And you're going to need them.'

He snorts as I shake my rolling pin at him and bits of uncooked pastry go flying. I'm making Zac some mince pies as a treat, because he loves them. But they're not quite going to plan. The pastry has gone all flaky and keeps cracking as it's rolled.

'Also,' I tell Zac, pushing the pastry together with my fingers. 'Dick has said he'll be Father Christmas at Logan's party, but now Stanley is insisting on being an elf. I bet he'll wear a pointy hat and everything.'

'Stop it!' Zac is bent double with his arms across his stomach. 'All this laughing is making me hurt. Oh, boy! I can just imagine Stanley all dressed in green with elf shoes on. You know, the ones that roll up at the end.'

He starts roaring with laughter again, pain etched across his face.

'Take it seriously or I won't make you any mince pies. I could have brought some home from work but instead I'm going to the not inconsiderable effort of making them myself.'

'And I'm very grateful,' says Zac, composing himself and poking at the pallid pastry with his finger. 'I'm sure they'll be very nice, as always.'

Ignoring his obvious sarcasm, I start cutting out pastry shells and placing them in the baking tray. Why are bits still flaking off?

Zac is heading out of the kitchen but pauses by the door and looks back, suddenly serious.

'Did I mention that I got an email today from Jasmine?'

'No, you didn't.' I wipe flour from my cheek with the back of my hand and start spooning fruity mincemeat into the rubbish pastry cases. 'What did she want?'

'She asked me to go with her to her work's party before Christmas. I was quite surprised to hear from her but she said her date had cancelled and she knows I'm interested in PR, so she wondered if I'd like to go along instead.'

'Like second best,' I say, and then wish I hadn't. Zac's face clouds over.

'I suppose so. But it was nice of her to ask me.'

'It was very nice. And Jasmine doesn't do second best. It's a shame that it's not really your thing.'

'Parties? Not usually. But maybe, like you, I ought to shake things up a bit and do something new – put some zing into Zac.'

Is he seriously considering going on a kind of date with my sister? A dollop of mincemeat splodges onto the worktop because I'm not concentrating.

'What do you think about me going with Jasmine?' asks Zac, not catching my eye. 'Would you mind?'

Of course I'd mind. It's weird and… inappropriate. Though I'm not sure why because Zac and I share a house. That's all. But I can hardly say 'No, don't go,' for no good reason, can I? He's a grown man who can do what he likes. I mop up the spilled mincemeat with kitchen roll and plaster on a smile.

'Why should I mind?'

'I just thought maybe 'cos it's Jasmine…' He shrugs his broad shoulders.

'I don't mind at all. In fact, you're right. You should get out there and do new stuff. Like what I'm doing with Logan's party.'

'Ah, yes. Lovely Logan.' Zac sucks his lower lip between his teeth for a moment. 'I think I will go to Jasmine's party. I'll give her a ring and tell her it's on.'

'She'll be delighted,' I call after him, slamming a spoonful of mincemeat so hard into a case, candied peel sprays everywhere.

I'm being ridiculous, I tell myself, once the pies are in the oven and I'm sitting in front of the fire with my feet up. Jazz fancies lots of men and she's not settled down with a single one of them yet. I'm leaping ahead. It'll be one date that will probably go really badly. And even if it doesn't, I want Zac to be happy, don't I? And Jasmine too. It's a bit hypocritical of me to deny them that when I'm doing my very best to secure a date with Logan Fairweather.

In fact, the only problem I can foresee is that if Jasmine hurts kind, trusting Zac, I'll have to kill her – and Mum would never forgive me. I'm so busy trying to make everything OK in my head, I don't realise the mince pies are well and truly cooked until the smoke alarm starts screeching.

Chapter Nine

It's two days later, Logan is coming into The Cosy Kettle any minute for a party planning meeting, and I can't keep still. It's late afternoon and the café is quiet so I'm pacing up and down in the shop. This is the fourth time I've walked back and forth past Flora, who's sorting through customers' orders that have just been delivered.

She looks up from the large pile of paperback and hardback novels. Books are a pretty safe Christmas present and people are starting to panic-buy. I should be panic-buying because we're into December and I haven't bought a single present yet.

'Are you all right, Becca?'

'Yes, thanks. I'm just waiting for Logan so we can sort out his party.'

'That Logan is rather good-looking, isn't he?'

Don't blush! Don't blush!

'Yeah, not bad, I suppose.'

Flora's beautiful violet eyes twinkle when she grins. 'You look rather nice today.'

'Thanks.' I grin, ridiculously pleased with the compliment from Flora, who looks fabulous all the time. I wouldn't wear what she does – fitted dresses in bright colours, smart chinos and silk blouses. I could never carry them off. But my boss always looks a picture of sophistication.

My clothes are far less smart, but I've made an effort today and am wearing my best jeans and a long-sleeved top that I bought ages ago and then shoved into the back of my wardrobe. It's fuchsia pink which is a colour Jasmine often wears, and it seems extra bright against my sapphire hair, but my complexion looks less wan than usual. It probably helps that I've also toned down my trademark black eyeliner and put blusher on my pale cheeks.

Flora peers out of the window into the darkness. 'I think that might be Logan coming now, along the High Street. I can see his blond hair shining under the street lights.'

'OK, thanks.' I scurry through into the café which is gorgeous at this time of the day. The last customer has left and the whole place smells of pine needles as I hit the switch and the Christmas lights flicker back on.

I open the back door and poke my head into the garden, to make sure no customers are loitering, and shiver because the temperature has dropped again. The weather app on my phone says snow is coming – more than the sprinkling we've had so far – and it certainly feels cold enough for it.

But here in the café it's cosy and warm. Lights are glinting off the strands of tinsel and the tree lights are shining in the corner. I lock the back door and feel a wave of pride rush through me. I helped Flora do this. Together, we've transformed a storeroom into this wonderful welcoming place.

'Becca?'

He's here. I take a deep breath, plaster on what I hope looks like a confident smile, and start channelling wish number one from my list. Assertiveness and confidence. That's what's needed right now.

Logan is standing in the café doorway wearing a navy double-breasted peacoat and carrying a sheaf of papers. He strides in and hesitates a moment before kissing me on the cheek. Hell's bells. There goes my vow not to blush in his presence. I really am pathetic! My cheeks start burning as he takes a seat at one of the tables and beckons for me to sit opposite him.

'Busy day?' he asks, glancing around the café.

I take another deep breath and pretend that I'm at home, all relaxed and talking to Zac.

'It's been manic. Everyone's after a coffee to warm up because it's so cold out there. And lots of cake to replace all the calories they've used up Christmas shopping.'

Phew, that came out OK. Channelling my relationship with Zac is obviously the way forward.

'Urgh.' Logan shudders. 'Christmas shopping is the pits. I leave all that kind of stuff to my assistant.'

'You have an assistant?'

'Ha, I wish.' He winks. 'I mean my mum. She sorts out presents from me for all the family.'

'Gosh, she sounds useful.'

'She is.' Logan grins, spreading his papers across the table as I wish my mum could sort out my gift dilemmas. Though Logan is a bit old still to be relying so much on his mother.

'So tell me how the planning's going,' says Logan, sitting back in his chair, folding his arms and looking at me. His blue eyes are crinkled in the corners as though he's amused.

'Well,' I gulp, suddenly feeling out of my depth. 'I've sourced some outside heaters to hire for the garden and I've had a word with our baker, who's happy to provide the food.'

'Hmm.' Logan leans forward, frowning slightly.

'Is there a problem with that?'

'I just wonder if a local baker is up to the job, really? I've had a bit of a rethink about the party and I'm considering hiring a chef I know to sort out the food.'

'OK, if that's what you want, but the cakes here are fabulous.'

'I know but they're not very… sophisticated. After having a chat with my boss about the calibre of guest we're expecting, I've decided that we should be going for a sophisticated vibe. That's what our French clients will be expecting. A particular blend of festive fusion: sophistication melding with tradition.'

'Festively cosy' was the vibe I had in mind but 'sophisticated festive fusion' works too. I push a vision of Stanley in full elf get-up out of my head. And maybe Dick's Father Christmas will have to go too. That might be seen as a bit naff by Logan's fancy French guests.

'Anyway, these are the people who need to be invited.' Logan pushes two sheets of paper across the table. They're covered in lists of names and email addresses. 'We're all so busy at work, it would be great if you could send out the invitations and keep a tally of who's coming and who isn't. And this is all a bit last minute so they'll need to go out as soon as possible. My boss asked them all a while ago to save the date, but they need to receive a formal invitation via email. Would that be OK?'

'Of course.'

'When you've designed the invitations, could you run them by me before they go out? I need to make sure they have the right kind of feel.'

'What kind of feel are you after?'

'You know… classy, upmarket, not very café-ish, that kind of thing.'

'OK,' I say slowly. 'Though this is a café.'

'Absolutely. But it's going to be transformed on the day, isn't it? For example, it would be great if we could tone down the decorations a bit, and perhaps replace a fair few of them. They're lovely for day-to-day customers but maybe not for our clientele.' He taps his finger against his lips. 'Oh, and we're going to need some music.'

'If you let me know what sort of background music you want, I can make the right kind of playlist on the speakers.'

'Oh, we don't want a playlist!' says Logan, his generous mouth curling into a smile.

'Don't we?'

'Definitely not.'

'What about some carols in the garden from Honeyford's community choir? I can make some enquiries and see if they'll sing for us. That would be lovely and Christmassy.'

Logan grimaces. 'I was thinking more along the lines of live music from professionals, such as these.' He pushes another sheet of paper towards me, this one bearing a photo of four middle-aged people in Elizabethan clothes. 'They sing a range of musical styles – from madrigals to excerpts from opera classics.'

'Madrigals?'

'Yeah, you know,' he says, waving his arm dismissively, 'songs from ages ago.' I get the feeling that Logan isn't quite sure what madrigals are either. 'Anyway, this lot are rather more upmarket than your average carol singers. Maybe you could see if they'd be free on the night? Do you have any other ideas?'

He watches me while I scan down the list of ideas I'd jotted down before he arrived. I'm a bit loath to share them now. I have a horrible feeling that he'll consider serving punch to his guests – assuming I can get a temporary drinks licence – far too plebeian. He'll probably insist on champagne. And as for having a lucky dip of gifts from Dick's Santa… I pick up my pen and score a thick blue line through that idea.

Logan suddenly glances at his watch, grabs his coat from the back of his chair and starts shoving his arms into it.

'Sorry, Becca. I didn't realise how late it is and I've got to be somewhere else in half an hour. Why don't you send me your ideas? Here you go – that's my private email.' He scrawls his address on the back of the guest list. 'I love your top, by the way – that colour really suits you.' Leaning forward, he peers at me more closely. 'And I've just noticed that you have the most amazing cheekbones.'

Logan Fairweather thinks I have amazing cheekbones! I suck my cheeks in as he gives me a wave and rushes off. He's almost reached the café door when he looks back and adds, nonchalantly: 'Do feel free to invite Jasmine to the party if she'd like to come along. She had a touch of French chic about her so I'm sure she'd fit in with my VIP guests.'

I stop sucking and sigh quietly. 'I could ask Jasmine but she's usually out with one of her boyfriends.'

Great! Not only have I invented a romantic partner for Jasmine in a rather pathetic attempt to put Logan off, I've made it romantic partners plural.

'In that case, never mind.' Logan hesitates. 'Thanks for coming to my rescue, Becca. I'm really excited about the party – it's going to blow everyone away.'

I nod and smile because blowing everyone away with my party planning skills is exactly what I have in mind. Though Logan has quite grand ideas for a small community café.

Anxiety starts gnawing at the pit of my stomach as Logan disappears into the gloomy bookshop, but I'm going to make this work. I have to if I'm serious about making my Christmas wish come true. Pull off the perfect party and my parents will be proud of what I've achieved for a host of fancy French guests; Logan will be delighted, and The Cosy

Kettle will benefit. Plus, I'll get a much-needed confidence boost – and possibly even a date, now Logan thinks Jasmine is already taken.

Should I be making up stuff about my sister? I wonder, as my conscience starts prickling. Nah, it's fine – she has her pick of eligible men. So it's win-win all round.

Chapter Ten

By the time I get home, it's started spitting with rain – so much for the snow forecast – and I'm damp, chilly and agitated.

The meeting with Logan didn't go exactly to plan, I've spent the last hour trying to work out how to make The Cosy Kettle more sophisticated, and my confidence is draining away. At least a chat with Zac will cheer me up. I've got a slice of Christmas pudding wrapped up in my handbag for him, seeing as my home-made mince pies were a culinary disaster. He ate the least burned ones but I'm pretty sure that was only for my benefit.

He's a very kind man, I think, putting my key in the lock. And the only person who really 'gets' the authentic, unimproved me. It suddenly strikes me that, in many ways, he'd be my perfect partner, but it's just as well we don't fancy each other. Sexual attraction, particularly if it was one-sided, could wreck our friendship that means so much to me.

Murmured voices are coming from the kitchen when I step into our tiny sitting room and close the front door behind me. It sounds like the radio's on until I get closer and recognise Zac's deep voice. Then I hear a woman talking, and tinkly laughter that sounds a lot like Jasmine.

I hurry into the kitchen and stop dead. Zac is spooning coffee into two mugs and Jasmine is standing very close to him, reaching into the cupboard above the worktop. Seeing her here, unexpectedly, makes me feel slightly disorientated, as though two separate worlds are colliding.

'Hello. What are you doing here, Jazz?'

She spins around, almost dropping the tea plates she's holding.

'Becca, you've got to stop creeping up on people like that. You're going to give someone a heart attack.'

'I didn't realise you were calling round.'

Zac starts pouring water into the mugs and doesn't catch my eye.

'I was passing and thought I'd call in to give you that.' She points at my grey jumper which is draped over a kitchen chair. 'You left it at Mum and Dad's on Sunday so I thought I'd drop it in for you.'

'That's kind but there was no need. I could have picked it up the next time I was round at theirs.'

'It was no problem. Anyway, I wanted to sort out a few arrangements for Friday with Zac.'

'Friday?'

'That's when we're going to my work do together. It's black tie, Zac. Is that OK?'

'Yeah, of course,' says Zac, though I'm not sure he owns a decent suit.

'Plus, I wanted to see where you're living now, Becca, seeing as you've been here for ages.'

She says it as though she's never been invited, even though I issued an open invitation when I moved in months ago. But I always end up going round to her modern, minimalist flat on the outskirts of Oxford.

'Perhaps you could show me around your cute little cottage, Zac,' says Jasmine, giving him her best angelic smile.

'Why don't I give you a tour while Zac's making you a coffee? We can start in the sitting room.'

Before Jasmine can protest, I link my arm through hers and guide her out of the kitchen.

'This is the very functional passageway that leads to the kitchen. And this is the sitting room which you'd have already seen when you came in.'

'Yeah, it's very old. I like the wood on the walls.' Jasmine points at the carved oak panelling that covers the wall behind the sofa. 'It looks a bit like a museum in here. Don't you find it a bit...?' She wrinkles her nose.

'A bit what?'

'Spooky.' Jasmine blows air through her cherry-red lips and wraps her arms around her waist. She's wearing a long black skirt and a fluffy blue angora jumper. Next to the pale, soft wool her face looks luminous, like a model in one of Flora's fashion magazines.

'I've never been spooked here. It's a happy house – a bit draughty and creaky, but that's all. If you think downstairs is spooky, upstairs will really freak you out. Follow me.'

She follows without a word up the narrow wooden staircase and along the landing with its old uneven floorboards. The dim light swinging from the beamed ceiling casts moving shadows and Jasmine shudders.

'This is where I sleep,' I say, flinging open my door and wincing because the room is a mess. I quickly make the bed and pick my dressing gown up off the floor.

'This is nice.' Jasmine wanders over to the window and looks out into Weavers Lane. 'And you've got a good view. You can see right across the park and down to the river. But I bet it gets really cold with no double glazing.'

'A bit chilly but the walls are pretty thick so it's not been too bad so far. We'll see what it's like when we get snow.'

'Let's see the rest then.'

Jasmine follows me out of my room and into our small bathroom with its enamelled tub and old-fashioned basin. It's nothing special, and the shower over the bath is ancient, but it's functional and clean.

'This is fine,' she says, running her fingers across Zac's shaving cream on the shelf. She picks up his deodorant, takes off the top and gives it a sniff. 'You couldn't swing a cat in here, but the bath looks nice and deep. So what else is on this floor?'

She wanders onto the landing and nods at the only other door. 'What's in there?'

'That's Zac's room.'

'Let's have a look, then.'

Before I can say anything, Jasmine has opened his door and gone in. I follow behind, feeling faintly uneasy. This is Zac's space and I tend to keep out of it. It's such a small cottage, it's become a kind of unwritten rule that our bedrooms are off limits.

'Well, I say. This is very macho.' Jasmine sits on Zac's bed and looks around the room. It's much tidier than mine and more bare, with no prints on the walls. His duvet cover is white with grey stripes, and there's an open book on his pillow – a thriller by Robert Harris.

'Good heavens, what's this?' asks Jazz, pulling her hand out from under the duvet cover and holding up a pair of blue checked pyjama shorts.

'Stop it, Jazz. Put them back.'

'Have you seen Zac wearing these?' she teases.

I have actually because I occasionally bump into him on the landing, early in the morning. Though I'm always too half-asleep to take much notice.

'Well, have you?' she asks, waving them at me.

'Of course not.'

'Shame.'

'Please put them back and let's go downstairs. Your coffee will be getting cold.'

'If you insist, spoilsport. I was just about to root through his knicker drawer.'

Jasmine shoves the shorts back under the duvet, with a grin, and gets up off Zac's bed. She's almost reached the door when I push it closed and stand, arms folded, with my back to it.

'Why are you here, Jazz?'

'I told you – to drop off your jumper, check out Friday with Zac, and see where you're living. Why are you being so weird all of a sudden?'

'I'm not. It's just that you've never seemed interested in where I live before.'

'Bit harsh. Of course I was interested but I'm a super-busy person. Are you really going to barricade me in a man's bedroom while you diss me for doing a good deed?'

Hmm, Jasmine has many positive qualities but doing good deeds with no ulterior motive is not one of them.

'Come on, Beccs. I don't want to have to fight you 'cos you know I'd whop your arse.' Jasmine raises her fists and I have to grin as I remember the scraps we had as children. We got on pretty well as kids, most of the time. We weren't as close as everyone expected us to be – they thought, being twins, we'd be joined at the hip. We were never *that* close, but we were good friends, until our teenage years when hormones kicked in. I wish we were closer now.

I step back from the door and unfold my arms. 'Sorry, and thanks for bringing my jumper back. It was just a bit full-on at work today. How's your job going?'

'Oh, you know. Good. Though it always takes a while to settle in to somewhere new.'

'Especially when you've got lots of new clients to impress?'

'Yeah, that kind of stuff.' Jasmine suddenly doesn't look quite as glowy as usual. Her eyes aren't as sparkly and there's something missing – as though she's been slightly flattened.

'Is everything all right, Jazz?'

'Of course. Why wouldn't it be?' she says, snapping back into mega-watt golden mode.

'I just thought it's probably tiring, pitching to all those high-level clients.'

'It's exhausting. But did I mention that my boss thinks I have massive potential?'

'Yep,' I tell her, opening the door to Zac's bedroom wide, to let her out. 'I think you might have mentioned it once or twice.'

Jasmine sits on our sofa drinking coffee, chatting with Zac and flicking her hair back over her shoulder for ages before she heads off. And she's only been gone a few minutes when Zac's mobile phone dings with a text.

He puts down the dirty coffee mugs he was carrying and ferrets in his pocket for his phone. He reads it and grins.

'Who's that from?'

'Jasmine.'

'Really? What does she want?'

'Nothing. Just stuff about the do we're going to.'

He shoves his phone back into his pocket and heads into the kitchen with the mugs.

A couple of hours later, after we've pigged out on chops and mixed veg, I notice Zac's phone on the coffee table. Zac has nipped into the kitchen for another lager and I'm supposed to be setting up the next episode of *Modern Family* on the Sky box.

I put the remote down and pick up his mobile. I shouldn't. I really shouldn't. Spying on your housemate is all kinds of wrong. Though is it wrong when it involves your twin sister who might be leading said housemate astray? I quickly key in Zac's passcode and click on his text messages.

There it is. With a nervous glance towards the kitchen, I open the text from Jasmine and quickly read it.

Hope you are OK with do being black tie. It'll be a bit posh, but it should be fun. Thanks so much for coming with me. I'm really looking forward to it x

She texted him a kiss... but Jasmine puts kisses on the ends of all her texts, even her passive-aggressive ones to me when we're in the middle of a barney.

Becca, you really need to grow up x

Becca, you really need to sort your life out x

Becca, you really need to stop being such a wuss x

Jasmine thinks I really need to do quite a lot of things. And the kisses are always there, whatever the tone of her message. So it doesn't matter that she's texting Zac kisses. It doesn't mean anything in particular. And what does it matter if it does? Urgh, my head is all over the place and I'm turning into a horrible person who selfishly wants to keep her best friend all to herself.

I close my eyes, cross my fingers and make an extra Christmas wish for Zac, who deserves nothing but the best in life. *I wish for Zac whatever will make him happy. And if that happens to be my sister, so be it.*

Chapter Eleven

'So that's how I'm thinking of changing The Cosy Kettle for the party.' I look up from the plans I've listed on a spreadsheet and wait for Flora's reaction. A wave of anxiety swooshes through me as she studies the A3 sheet I've laid out across the counter in the café. What if she hates what I've planned and thinks I'm over-reaching myself? I want to impress her, not worry her.

Flora smiles. 'You've really thought this through, Becca. It sounds great but quite different from what you mentioned the other day. I thought Dick and Stanley were helping you by getting all dressed up and there were going to be carols in the garden?'

'I've had a bit of a rethink after my meeting with Logan. He's looking for sophistication because his VIP guests are French, and I don't think Dick and Stanley quite fit the bill.'

'Probably not,' says Flora, giving me a straight look that's hard to interpret. 'Madrigals – whatever they are – certainly sound far more upmarket and I can't wait to see a transformed Cosy Kettle. I noticed it's looking a little bare in here.'

She frowns at a large box in the corner. Strands of shiny red tinsel are snaking from underneath the cardboard lid, and a heap of paper chains are piled on a table nearby. Next to them is the rolled-up poster of the snow-encrusted fir tree.

'I've started taking some of the tackier Christmas decorations down so I can replace them with more upmarket decs and make the café look a little more elegant.'

'Ah, I see.' Flora sucks her lower lip between her teeth.

'So, um… are you're happy for me to carry on?'

Flora carefully folds the spreadsheet and hands it back to me. 'This is your party, Becca. You got the booking and you're arranging it and I know that The Cosy Kettle is in safe hands. I have every faith in you.'

If only I had faith in myself. I catch the thought as it swirls around my head and do my best to damp it down.

'Did you say you're having problems tracking down the madrigals quartet?'

'Their website doesn't seem to be working at the moment.'

'You ought to have a chat with Luna. She might be able to help.'

'How?'

'I'm sure she knows the woman who sings in the madrigal group and, as it's all a bit late notice, she can probably put a good word in for you too. Why don't you nip along and see her now? I can keep an eye on the café for you.'

'What, see Luna in her shop? Now?'

'Yes, it'll only take you a few minutes. Have you ever been in her shop?' When I shake my head, her mouth lifts in the corner. 'It's definitely worth a look, and it's nothing to be frightened of.'

'I'm not frightened. I've just never needed anything she sells.'

I'm lying, and my nerves increase as I rush along the High Street towards Luna's Magical Emporium. Rumour has it that Luna is a white witch, which is ridiculous. But anything supernatural gives me the creeps which is why I've never been into her shop. I went to Luna's home, Starlight Cottage, once, when she hosted a book club meeting for Flora, and that was quite enough for me. The creepy cottage, in the middle of nowhere, was mega-spooky, with candles and incense, gloomy cobwebbed corners and paintings of women with third eyes in the middle of their foreheads. I don't know how Flora can live there. But I can hardly admit to Flora that I'm too nervous to go into her prospective mother-in-law's shop – not now I'm trying so hard to impress her with my confidence and business acumen. Old fears that have held me back for ages aren't going to scupper my Christmas wish.

Before I have time to think any more about it, I burst through the doorway into Luna's shop and stand there, like an idiot.

Luna slowly looks up from the counter, where she's sitting doing her knitting, and her strange amber eyes open wide. 'Heavens, are you all right, Becca? You rushed in like a bat out of hell and you seem rather distracted.'

She comes out from behind the counter and starts waving her arms around in front of me. Ooh, I hate it when she does this. Flora says she does it to read my energies. I think she does it to spook the hell out of me.

'You're changing, child,' says Luna, tilting her head to one side. 'How interesting. Your energies are in flux and the colour of your aura is pulsing from shade to shade. There's a huge transformation in progress.'

OK, I'm really spooked now. How can she possibly know that I'm trying to change myself? Unless…

'You've been talking to Stanley about me, haven't you?'

Luna shrugs and pushes her sheet of silver hair over her shoulder. 'If you like. If that makes you feel more comfortable. How can I help you, Becca? Do you have a message from Flora or are you here looking for something?'

I glance around me at Luna's Magical Emporium which is just as I imagined it would be. Dozens of dreamcatchers are hanging from the ceiling, one row of shelves is covered with geodes filled with amethyst crystals, another shelf is full of plastic unicorns, and there are pink faerie wings, and drawings of wood nymphs and wizards. In the corner of the store is a huge stone statue of a witch in flowing robes. She looks a lot like Luna, actually. I shiver and thrust the photo of the madrigal singers into Luna's hands.

'I'm here to ask for your help, actually. I'm hoping to hire these singers for a Christmas party that's happening in The Cosy Kettle in a couple of weeks' time and Flora said you know the lady involved? Their website isn't working at the moment.'

Luna looks at the photo and smiles. 'I do know Geraldine. She lives in Oxford but often comes into the shop when she's passing Honeyford, for potpourri. I make my own using dried flowers and herbs. Here, have a sniff of my festive special.'

When she picks up a bowl on the till counter and wafts it under my nose, a rich blend of orange, star anise and cinnamon fills the room.

'That's really nice.'

'I think so and my customers love it.' Luna leads me to a bean bag in the corner of the shop and beckons for me to sit down. 'Why don't you take the weight off your feet for a while. Have you ever tried meditation, Becca?'

'Sort of.'

The truth is, I've tried it on and off for years in a bid to promote serenity and calm my agitated brain. It seems to work for a while but I can never keep it up.

'Did it help you?' asks Luna, playing with the ends of the pink scarf wrapped around her head. It matches the chunk of pink crystal on a leather thong around her neck.

'Not really. I can never keep still for long enough.'

Plus my thoughts seem louder than ever while I'm meditating. And my mind strays to all sorts of things I'd rather forget, like Charlie and Chloë wrapped in a tight embrace, and my mum's expression when I told her I'd jacked in my high-flying job.

'It takes practice but meditation can be very useful, especially for people with radiant souls who are shackled by fear and feelings of inadequacy.'

She gives me one of her weird knowing smiles as I wonder if she means me. *Shackled by fear and feelings of inadequacy,* I understand. But there's no way I have a radiant soul. She's getting me confused with Jasmine.

'Let me get you a cup of herbal tea,' says Luna. 'What would you prefer – I have soothing chamomile, lemon balm or peppermint?'

'That's really kind of you but I'm afraid I need to get back to the café.' I struggle off the bean bag and onto my feet, way out of my comfort zone and keen to leave. 'I'd be really grateful if you could mention the party to Geraldine and ask her to give me a ring at the bookshop. Would that be OK? Or I can call her myself if you could give me her phone number.'

'It's probably better if I contact her initially. That's not a problem at all. Madrigals in The Cosy Kettle – how marvellous.' She pauses. 'Your café has a wonderful vibrancy. I feel it emanating from the back of the bookshop whenever I call in to speak to Flora. It oozes friendliness and warmth which is testament to your sensitive spirit, Becca.'

'Thank you,' I reply, genuinely touched by such an unexpected compliment. 'How is Caleb doing now?'

'My grandson is back at school with his energies restored and looking forward to Christmas. Thank you for asking about him. And how is business in the café? I imagine The Cosy Kettle must be very busy at this time of year.'

'It is, and I've got the party to organise on top of everything else. Not that I'm complaining. I'm looking forward to it and hope Geraldine and her friends will be able to come along and sing for us.'

'If the universe wills it, then it will happen,' says Luna, with a beatific smile. 'And I will light a candle to wish you well with your party plans and your… personal endeavours.'

Aw, that's a bit woo-woo but very kind of her. I suddenly realise why Flora likes living with Luna – get past the spooky supernatural stuff and she's just a lovely lady with a very eccentric fashion sense. Today, her floor-length oatmeal linen tunic is tied at the waist with what looks like a length of rope and her earrings are basically huge chunks of amber glass suspended on silver chains. She looks totally at home in this shop but quite how she sells enough of her weird stuff to keep a roof above her head is beyond me.

'Could I buy some of your festive potpourri?' I ask, keen to repay her in some way for helping out with Geraldine. 'It'll smell gorgeous in our little cottage.'

'You live in Weavers Lane, don't you?' asks Luna, pouring dried fruit and herbs into a cellophane bag and sealing it with a twist of red ribbon. 'Those cottages are even older than mine and so steeped in history. So many souls. So many stories.' I pay quickly before she can start spooking me out about ghosts wafting round my head at home.

When I get to the door, she waves as though I'm about to embark on a long journey, and calls: 'You are surrounded by love, Becca, and you're worthy of it. Never forget that.'

'Um, OK, I won't? Thanks again for all your help.'

I feel slightly punch-drunk as I stumble out of Luna's shop, as though I've been zapped by weirdness. That's why I don't notice Logan until he grabs my elbow.

'Hey, watch where you're going, Becca babe. You're my VIP party planner and I don't want you falling and breaking something.'

'Sorry.' Logan is standing so close to me with his hand supporting my elbow, the rough fibres of his navy-blue coat are grazing my cheek. Fortunately, there's a biting wind blowing off the hills and the bracing temperature keeps my over-heated blushing in check.

He grins and lets me go. 'So what are you doing coming out of the most bonkers shop in town?'

'I was asking Luna to contact Geraldine who sings with the madrigal quartet. She and Geraldine are friends, apparently.'

'Awesome.' He gives a low whistle. 'Actually, bumping into you is very fortuitous. I could do with your help because you're a woman, aren't you?'

'I was the last time I looked.' When Logan laughs, my shoulders drop and I start to feel more relaxed. More like the person I want to be when my Christmas wish comes true. 'How can I help you?'

'I need to get a Christmas present for my mother and I haven't got a clue. She's sorting out my presents for other members of the family but I can hardly ask her to buy her own Christmas gift, can I? Although…' He grins when I shake my head. 'Nah. Probably not. In which case, you need to help me choose something for her, unless you have to get back to work.'

I *should* get back to work. I told Flora I'd only be a little while. But Logan needs me.

'No, it's fine. I can spare a bit of time to help with your gift dilemma.'

'Thanks, Becca. I just knew you wouldn't let me down.' Logan smoulders, running his tongue across his upper lip. He must have twigged I have a crush on him. Either that, or he smoulders at women indiscriminately.

Before I can work out which, he grabs my hand and starts pulling me towards the town square.

'Let's check out the Christmas market for present ideas, and we might get some inspiration for the party too.' He clocks my expression and grins. 'Had you forgotten that the market starts today? I can't believe that the most exciting thing to happen in Honeyford for months has slipped your mind.'

It is pretty exciting actually – I love a festive market – but I had completely forgotten it, even though Honeyford Heritage Trust has been shoving flyers about it through my door for weeks. Party planning, while I'm also making my wishes come true and turning myself into a whole different person, doesn't leave much headspace for anything else.

There's a hubbub of noise as we get closer to the square and, when we turn the corner, I gasp. Honeyford has excelled itself. The square, edged by ancient Cotswold-stone buildings, is ablaze with hundreds of fairy lights strung around dozens of stalls. They're glowing in the gloom of a cloudy December day, and the air is thick with the smell of cinnamon and cloves.

'Wow, this is lovely,' I whisper, my hand still in Logan's.

'It's certainly festive, though rather over the top. Christmas markets are always a bit naff.'

He laughs at Santa, who looks remarkably like Vernon, in a tragic cotton-wool beard. But tiny children are clustered around him, their faces turned up to him in awe. They don't think it's naff and neither do their parents, who are enjoying seeing their youngsters experience the joy of Christmas.

Logan drops my hand and together we wander around the stalls, past striped candy canes and golden toffee apples, brightly painted tree decorations, glinting jewellery and bars of handmade soap that smell of pine needles.

'What about a necklace for your mum?'

I pick up a pretty silver pendant that feels heavy in my hand, but Logan scrunches up his nose. 'I don't know the kind of jewellery she likes.'

'What about a jumper? I saw some gorgeous Aran jumpers on a stall near the Christmas tree.'

Logan shakes his head. 'I don't know what kind of clothes she likes.'

Logan doesn't seem to know his mother very well at all. 'Does she enjoy reading? I'm sure Flora could recommend some suitable books.'

'I have no idea what books she's read already. Urgh, this present-buying is a nightmare.'

'It's a good job you only have to buy one whole present then.'

Oops, that's the kind of sarcastic comment I'd make to Zac. He'd laugh and come back with a witty retort, but Logan might take offence. When I glance nervously at Logan, he blinks at me for a moment before raising an eyebrow and grinning. 'I do believe there's more to you than meets the eye, Becca.'

Phew, he's not annoyed and, on the plus side, he's getting much better at remembering my name. On the other hand, his comment might imply that my face is no great shakes. Let's see how he feels when I achieve wish number six and am transformed into a Jasmine lookalike.

'What about a voucher for a massage or a facial?'

When I point at the tiny beauty clinic that's recently opened in a corner of the square, Logan punches the air. 'Yes, that's perfect! She'll love it. I knew when I saw you that you'd rescue me – for the second time. Shall we nip to the pub so I can buy you a drink to say thanks?'

It's very tempting, especially if it might bring me a tad closer to achieving wish number five and securing a date with Logan. But The Cosy Kettle is calling, Flora will be wondering where I am, and who am I kidding about wish number five anyway? Logan is currently waving at a stunning blonde buying cinder toffee from a stall nearby. She looks familiar and I'm sure I've seen the two of them pictured together on his Instagram account. She giggles and waves back.

'I'd better get back to the café so maybe another time.'

'Yeah, definitely,' says Logan, wandering off towards the giggler. 'Thanks again, Becca,' he calls over his shoulder. 'You're the best.'

Chapter Twelve

It's Friday morning, Zac and Jasmine are going on a 'date' in twelve hours' time, and I'm so busy giving myself a pep talk on the way back from the shops, I don't notice there's someone sitting on my doorstep until I almost fall over her.

'Mum, is that you?' I ask, as a carrier bag holding a pint of milk and packet of Jammie Dodgers bangs against my thigh.

The huddled figure stands up and stretches out her legs.

'Of course it's me, Rebecca. Don't you recognise your own mother? And why are you talking to yourself in the street? People will think you're mad. Not that I... I mean, I don't really think you're... oh, whatever.'

Whatever? Mum really isn't herself. It's obvious because she's dressed in old leggings, a thick woolly jumper and a big hat pulled down low over her eyes. I've never seen her looking so scruffy.

I take my key out of my pocket and open the front door. 'Of course I recognise you, Mum, but I didn't expect to find you on my doorstep first thing in the morning. Why are you here? Is Dad all right?'

'He's the same as usual,' she sniffs. 'And why are you out so early? It's only just gone eight o'clock.'

'We're low on milk and I was up early because I couldn't sleep. You could have knocked on the door, you know. Zac would have let you in.'

'I saw you disappearing around the corner as I got here and hoped you wouldn't be long. I didn't want to disturb Zac. I thought he might still be asleep.'

'Probably 'cos he's working from home today, but he wouldn't have minded if you'd knocked. He'll be up and about soon.'

'In which case, we need to go for a walk,' she says, lowering her voice though there's no one nearby. 'I don't want Zac around because I need to talk.' This is a first. Mum and I talk, of course, but she never 'needs' to talk. Not to me, at any rate. 'Of course, if you have to get to work…'

'No, I've got half an hour before I need to head to the café. Let me shove my carrier inside and we can have a quick walk through the park, if you're sure you're not too cold.'

'I'm absolutely fine.' She buries her chin in the polo neck of her thick jumper as I peer at her face. She looks different today – the deep furrow between her eyebrows hints at anxiety but her eyes are alive with excitement. She looks slightly wild, as though she's not quite in control.

I drop my groceries inside the front door and pull it closed. Then I grab her arm and steer her towards the park.

Honeyford Memorial Park is gorgeous, whatever the season. It's pretty in the spring, as flowers poke through the dark earth, and beautiful in summer with the trees in full leaf and sunlight glinting on the winding river. In autumn, the park is crisp with fallen leaves in rich shades of red and gold. But I like the park best in winter, when it seems to be sleeping as plunging temperatures coat the ground with frost.

Today, the rising sun is a lemon orb in a pale blue sky and the cold grass crunches quietly under our feet.

'Are you sure you want to walk?' I ask Mum, as I spot scattered flakes of snow on the path. It must have snowed slightly in the night.

'Why don't we go back and have a coffee and I can ask Zac to give us some privacy?'

'No, I like walking. The fresh air will do us good and we'll soon warm up.' She bangs her gloved hands together, her breath hanging white in the air. 'What were you talking to yourself about when you came down the road? You looked cross.'

'That's just my normal resting bitch face,' I say, because there's no way I'm admitting that I was giving myself a good telling-off. *Honestly, Becca, so what if Zac and Jasmine are going on a date this evening? You want your best friend and your sister to have a good time, don't you? It's totally selfish and frankly weird to want to keep your best friend all to yourself. He doesn't belong to you, you know. And soon your Christmas wish will come true and you'll be uber-confident and possibly going out with Logan and staying at his place most nights anyway.* Thank goodness Mum can't lip-read.

'Where to now?' asks Mum as we reach the shallow river and the path forks two ways.

'Let's follow the river along for a while. It looks lovely with the sunshine glinting on the water.'

We start walking along the bank, side by side, our feet slipping on ice-covered puddles. It's nice being outdoors with Mum, on her own. Usually, she's chained to the kitchen sink with Dad nearby, or Jasmine's around, trying to hog all of her time.

'So what brings you to my door at the crack of dawn?'

Mum gives me a sideways glance. 'Nothing really. I'm just being silly. But I've been tossing and turning all night and needed to talk to someone before I went mad.'

'You can talk to me about anything, Mum,' I tell her, touched that Mum chose me to turn to when she could have picked Dad or Jasmine or her best friend, Lesley, instead.

'I know it's early and I don't want to take up your time,' says Mum, grabbing my arm when she almost slips over. 'I wouldn't have bothered you at all, but Lesley's gone to visit her daughter in Salisbury, it's not something I can talk to your dad about, and I'd never bother Jasmine because she's far too busy with her important job.'

Hmm. It sounds like I was not so much the best person to turn to as the only person available.

'Also,' adds Mum, walking under a tall oak tree whose stark leafless branches arc into the pale, lightening sky. 'I know I don't often say it but you're far more like me than Jasmine is.'

'In what ways?'

'You're more anxious and less ambitious than Jasmine. And you haven't lived up to your potential, which is just like me. Oh, I'm so sorry, Becca. That came out wrong. I didn't mean that to sound awful.'

I'm not sure how else it could possibly have sounded, but I give a wobbly smile. 'That's all right. So what's the problem, Mum?'

She stops abruptly and turns to face me, her face pinched against the cold. 'I've been offered a place on the art course that I told you about.'

'But that's brilliant, isn't it? I bet they had loads of applicants and they've chosen you which just proves how talented you are. Aren't you pleased?'

'Of course I am. It's amazing because I never thought in a month of Sundays that they'd want me. But I can't take up the offer.'

'Why not?'

'Because your Dad says it's daft. Because I work full-time. Because I don't have confidence in my artistic abilities. Because I'm scared of life and I know you understand that one.'

Is that how my own mother sees me? Scared of life? That's pretty depressing.

I rub my frozen nose for a moment until the feeling starts to come back. 'I used to be shy and a bit of a wuss, Mum, but I've changed since I came to Honeyford. And I'm still making lots of big changes. You can too.'

'Changing in what way? You're not changing your job again, are you? You can't keep chopping and changing, Becca. Not after what happened in Birmingham.'

I sigh. 'I left my job in Birmingham because it all got too much. And I moved to Honeyford and I've got another job in The Cosy Kettle. So it's all good.'

'But you had such a good job in Birmingham, Becca. We were all so proud of you.'

'It was a good but stressful job in a high-powered office that almost drove me nuts.' I think back to how I was then – a bag of nerves, prone to panic attacks, who fled the big city for Honeyford. Gradually, this gorgeous little town has worked its soothing magic on me. 'Anyway, managing The Cosy Kettle is a good job too, and it's far less stressful.'

Except when I'm trying to organise an upmarket event for a drop-dead gorgeous bloke, while also transforming into a better version of myself.

'So how are you changing, then?' asks Mum, with a frown.

'I'm trying to be more assertive and be, um, my best self,' I say, channelling Stanley, who's taken reinvention to a whole new level. 'What I mean is, it's never too late to try and ditch the bits that aren't working and focus on what will make your wishes come true.'

'Hmm,' sniffs Mum. 'I'm a bit old to start being what I'm not.'

'But what if what you are now *is* what you're not? What if your potential is hidden under years of looking after us and being what Dad expects you to be?'

Mum scrunches up her face as though I'm talking a foreign language she doesn't understand.

'What if really you're a great artist who should be spending her time painting and creating and feeling fulfilled? That's the life path you could have taken. But you've been side-tracked by cooking and cleaning and working, and your confidence has drained away.'

'I'm fulfilled by my family, not side-tracked,' says Mum, looking rather put out. 'There's nothing wrong with being a wife and a mother.'

'I'm not saying there is. But what if you've done the wife and mother thing for years and now it's time to give free rein to your more artistic side?'

'You girls might have left home but there's still your father to look after.'

'He's an adult and capable of looking after himself.'

'Do you really think so?' Mum raises her eyebrows and she's got a point. Dad has always expected to be looked after and she's made a rod for her own back by going along with it.

'When do you have to let them know whether you're going to take up your place on the course?'

'By the new year.'

'So at least you've got some time to consider it and how you might make it work.'

'There's nothing to consider. Dad doesn't want me to go part-time at work and spend money on something frivolous.'

'But it's not frivolous if it will make you happy.' My voice is getting louder and a woman jogging under the trees glances over at us.

'But *would* it make me happy?' hisses Mum, pulling me along the path, away from her.

'I don't know, Mum. Are you happy now?'

She thinks for a moment. 'I'm not unhappy, not really. But I'm feeling more and more that there's a huge unexplored part of me that's gradually withering away.' She blinks as though her words have taken her by surprise.

'That's sad, Mum.' I put my arm around her shoulders and squeeze tight as we walk along. 'If you could make a wish, right now, what would it be?'

'For you and Jasmine to be well and happy.'

'No, a Christmas wish that's just for you. It can be anything.'

'I suppose I would wish that I could pursue my art before it's too late.'

'Then have a think about the actions you need to take. Wishes don't come true by magic. You have to make them happen,' I tell her, parroting Zac's wise words.

'You're sounding very insightful all of a sudden.' Mum sighs. 'Thank you, Becca. I have some more thinking to do.' She stops and pulls up her sweater sleeve to check her watch. 'Heavens, time's getting on. We'd better get back before your father sends out a search party and you're late for work.' Her woolly gloves scratch my face as she cups my cheeks in her hands, bends my head towards her and kisses me on the forehead. 'Thank you, Becca. You're a good daughter.'

Together, we crunch back along the path in companionable silence as a tiny robin redbreast hops ahead of us.

Zac is wandering around the kitchen with a bad case of bedhead hair when I rush in after seeing Mum to her car.

'I thought you'd gone in to work early,' says Zac, absentmindedly scratching his stomach. 'I couldn't find you but there was a carrier bag full of milk and Jammie Dodgers by the front door. Cheers for that. There's nothing better than biscuits for breakfast.' He pulls a Dodger from the pocket of his trackie bottoms and has a nibble.

'I was out having a heart to heart with Mum and now I'm going to be late for work.' I grab a bowl and start pouring cereal into it. Stray cornflakes bounce off the worktop and disappear down the gap next to the cooker.

'Jasmine pays us a visit earlier this week, then your mum… it'll be your dad calling in for fish and chips next.'

'I doubt it. Dad rarely strays far from home territory. He's like a homing pigeon that never actually flies anywhere. He doesn't much like his family flying away either.'

'Was your mum all right?' asks Zac, pushing his fingers through his wild curls as I splosh milk into the bowl. 'What was the heart to heart about?'

'We went for a walk in the park and she told me she's been accepted onto that art course she was telling me about.'

'That's fantastic news! Do you want a coffee?' He waves the kettle at me.

'No thanks. No time. Yeah, it would be fantastic news for Mum if she wasn't going to turn it down.'

Zac pauses with his finger on the kettle switch. 'Why's she going to do that? Her paintings are really good.'

'I know.' I pause to shovel in a large mouthful of cornflakes, chew and swallow. 'But Dad's still not keen on her going part-time at work, and spending her time and money on what he sees as a frivolous hobby.'

'That's such a shame. It's not frivolous when she has real talent.'

'That's what I told her.'

'Do you think it helped?'

'I'm not sure. I told her a bit about the changes I'm trying to make and suggested she could change her life too. I even got her to make her own Christmas wish, which was to take up the art course offer.'

'I bet you sounded inspirational and wise.'

'What, me?' I laugh. 'Probably not. But I hope our chat might help her to make up her mind.'

'Are you going to speak to your dad about it?'

'Do you think I should? Maybe that's something Jasmine should broach with him.'

'Why Jasmine and not you?'

'I dunno. She gets on better with him than I do and I can't remember the last time Dad and I had a proper chat.'

Truth be told, I find Dad a bit intimidating. Not physically, because he'd never lift a finger against me or Jazz. He's more intimidating mentally, because he's such a bombastic character who views shyness as a personality flaw.

'Does your sister understand your mum's emotions as well as you do?' asks Zac, rootling round in the cutlery drawer for a teaspoon. However many we buy, they mysteriously vanish into the ether.

'Probably not.' I think for a moment about my goal to be more assertive. 'Yeah, maybe I'll get Dad on his own and have a word. Good idea.'

'Poor Pauline,' says Zac, waving a clean teaspoon in triumph. 'That's really hard if she has to give up her place. It's nice that she confided in you, though.'

'Yeah, she didn't want to bother Jasmine, who's busy with her important job. And Mum and I are the same, apparently – nervy types with no ambition.'

'Ouch.' Zac grimaces. 'I'm sure she didn't mean it like that.'

'I'm sure she did, but it's OK. She'll be impressed when my sophisti-cated Christmas party is a huge success. So will Flora, and I already feel more confident and assertive than I did. My Christmas wish is coming true which thankfully means I'm not going to be a screw-up forever.'

Zac grins. 'I'm very pleased for you, Beccs, though I never thought you were a screw-up in the first place.'

'Not even a leetle bit of a screw-up?'

'Never! Annoying, argumentative and an occasional pain in the arse, absolutely. A screw-up? Nope.'

He ducks when I pick up the local takeaway menu and chuck it at his head. 'Oh, and talking of my Christmas wish, did I mention that Logan Fairweather reckons I have amazing cheekbones, and he's thanked me for rescuing him, twice?'

'Has he indeed? How are things going with Mr Fairweather?'

'I'm not sure. He's been quite complimentary about me a couple of times and he smouldered a bit when he bumped into me outside Luna's.'

'Smouldered?' snorts Zac. 'What, like a cigarette that's been dropped down the back of a sofa?'

'Exactly like that.'

'Was he complimentary about all of the hard work you're putting in on his party?'

'Kind of. He was more wowed by my sparkling personality.' I grin but Zac says nothing and shoves a Jammie Dodger into his mouth, whole. While he's crunching, I finish off the cornflakes, though I'm eating so fast I hardly taste them. 'What time are you and Jasmine going out later?'

'Eight o'clock,' he replies, spraying biscuit crumbs everywhere. 'Oops, sorry.'

As he brushes crumbs from my shoulder, hair flops across his face and I stroke my hand across his forehead to push it back. His tangled hair catches in my fingers and for a moment we're caught together: best friends who are totally comfortable with each other. Only I don't feel comfortable now. I feel awkward and embarrassed, as though I'm doing something wrong.

When I pull my fingers away, Zac turns and starts spooning coffee into his mug. 'You'd better get off or you'll definitely be late,' he says, gruffly.

'Shit, it's almost nine o'clock!' I run upstairs and am about to change out of my scruffy jeans into black leggings when I spot a flash of green at the back of my wardrobe. It's the dress that I last wore to my job interview in Birmingham – the only dress I possess. I pull it from the wardrobe and smooth it out across my duvet. Jasmine wears dresses and I wear jeans or trousers; that's how it's been for as long as I can remember. But everything's changing now. I'm changing. And Logan emailed last night to say he'd be calling into The Cosy Kettle at lunchtime. I step out of my jeans and pull the scratchy woollen dress over my head.

A few minutes later, I thunder back down the stairs and rush to the front door. 'What are you doing today?' I shout over my shoulder towards the kitchen, as I grab my jacket.

'Lots of work,' Zac shouts back. 'And then tarting myself up for the do this evening.'

'Jasmine will appreciate any tarting up you can manage,' I call back, because that's the kind of thing I'd usually say. But I still feel uneasy as I wrench open the front door and hurtle through it.

Chapter Thirteen

Flora gives me a hard stare when she spots me barrelling through the bookshop doorway. I almost take out a high display of Christmas-themed thrillers because I'm in such a rush.

'Sorry I'm late.' I'm puffing, having run all the way up the High Street, my open jacket flapping around me. 'My mum called round unexpectedly first thing and by the time I'd sorted her out it was almost nine o'clock and I had to—'

'Breathe, Becca!' commands Flora, walking over and putting her hand on my shoulder. 'It doesn't matter that you're a few minutes late. The Cosy Kettle doesn't open until nine thirty so you've got plenty of time.'

'OK.' I breathe out heavily. 'Thanks. I thought you were annoyed with me.' I giggle, which is what I sometimes do if I'm in a flap and feeling self-conscious, even when laughter is totally inappropriate. My brain says, 'Hey, what can you do to make your current situation even worse?' and then does it. Thanks, brain.

Flora walks slowly around me and smiles. 'I'm not annoyed at all. I was only staring because you look different. You look really nice actually. Becca in a dress! Wow. I never thought I'd see the day.'

Is wearing a dress overdoing it? I wonder, as I hurry into the café, switch on the coffee machine and start putting out the cakes that local baker John has delivered – they're standing in stacked wooden crates smelling delicious. Maybe, but I need to start practising dressing up if I'm going to achieve my wish of becoming a Jasmine lookalike.

Regular customers keep commenting on my new look, and the book club stare at me and nudge each other when they wander in mid-morning. Stanley gives me a huge wink as he saunters up to the counter.

'You're looking pretty dope this morning, Beccs. I love the black tights and ankle boots combo.'

'Thanks. What are you lot doing in today?'

'It's a free country, dude. Mary can't make it because she's up to her eyes in domestic detail but the rest of us are free spirits.' He grabs an iced gingerbread man and plonks it on the counter. 'That's for Millie, who's partial to a biscuit. It'll keep her sweet. She reckons she doesn't want cake this morning but she gets hangry when her sugar levels drop and it's in all our interests to keep her topped up. The rest of us will have our usual drinks and cakes, ta, love.'

As I make their coffees, he leans against the counter and spins the gold hoop in his earlobe. 'What have you done to this place?' He stares around him and frowns. 'It seems a bit different in here today.'

'I've started thinning out the decorations so the place looks less like a fairy grotto.'

'Where have those flashing rainbow lights gone?'

'Back in their box while I get ready for the party which is getting quite close now.'

'And the tinsel?'

'That's back in the box with the lights. It was over the top and a bit naff really. Don't worry, I'm going to replace everything with more upmarket decorations.'

'Upmarket?' Stanley curls his lip. 'It doesn't feel as cosy in here as it did.'

'The café's mid-transformation at the moment. You'll love it once it's finished. Why don't you go and sit down and I'll bring your coffees over?'

Stanley grumps off to his seat, and Millicent applauds when I approach them with their drinks and cakes on a tray.

'Well done on making an effort with your appearance,' she says, as I set down fat slices of lemon drizzle cake, honey sponge and apple tart in front of them. It's a teensy bit condescending, being congratulated for putting on a dress, but I take it in the spirit it was intended.

There's a triple-layer red velvet sponge under a glass dome on the counter that's calling out to me, and at half past eleven I opt for an early lunch and cut myself a slice. I don't usually start my lunch with cake but it's been a trying morning – as well as getting used to my scratchy wool dress, and handling the book club's grumblings about the café's new look, I can't stop worrying about Mum, or thinking about Zac and Jasmine's date this evening.

I've only taken one large sweet mouthful when Logan strides into the café. Damn it, he's early! He scans the room, looking ridiculously handsome in tight jeans and a moss-green puffa jacket, and strides across when he spots me.

'Hi, Becca. I know I said I'd nip in at twelve but I was in town earlier than expected. Is now all right to catch up about any replies to the invitations?'

I nod because Flora volunteered her partner, Daniel, to design the invitations, and he did such a good and swift job in his lunchbreak, I was able to email them out yesterday afternoon. Invitees were encouraged to round off their trip to the UK, hosted by Logan's firm, with an upmarket evening of Christmas celebration, rather than heading straight for home.

'Of course. We've had loads of replies already.' I self-consciously check the corners of my mouth for crumbs. I reapplied my lipstick an hour ago but I bet I've eaten it off. 'We've heard from almost twenty people so far and all but two have accepted.'

'That's great.' Logan leans across the counter. 'You've looking pretty special today, Becca. Nice dress.'

'Thanks,' I reply as, out of the corner of my eye I spot Stanley barrelling down on me. Great! Logan is paying me a compliment and for once I haven't erupted into a blaze of blushing, but we're about to be interrupted by Honeyford's oldest eccentric.

I would say *only* eccentric, but there's Luna with her crystals and dreamcatchers, and butcher Vernon has his moments. Last week he announced to a full café that he and his dog have full-blown conversations because he's able to understand the language of barking.

'You dropped this, hun,' says Stanley, waving a beer mat at me. 'When you were leaning over me with my coffee. I found it on the floor.'

It's my Christmas wish list which I've been carrying around in my apron pocket like a good luck charm. My heart sinks as I remember number five: *Secure a date with Logan.* Fingers crossed, Stanley hasn't read it.

'Who's this young dude, then?' asks Stanley, as I grab the beer mat with a murmured thanks, and shove it into my pocket.

'I'm Logan Fairweather. Pleased to meet you.'

'*Logan,* you say? Interesting. What do you reckon to our gorgeous Becca, then?'

Oh, God. He has read it.

Stanley slips behind the counter and stands beside me. 'She's young, unmarried, with good childbearing hips and she makes a cracking cup of coffee. Plus, she's actually wearing a dress today. What more could a thrusting young buck in the prime of life possibly wish for?'

My only wish right now is for the ground to swallow me up. Me and Stanley, who deserves to plummet to his doom for being so unutterably crass. Childbearing hips? He tries to be modern with his skinny jeans and yoof slang but scratch the surface and there's a matchmaking octogenarian underneath.

'Um, she certainly makes a great cup of coffee.' Logan is smiling at me. 'And I approve of the dress. It shows off your lovely legs, Becca.'

I give a faint smile back and make a big show of scrabbling under the counter for the list of people who are coming to the party. 'Here are the people coming so far,' I announce, waving the list in the air. 'Why don't we go and sit in the garden, Logan, while you go through it? I'll make you a cappuccino.'

'O-K,' says Logan, slowly, pulling his jacket tighter around him. 'Can I have a latte instead?'

'No problem.' I make the fastest latte ever while Stanley wanders back to the book club, who are huddled in a corner near the Christmas tree. 'Oh, Stanley,' I call across the café as he sits down and starts chatting, 'Please don't say anything about…'

Too late. They have their heads bent together, and Phyllis glances at me with a perfect *ooh* on her face. Not only are the Cosy Kettle Afternoon Book Club supporting me with my metamorphosis into a better person, they may have just entered the matchmaking business. I have a very bad feeling about this.

*

Outside, the garden is empty for the very good reason that it's absolutely flipping freezing. The sky is pearly white and threatening snow and the garden is bleached of colour. A sharp wind is blowing through the bare branches of our apple tree and even the café's adopted stray cat has taken shelter inside.

'Aren't you going to be chilly out here?' asks Logan, sitting on one of the filigree iron chairs and wincing as cold leaches through the denim of his jeans.

'No, I'm fine,' I tell him, perching on the chair on the opposite side of the table. 'I don't tend to feel the cold.'

This is a big fat lie. I walk around at home swaddled in thick jumpers while Zac's wandering round in T-shirts. But it's said now and I'll look a right idiot if I suddenly rush inside for my thick coat. Especially as I was the one who suggested coming out here in the first place, to get away from Stanley.

'If you're sure.' Logan doesn't look convinced but he scans the guest list and smiles broadly when I tell him that Geraldine has been in touch and the madrigal singers have agreed to perform at the party. He drinks his coffee, all wrapped up in his thick jacket, while I try to look interested, and warm.

By the time we start discussing what's going to happen during the evening, my mouth is starting to seize up with the cold so I've taken to nodding vigorously at Logan's suggestions – even though they seem increasingly over the top, and he keeps talking about ensuring the café has the right upmarket ambiance.

As he works his way down a checklist on his phone, he keeps mentioning how important the party is until my heart starts hammering with anxiety. He's not the most soothing of people to be around.

At last he reaches the final point on his list – something to do with a dry ice machine wafting mist through the bookshop as people arrive – but he hesitates mid-sentence and shakes his head. 'Are you sure you're OK out here? Only you've started going a bit blue. Here, have my coat.'

He takes off his jacket and places it gently around my shoulders. The jacket is warm and smells all musky, like him.

'M-m-might be a good idea to go in now actually,' I stammer through my frozen lips.

'You're probably right,' says Logan, putting his phone into his jeans pocket, 'and it sounds as if things are in hand. So let's call it a day before you turn into an ice sculpture, though I think you'd make a very fetching ice maiden.'

Is he flirting with me? I'm too frozen to the bone to care right now. My teeth have locked so tight, my mouth is stretched into a thin line, and the muscles in my neck are rigid.

I follow Logan through the back door and sigh with pleasure as I ram my bum up against the nearest radiator and a wave of heat envelops my nether regions.

'It's looking good in here. Far less festively rustic,' says Logan, taking in the spaces where the fairy lights and tinsel used to be.

'I've got some nicer decorations to put up over the next few days, before the party.'

'That's great. Not too many, though. It was a bit cluttered before. Less is more when you're going for sophisticated and… hang on a minute.' He pulls his ringing mobile from his pocket and frowns at the screen before rejecting the call.

'Someone you're avoiding?'

'Just my flatmate, who's being a bit…' Logan suddenly rams his hands into his pockets and starts shifting from foot to foot.

'Can I ask you something? I wouldn't normally ask about this kind of thing but you seem to be quite a… sensitive person, with the blushing and everything.'

'Mmm.' I nod, rather gutted he's bringing up my tendency to go beetroot red. I'd kind of convinced myself he'd never really noticed.

'It's about my flatmate, Liam. He's always up for a laugh but he's different these days. It's hard to put my finger on it but he's a bit miserable and quieter. Not his usual self.' He shakes his head. 'I'm not sure what's wrong with him.'

'Have you spoken to him about it?'

'Spoken to him?' Logan laughs as if the thought of communicating with his flatmate about emotions is preposterous. 'Is that a good idea?'

'I think so. He might be anxious or depressed or stressed.'

'About what?'

'I don't know. He might tell you if you ask.'

Logan grimaces. 'What if he is any of that stuff? What then?'

'Let him talk, if he wants to. Maybe, underneath all the being up for a laugh, he's quite a sensitive person too.'

'I'll have to choose the right time to tackle him about it.' Logan stares into my eyes and gives a slow, sexy smile. 'You're a woman of many talents, Becca – café manager, party planner, and now counsellor too.'

'I have my moments,' I say, swallowing loudly.

Oh no, Stanley is homing in on us again. He wanders over, trying to look nonchalant, and stands in front of me.

'How's it going, Becca?' he asks, placing his empty coffee cup on a table nearby. 'I'll have another drink when you get a chance. Oh, and I meant to ask, how did your date go last night?'

'Date?' I say, giving Stanley the evil eye.

'Yeah, your hot date with Thor.'

Thor? I stare at Stanley in horror but he's already turned to Logan.

'Thor's just asked her out. Is he a bodybuilder, Becca? Anyway, he has muscles to die for and he's so handsome. Incredibly handsome. One of the most handsome men I've ever seen. So did your date with Thor go well then?'

'It was fine,' I mutter, putting my cold arm through Logan's and pulling him away. 'I'll sort you out with your coffee and everything else in a minute, Stanley.'

'That old guy's quite a character,' says Logan, as I pull him through the café. 'Is he gay?'

'I don't think so.'

'Only he seems rather taken with your new boyfriend.'

'He's just looking out for me.'

'I'm not surprised. Who wouldn't? Well, thank you for the party update and the lovely coffee, and the chat. I hope to see you soon.' Logan takes the jacket I hand over and winks at me before disappearing into the bookshop.

As soon as he's out of sight, I hurry back to Stanley, who's standing in the middle of the café.

'What do you think you're doing, saying that stuff to Logan?'

'I'm pimping you out.'

'You're… what?'

'I'm trying to secure you a romantic date with Logan and help make one of your Christmas wishes come true.'

I wipe my hands across my face, probably smearing make-up everywhere.

'One, you shouldn't have read my list, Stanley. Two, it's not your place to interfere in my life like that. And three, that's not what pimping out means. You'd better not use that term again until you've looked it up in the dictionary. You'll get yourself into all sorts of trouble. Also, who the hell is Thor?'

'Keep your hair on, Beccs. I was just making sure that Mr Fair-weather knows he's only one person in a long line of men wanting to go out with you.'

'What line? What men? And why did you call my imaginary boyfriend Thor? You made it sound like I was going out with an idiot.'

'I made it sound like you're going out with a superhero who's totally ripped. Logan will be so jealous.'

'You think? And what about you?' I turn towards Dick, who, along with the rest of the book club, is listening in, agog. 'You're Stanley's best friend. Can't you keep his more madcap ideas in check?'

Dick sounds like a braying horse when he puffs air through his lips. 'Quite honestly, there's a limit to what I can do, love.'

'I must say, Becca,' interrupts Millicent, 'you appear to be achieving your goal of becoming more assertive. Your telling-off of Stanley was most impressive.'

'I wasn't really telling him off,' I say, sinking onto a spare chair. 'I'm cold and I'm not really feeling myself today. Sorry, Stanley, if I was rude or—'

'And usual Becca is back,' sighs Millicent. 'He deserved a telling-off after behaving so crassly in front of your young man.'

'He's not my young man,' I say, wearily, but no one's listening. Their attention has turned to a piece of paper that Stanley has placed on the table.

'We had an inaugural meeting a few days ago, as you know, about getting your transformation rolling,' he says, cheerfully, as though our altercation never happened. 'We're here today to give you an update and, as luck would have it, we've been able to spend the last ten mins working through your actual bona fide wish list, which is totally rad 'cos now we've got a proper plan to help make your wishes come true.'

'How did you remember the whole list, which was totally private and not for sharing, Stanley?'

'I took a photo of it,' he says, waving his mobile in my face. 'So let's see who's been allocated what.' He clears his throat. 'I'm all over the date with Logan and Millie can help with pointers on increasing your assertiveness. She seemed the obvious choice, seeing as she's the most arsey amongst us.'

He grins and rolls his eyes as Millicent harrumphs quietly beside him. 'Next, Phyllis has volunteered to provide moral support and counselling as required when it comes to impressing Flora and your parents. Phyllis is the woman for that job because she knows more than most how important family is, don't you, Phyllis?'

When Phyllis nods, tears fill her eyes and I gently squeeze her shoulder. Poor Phyllis. She misses her family in Australia so much.

'I'm happy to help,' she gulps, 'though I'm sure your parents are very proud of you already. You're a very kind girl.'

Stanley runs his finger down the sheet of paper. 'One question – who's Jasmine?'

'She's my sister.'

'Really? Well, we think you're fine as you are but, if you're after changing how you look, Mary can help you with that. She's already offered and she's a youngster who knows all about fashion and contouring and stuff.'

'Contouring?' asks Dick. 'I thought that was something to do with outdoor activity centres.'

'You're thinking of orienteering,' says Millicent, with a sniff.

'Contouring is using make-up to highlight, shadow and show off the best bits of the face. It can enhance a delicate bone structure like Becca's,' says Stanley. He holds out his hands when we all stare at him. 'What? Don't forget I live with my granddaughter, who's got a make-up bag the size of a small golf trolley even though she hardly wears any.'

'And don't forget that I'm also in charge of hair,' says Millicent, picking up a strand of my bright blue hair before dropping it as though it's red hot. 'I'll see if my hairdresser can rescue your hairstyle in time for the Christmas party. She owes me a favour so I'm sure she'll fit you in somewhere.'

'So how does that sound?' asks Dick. 'None of us knows much about public speaking, so you're on your own with that one.'

How does that sound? I look at the four people in front of me who are so keen to help make my wishes come true. Their involvement is rather terrifying – heaven knows what Stanley has in mind to top 'Thor' – but it's also sweet and kind. Not to mention a little ironic, seeing as they've already pretty much accepted me as I am right now.

I take a deep breath as they wait for my reply. 'Thank you, everyone. It turns out that changing yourself is quite hard so I can do with all the help I can get. Though I'd rather deal with Logan on my own, Stanley, if that's all right with you.'

'Ooh, here's your other young man.' Phyllis gestures over my shoulder to where Zac is silhouetted in the café doorway. He waves and my stomach does a weird little flip because I'm so pleased to see him: a nice, normal bloke who doesn't behave inappropriately or make me nervous.

'You're wearing a dress!' says Zac, when I wander over.

He couldn't sound more surprised if I was in full Star Trek costume. Actually, he'd probably like that because he's a sci-fi nerd. We first bonded over our shared love of the Starship *Enterprise*.

'So what if I am in a dress today? I've got a bit fed up with people commenting on my clothes. It's not like I usually wear rags.'

'They're just surprised that you've got legs!' laughs Zac, walking round and round me.

'OK. Pack it in. I decided to wear a dress, in the spirit of looking more like Jasmine, and I don't need you taking the mick. It's been a trying morning.'

'Why?'

'Stanley tried to pimp me out.'

Zac's jaw almost hits the floor. 'Stanley did what?'

'He tried to pimp me out to Logan.'

'Ah. I just bumped into Logan outside the bookshop.' Zac's face clouds over. 'Did Stanley succeed?'

'No, of course not.'

'So why was he trying to pair you off with him, anyway?'

'I dropped my wish list and Stanley found it and read it, including wish number five which is—'

'Secure a date with Logan. Yeah, I know.'

'And now the whole book club knows too. I've told Stanley to back off but I expect it'll still be pimp central in The Cosy Kettle from now on. It's not funny,' I wail, as Zac starts sniggering. He's not being at all supportive.

'You never know, it might help you to get off with Logan. If that's what you still want.' Zac stops laughing and looks around the café. 'You've been busy in here. This place looks different. It's less—'

'Cosy?' interjects Phyllis, coming over with the rest of the book club, who seem to be going home, at last. 'What have you done to the place, Becca?'

'She's making it more upmarket, for the party.' Stanley sniffs. 'Less tinsel. More classy stuff. What do you think, Zac?'

Zac sucks his bottom lip between his teeth. 'I think it'll look more sophisticated, which is the vibe Becca's going for. I agree that it doesn't seem as cosy.'

'Don't you approve?' I ask. 'I've still got to put up the new decorations.'

He shrugs. 'I didn't say I didn't approve. I just said it looked different. Was Logan happy with the changes?'

'Yeah, he told me the café was looking less blingy and more in keeping with his party plans. Did he say anything to you?'

'Not much 'cos he was in a hurry. He asked me if I'd ever met someone called… Thane, Theo?'

'Thor.'

'Thor?' Zac starts laughing again. 'Who the hell is Thor?'

'My boyfriend, apparently. One in a long line of boyfriends queuing up to take me out.'

'Stanley?' gasps Zac, laughing quite hard now.

'Yep, it was a Stanley Special.'

'Nice one, mate.' Zac grasps Stanley's hand and gives it a shake. And he's still laughing when he heads off with his takeaway macchiato.

Chapter Fourteen

Seven hours later, and I'm glad to be home. I spent half the afternoon un-decorating the Cosy Kettle Christmas tree, so it's ready for the new decorations I've ordered, and the rest running around making coffees and selling cake. We had so many customers at one point, a couple of the hardier ones braved the freezing garden. They said they didn't mind, and at least it gave me a chance to test out the hired patio heaters which arrived just after lunch.

'What do you reckon, then?' asks Zac, stepping into the kitchen where I'm refilling our tiny dishwasher after his earlier efforts. He's pretty good at vacuuming and cleaning the bath, but his dishwasher-filling technique leaves a lot to be desired.

I look up from a muddle of crockery and gasp. I can't help it. Zac looks... amazing!

I've never seen Zac in a dinner suit before. He's got a cheap suit that he drags out of the wardrobe for interviews and meetings with new clients – it's slightly too big and hangs on his frame. But the rented black dinner suit he's currently wearing fits him like a glove. He looks like James Bond... with curling hair and horn-rimmed glasses.

He runs his finger under the collar of his snow-white shirt and stretches his neck from side to side. 'Tell me the truth, Becca. Do I look like a total muppet?'

'No, that really suits you. You still look like a muppet, obviously, but not a total muppet.'

I duck as Zac picks up a handful of potato peelings that are sitting on the counter and chucks them in my direction.

'Missed! What time will Jasmine be here?'

Zac shoots his cuffs and glances at his watch. 'In about ten minutes.' He breathes out in a loud *oof!* 'I'm not sure about this evening, Beccs. It feels strange going to some posh do with your sister. Are you sure you don't mind?'

He twists his mouth and chews the inside of his cheek, suddenly resembling a child playing dress-up in his dad's clothes.

'Of course not. Why would I mind?' I swallow hard and slot a greasy knife into the cutlery tray.

'I just thought that maybe…' Zac studies his polished black shoes. '… maybe you…'

'Good grief!' The spoon I'm holding falls onto a plate with a clatter as the doorbell rings. 'That bell is stupidly loud! You'd better let Jasmine in and I hope the two of you have a lovely evening. I'm so happy you're going out together.'

Why did I say that last bit? In reality, the whole thing feels a bit wrong. Zac catches my eye and holds my gaze until the doorbell rings again and I look away. 'Yeah, thanks. I'm not sure posh dos are my thing but it'll be different. Suppose I better had let her in 'cos it's freezing out there.'

I hear him opening the front door and a murmur of conversation as I close the dishwasher and wipe my hands down my dress. Catching sight of myself in the shiny chrome of the kettle, I realise that I look flushed and untidy, but it can't be helped. And Jazz has seen me looking worse.

When I walk into the front room, I stop dead. Jasmine and Zac are standing close together by the open front door. A cold draught is snaking across the layer of snow outside and through the room, but Jasmine has taken off her coat and is standing with her hands on her hips.

'Hey, Becca. I was just showing Zac my new dress and admiring him in his fabulous suit. What do you reckon?'

Jasmine does a twirl for me and I catch my breath. She looks amazing in a shimmering bronze dress that's clinging to her slim body in all the right places. Fat flakes of snow are caught in her golden hair, which is tied up in a messy bun, with tendrils framing her face. She's gone overboard on the highlighter and her whole face is glowing – not like mine glows when I'm feeling insecure and blushing, but glowing with confidence, vitality and beauty.

'You look wonderful, Jazz,' I say, wondering again how twins can be so different. What a cosmic cock-up!

'Cheers, Beccs. What do you think, Zac?' She gives him her prettiest pout and he smiles down at her.

'You look absolutely wonderful.'

He's only telling the truth, but his words hit me like a blow. This is stupid. I'm feeling out of sorts because my sister is going out for the evening with my best friend. But I love them and want the best for them, so what's my problem? I shake my head to get rid of the thoughts and Zac frowns. 'Is everything all right? Have you got a headache?'

'Nope,' I say brightly, my brain buzzing. 'I'm just dazzled by how fabulous the two of you look together – a proper golden couple.'

Adorable dimples appear in Jasmine's cheeks when she smiles. 'We are, aren't we? Hey, Beccs! I've just clocked that you're wearing a dress!'

'Yep, I thought I'd get my legs out for a change.'

'All for Logan's benefit,' says Zac, sounding faintly annoyed, as though I've let the side down by being interested in a man he doesn't approve of.

'Logan? Oh, that man who was in the café when I came in? I could tell you liked him.'

'I didn't wear the dress solely for Logan's benefit,' I insist. She doesn't believe me, but what else can I say? *An integral part of achieving my Christmas wish involves looking more like you, Jasmine, because I'm not good enough the way I am.* Gosh, that's depressing.

Jasmine sniffs. 'Whatever. It's good to see you out of your jeans and Doc Martens, anyway.'

'Thank you.' I take a deep breath and let the air out slowly. 'Hadn't you two better be getting off or you'll miss the champagne?'

'Hell, yeah, we don't want to miss that,' says Jasmine, slipping her arms into her coat that Zac is holding up for her. 'I'll leave my car there and we can get a taxi back. Is that OK with you, Zac?'

'That sounds fine. So we'll see you later then, Becca.'

'Yeah, have a brilliant time and don't do anything I wouldn't.'

I wink. I actually wink. It's like my whole body has been taken over by an alien.

'OK, if you're sure you're all right.' Zac smiles, looking extra handsome in his amazing suit. He puts out his arm and Jasmine slips her arm through his. 'Let's go.'

The cottage seems quiet and full of shadows when I close the front door behind them. What on earth is the matter with me? My brain is in meltdown. I slide down the door and sit on the cold flagstones, with my legs splayed out. It's not that I feel left out and want to tag along to Jasmine's work do. My idea of hell is making small talk with people I've only just met. But thinking of Jasmine and Zac, arm in arm, at their posh event makes my head hurt. No, not my head… my heart. *Of course it does, you idiot,* says the little voice in my head, the one that's always telling me terrible things are about to happen. *Your heart hurts because you're in love with Zac.*

I take in short, shallow gasps of air. That can't be right. Obviously, I love spending time with Zac. Who wouldn't? He's a fabulous human being. He's kind and caring, and the only person I feel truly comfortable with. We've always been able to talk frankly about everything, and he's the sole person on the planet who thinks I'm totally fine as I am and don't need to change. After work, I can't wait to get home to see his wonderful smile, and the thought of him not being here with me, and putting his arms around someone who isn't me, makes me feel… like I can't breathe.

'Oh, for goodness' sake!' I say out loud to the empty room, putting my head in my hands. Everything is suddenly crystal clear. I *am* in love with Zac. But when did that happen? When did loving Zac turn into *really* loving Zac, and what the hell do I do now? We're nothing more than platonic best friends in his eyes – he once described me as 'the sister he never had' – and he's out right now on a date with my perfect sister, after I told him that was fine.

My words in the kitchen, just after Jasmine rang the doorbell, sound in my head. *I'm so happy you're going out together.* Why did I say that? I close my eyes as hot tears roll down my cheeks and plop onto the neckline of my dress. This is the mother of all screw-ups, and a perfect storm of impossibility, because telling Zac how I feel risks ruining our precious friendship. We'd never recover from the embarrassment of him giving me the brush-off. Just imagine how horribly sad and heartbreaking that brush-off would be! Our comfortable, easy friendship could never survive it.

I sit on the floor for ages, listening to the house creak and groan around me, as I remember the first time Zac and I met, how he gives me hugs and makes me laugh, and the way he came to my rescue when the world went black a year ago. He is the very best of men and I can't imagine my life without him in it.

Brushing away tears, I stagger to my feet and pull down the dress which has ridden up my thighs. There's only one way to get through this and still have Zac in my life. I have to keep my mouth shut because I'm the one who's moved the goalposts and made our friendship so complicated.

I wander into the kitchen, grab a glass and the bottle of Chardonnay I forgot to take to Sunday lunch at my parents'. Then I throw myself onto the sofa, switch on the TV to drown out my thoughts, and prepare to drink my inner voice into submission.

Two glasses of wine later, the little voice in my head is still shouting at me – *you're in love with Zac* – and I'm feeling sad and confused. Another four glasses later, and my inner voice has collapsed in a heap and I'm googling *Logan Fairweather* on my computer to distract myself. There are loads of photos of him on his Instagram feed and I'm struck again by how gorgeous he is – stocky, blond hair, twinkling eyes. And I do think he likes me, just a little bit.

I squint at a summer picture of Logan, all tanned in swim shorts, and wonder if having him as my boyfriend would help me to get over being in love with my best friend. Very possibly. I take another swig of wine, which is damping down my feelings nicely, and click 'like' on several of Logan's selfies. I do like. Very much indeed.

Five minutes later, I'm half-slumped on the sofa when my phone rings, almost giving me a heart attack. Who's ringing at…? I try hard to focus on my watch but the stupid numbers keep moving around.

'Yeah. Hello. What d'you want?' I mumble into the phone.

'Becca, is that you?'

I recognise the voice immediately and sit up straight on the sofa, blinking rapidly.

'Yep, it's me. Most definitely me. My phone. I answered it. It's me.' I take in a deep whoosh of air, feeling sick.

'That's great,' says Logan. 'I saw on Insta that you were still up so I thought I'd call. Hope that's OK.'

'Of course,' I croak, trying to stop swaying back and forth because it's making my nausea worse. 'Did you want to talk about work, Logan? The party you're having? It's going to be so posh. Full of posh decorations, posh food, posh music and posh people. The Cosy Kettle is going to be so… posh.'

I clamp my lips tightly together because I have a horrible feeling that I might be embarrassing myself and number five on my wish list – which will make me feel so much better if it comes off – is about to go totally tits-up. But maybe I can claw things back if I say very little from now on.

Logan laughs. 'Have you been drinking, Becca?'

Oops, I've been rumbled!

'Just a bit.'

'I'm not sure now is the best time then.'

'Best for what?' I hiccup loudly.

'Best for thanking you for your advice about my flatmate, and for asking if you'd like to come with me to Tuckers, that new nightclub in Oxford, after the Christmas party. I'm crazy busy at work until then but I thought we could go out when the party ends.'

'You want me to go with you to Tuckers?'

'That's what I said.'

'Just you and me.'

'Well, there will be other people there but yeah, just you and me.'

'To talk about the party and do a shmort of debrief?' Oops, I think I'm slurring my words.

'We can talk about the party if you like but I'd just as soon treat it as a normal date and talk about me and you. Though I don't want to tread on Thor's toes.'

'Thor who?'

'Thor, your current boyfriend?'

'Oh, *that* Thor! Nah, he's very liberal 'bout stuff like that.'

'In that case, I'll look forward to it. Gotta go, but I'll see you soon. Sleep well, Becca.'

'Cool,' I say, before realising that he's already rung off. Which is just as well because I never usually say 'cool' because it's just not… cool.

I've slung the empty wine bottle into the recycling bin and staggered upstairs before I realise that Logan didn't actually wait for me to say that I definitely *would* go on a date with him. He just assumed that I would. Though I guess that's not surprising. I imagine very few women ever turn Logan down.

A date with Logan! 'That's wish number five ticked off the list, and defo before Chrishmas,' I mumble out loud as I climb into bed, still fully clothed. 'Tha's just what I need, and totally brill.'

It *is* brilliant. And exciting and scary. And it's given my confidence a huge boost, I realise as I lie in bed and the room spins. I just wish I felt happier about it.

It's the drink. *Alcohol does terrible things to the brain*, I tell myself, before switching off my lamp. It dampens down emotion and makes brilliant things seem a bit more… blah. Damn Chardonnay! In the morning I'll be delighted about my date with Logan and the excitement will distract me from my feelings about Zac, which probably aren't true feelings anyway. I snuggle under the duvet, imagine I'm in The Cosy Kettle counting a huge mountain of lemon chiffon pies, and fall into a deep, dreamless sleep.

Chapter Fifteen

I am never going to drink again. That's the first thought that crosses my mind when my eyes flutter open the next morning. Or rather, *eye* – one seems to be stuck down, along with my tongue which is flat against the roof of my mouth. It feels like sandpaper when I take a swig of my remaining water.

I'm in love with my best friend. That's the second thought that hammers its way into my poor dehydrated brain.

'Nope. Too complicated,' I croak out loud, clambering out of bed and walking to the window. I wince as I pull back the curtains because it's stupidly bright outside. The sun is shining in a crisp blue sky and a layer of snow on the grass verge opposite is sparkling with a crust of frost. How dare it be so dazzlingly beautiful, and what time is it anyway? I stare at the clock radio by my bed and sigh, as quietly as possible because my head is throbbing like it's about to explode. It's five past eight which means I need to get ready for work.

I stagger along the landing and pause for a moment to register that Zac's bedroom door, open when I went to bed, is now closed. That means he got home safely after his hot date with my sister. I go into the bathroom, switch the shower on full pelt and clamber into the bath.

As water streams over me, I fight off the clammy shower curtain which wraps itself around my thighs, and lean my head back against the tiles. I've bagged a date with very handsome Logan Fairweather, albeit while drunk and rather incoherent. I have vague memories of saying 'posh' over and over again. But it didn't put him off. Hooray! Logan wants to take me out, the party planning is going well, and I'm feeling more assertive these days – my wishes are coming true, so I'm happy. Aren't I?

An image of Zac and Jasmine last night, standing together by the front door, shining and happy, swims into my mind, along with the thought: *It should have been me.* Urgh. I slide slowly down into the tub and let the water bounce off my head, down my nose and onto the chipped enamel.

I'm definitely still in love with Zac, which is hardly surprising. Did I think my feelings would disappear overnight in a Chardonnay-fuelled puff of smoke? The water in our dodgy shower has gone cold but I carry on sitting in the bath, contemplating the irony of my situation and shivering. What seemed like an impossible wish has come true and Logan has asked me out – but, as it happens, he isn't the one I really want to go on a date with. I'd laugh if it wasn't all so terribly sad.

Right now, what I wish the most is that I could talk to Zac about how I'm feeling. I know that's impossible, and yet… a spark of bravery stirs in my poor, hungover soul as I hear his bedroom door open and footsteps going down the stairs.

I haul myself out of the bath and get dressed quickly in my jeans and a dark sweatshirt. Then I brush my hair, put on my eyeliner with a shaky hand, and take a deep breath. Wouldn't reinvented Becca have the confidence to speak her mind?

'I know it's early, Zac, but can we talk?' I ask, bursting into the kitchen. 'Oh, for goodness' sake, what the—?'

I swallow the rest of my words and hang onto the kitchen table, feeling nauseous. There in front of me are Zac and Jasmine leaning into the fridge, with their heads bent close together. They both look up at me, their faces glowing in the fridge light.

'Hell's teeth, Beccs. You look like the ghost of Christmas past!' laughs Jasmine, taking a yoghurt from the fridge. 'Sorry, we didn't mean to wake you.'

'You didn't. I had to get up to go to work.'

'Oh yeah, I forgot you work at weekends. What a bore.' Jasmine takes the teaspoon being offered by Zac and peels the foil top from her yoghurt pot. Then she stops and pushes her face towards mine. 'You look ever so ill.'

'You look ever so undressed.'

Why did I say that? Why did I draw attention to the fact that Jasmine is wearing nothing but one of Zac's shirts? She sits on the end of the table and swings her long bare legs.

'I stayed over because I'd had too much to drink to drive, and the taxi driver seemed a bit dodgy. Zac didn't want me travelling home with him on my own and I didn't fancy it either.' Uh-huh. I bet that wasn't all she fancied. But I nod. If she wants to be coy about it, carry on.

Zac, in a baggy T-shirt and jogging bottoms, runs his hands through his tousled hair. He looks sleepy and vulnerable and I so want to put my arms around him and my head against his chest. I grip the table instead and take a deep breath.

'Did you want to talk to me, Beccs?' he asks, closing the fridge.

'Nope.'

'Only you said you did when you came in.'

'Oh, yeah.' I try to think straight for one moment. 'I just wondered… if you'd both had a good evening.'

'Yeah, great. The party was fun and Zac made a very good impression,' says Jasmine, giving him a grin. 'I think that was due to his rather sharp suit.'

'Not due to my sparkling personality and ready wit then?' retorts Zac, splashing milk across the worktop as he pulls the tab off the new carton.

'That too,' says Jasmine, leaping up, tearing off a wodge of kitchen roll and leaning across him to mop up the mess. Her arm brushes against his chest but he doesn't step back. They seem very easy together, as though they know each other really well. Which they obviously do, after spending the night together. Another wave of nausea hits me and I close my eyes. Hangovers really are the pits.

'Are you sure you're all right? I'm making tea for us if you want one,' says Zac, gently, touching me lightly on the shoulder.

I open my eyes. 'No thanks. I need to get in to work 'cos there's lots to do. I'll have a paracetamol though, if there's one going. I've got a cracking headache.'

Zac reaches into the cupboard and pulls out a box of painkillers. 'Here you go, Beccs. You do look pale. You're not crying, are you?'

'Nah, crying's for wimps. I'm OK.'

'Can't you take the day off?'

'Honestly, I'm fine. I just had a bit too much to drink last night.' When I point at the empty wine bottle resting on top of the recycling bin, Zac does a double take and pours me a very large glass of water.

'It's not like you to drink on your own.' Jasmine licks yoghurt off her teaspoon with one eye on Zac. 'You're usually fairly sensible about that kind of thing.'

'I was celebrating,' I blurt out. 'Celebrating being asked out by Logan Fairweather, the bloke whose Christmas party I'm arranging in The Cosy Kettle. He rang me last night and asked if I wanted to go to Tuckers with him at the end of the party. It's a proper date.'

I stare at my sister as defiantly as my banging headache will allow. She might have just slept with the man I've very inconveniently realised I'm in love with, but hey, I've been asked out by the local heartthrob.

'Wow.' Jasmine looks properly impressed with me for the first time since… nope, I can't remember when. 'Are you going?'

'Of course I'm going. I'm crazy about him and looking forward to the start of a beautiful relationship.'

'Brilliant. That's really good news, then, isn't it?'

'It certainly is,' I say, as brightly as I can muster.

Jasmine glances at Zac, who's pouring Coco Pops into a bowl. 'What do you think about it, Zac?'

'Yeah, it's good news,' he says, without taking his eyes from his breakfast. 'If you're quite sure that's what you want.'

'Of course I'm sure! He's the man of my dreams.'

That's over the top but it's none of Zac's business who I'm seeing, not now he's so keen on my sister. I know Zac. He wouldn't spend the night with someone unless he really, *really* liked them. And he certainly wouldn't spend the night with my sister if he had even the slightest twinge of romantic feelings for me. A faint stirring of hope that my feelings for him might be reciprocated – so faint I hadn't acknowledged it until now – fades away. So that's that, then.

Another wave of nausea hits me and I gulp down two paracetamol.

'Right, I'd better be off and leave you to it,' I mutter, wondering if they'll be taking their cups of tea back to bed. I scurry into the sitting room, grab my jacket and charge out into the blindingly bright December morning.

Brrr! I have seriously underestimated how cold it is out here and I shiver as I crunch my way through the snow. Several small shops are already open and the High Street is bustling with Christmas shoppers who haven't been put off by the weather.

Zac and Jasmine are a couple. I try to push the thought out of my mind and keep walking. Ahead of me, the hills rising above Honeyford are coated in white and smoke is curling from cottage chimneys. A number of small stalls have been set up under the stone arches of the market house and trading has already begun.

Two of the people I love most in the world are together. I give up, as I walk past the town Christmas tree and the festive bunting looped from lamp post to lamp post, and let the thought take hold. It might not last – Jasmine's track record with relationships isn't great. But even if by some miracle Zac and I ever did get together, he chose Jasmine first which means I'd always feel more second best than ever.

It's hard to think straight with a banging hangover, but the way ahead is clear. Let Zac's relationship with Jasmine play out and keep quiet about my unrequited feelings. Push them down deep until they lose their painful edge, and keep myself occupied working to make my Christmas wish come true. I won't go to pieces like I did after Charlie left.

I crunch on through the glinting snow and past picture-perfect cottages, but the soothing magic of Honeyford isn't working on me today. It'll be OK, I tell myself. I'll get past these difficult feelings and become the person I want to be. Mary is helping me to update my wardrobe tomorrow, the Cosy Kettle party will wow everyone, and then I'm going on an actual proper date with super-hunky Logan. That thought does cheer me up a tiny bit, actually.

*

Two pints of water and three very strong cups of coffee later, I'm start-ing to feel much better – at least on the hangover front. We've been inundated with frazzled shoppers seeking warmth and a breather from the Christmas crowds, but I've still found the time to put up the new decorations that arrived in a big parcel yesterday. Keeping busy has been good for me because it leaves no time to dwell on the fact that I'm in love with my best friend.

Late morning, I stand behind the counter, next to the coffee machine, and look around the café. White frosted-glass baubles and macramé stars adorn the tree and I've tied white ribbon bows onto the branches. Large green wreaths dotted with fir cones are hanging on the walls and an arch of greenery dotted with tiny white fairy lights is pinned above the door to the garden. Logan's company has covered the cost of the decorations and they've certainly done the trick – The Cosy Kettle looks terribly tasteful.

There's just one more thing to do while there's a lull in customers. I pick up the cardboard box at my feet, walk over to the shelf that runs along one wall and stand with my hands on my hips. It's daft but I've not been looking forward to this bit. Carefully, I start taking down the copper kettles that gave the café its name. They belonged to Stanley's late wife, Moira, and have been on display since The Cosy Kettle first opened. The burnished copper catches the light and feels smooth under my fingers as I pack the kettles away and replace them with three large silver reindeer.

They're the only reindeer in the café now. The light-up reindeer on the counter was one of the first decorations to go. Kids coming in loved him and patted his glowing red nose with huge smiles on their

faces. But he's been banished to the shop's attic, along with the paper
garlands and flashing fairy lights and everything else considered too
tacky for Logan's sophisticated guests.

I bite my lip and take a deep breath to ease my churning stomach.
Even a batch of freshly baked cinnamon buns weren't enough to tempt
me this morning so I've had nothing to eat since last night.

'Good morning, Becca.' When I turn around, Luna is standing next
to the Christmas tree. Her long white tunic and white, wide-legged
trousers match the ribbon-bows tied to the branches behind her. 'My
word. Flora said you were busy changing things round and she was
right. It's quite the transformation.'

'Hello, Luna,' I say, feeling a familiar nag of unease as she steps
forward and holds out the palms of her hands towards me. 'Do you
like The Cosy Kettle's new look?'

'Do you?' she asks, her silver hair falling over one shoulder as she
tilts her head.

'Yes, I think so. The café has a more upmarket atmosphere which is
what Logan wants for his party. He's expecting sophistication.'

'Do you always do what people expect, Becca?'

'I do when they're paying to host an event here,' I snap, miffed that
Luna seems to be implying I don't have a mind of my own. Not long
ago I'd have immediately apologised for being bad-tempered but I don't
feel minded to today. My head's aching, Zac is probably snogging the
life out of Jasmine right now, and I don't have to be shy and quietly
spoken all of the time. My Christmas wish will never come true if I
keep being the same old anxious Becca.

Luna doesn't seem fazed by my unusual display of bad temper. In
fact, she smiles one of her mysterious smiles and lowers her hands.
'Could you make me a decaffeinated flat white with oat milk when you

have a moment? To go, because I need to get back to my emporium. You'd be surprised how many people come in to browse when they've run out of ideas for presents.'

She winks and follows me as I slip behind the counter and start making her coffee. She'll give me her verdict on my aura and energies and spiritual health any moment. I prepare myself for it as I get the oat milk from the fridge and pour her finished coffee into a cardboard cup. But it doesn't come. Luna stays quiet, running her finger along the counter as she considers the array of delicious cakes and pies for sale.

'Thank you, Becca,' she says, handing over her money when I place the cup in front of her. 'I wish you a happy and fulfilled day.' Then she turns to go.

'Um, and how are you doing?' I ask, feeling disappointed, for some strange reason, that Luna has kept the state of my aura to herself.

When she turns back to face me, her amber eyes lock onto mine. 'I and my family are very blessed. Flora has brought a new healing energy to Starlight Cottage. How are you?'

'I'm… bearing up. I had a bit of a heavy night with the Chardonnay 'cos of… stuff going on.' Oops, too much information. Why am I telling scary Luna all this?

I start drumming my fingers on the counter until she places her hand on top of mine. Her skin is soft and warm and I know it's bonkers, but I feel a sudden whoosh of calm envelop me from my head to my toes.

'All will be well, Becca, if you remain true to yourself,' she says, over the hubbub of conversation from café customers. 'You're rather lost right now but I'm sure you'll find your way.' She lets go of my hand and smiles. 'And so will the café.'

'Does that mean you don't like the new decorations?'

Luna glances around her and frowns slightly. 'They don't quite fit. Remember that even buildings have a soul, a unique ambience that resonates for good or ill with those who pass through it.'

Luna referring to The Cosy Kettle as if it's a living, breathing entity is starting to spook me out, and I take a step back – farther away from her weird cat-like eyes.

She smiles and clasps her coffee to her chest. 'I'd best be getting back to work, and it looks as if you have visitors anyway.' She nods towards the doorway which is filled with Phyllis's wheelchair being pushed by Mary. Behind them, I spot Stanley's glasses and Dick's white beard. 'Did you know the book club was coming in?'

'No,' I sigh, regretting my text an hour ago to Stanley. All I did was ask him to call me when he was free, so I could give him an update on the Logan situation to ensure he backed off on the matchmaking front. I don't want him scaring Logan off because, who knows, maybe our date will be a great success and my feelings for Zac will start to fade? But it looks as if Stanley, rather than simply calling me back, has rallied the troops.

'Good luck,' are Luna's parting words as she leaves and Stanley hurries over.

'Don't worry, Beccs. We're all here to help so bring over our usual order and we can get started. Here comes Millie, too. She responded to your call for help.'

'What call for help? I simply asked you to ring me for a quick chat.' But Stanley is already heading back to his friends, who have bagged a free table in the corner. Millicent joins them and gives me a brief wave before taking her seat.

I'm not sure I'm up to coping with the book club today, but I make their favourite coffees and carry them over on a tray.

'Take a seat,' says Phyllis, patting a spare chair next to her. 'Then tell us what the emergency is. Does it involve your Christmas wishes?'

'We're so happy to help,' butts in Dick. 'It's not often oldies like us – not including yourself, Mary – can be useful to youngsters like you.'

'Yep, all you have to do is say what the CK Crew can do for you,' says Stanley, doing some weird clicking thing with his fingers. He's wearing a tatty grey hoodie and hasn't put the hood down since he came in.

'CK Crew, Stanley?' Millicent's face is a picture of disdain.

'That's us. We are the Cosy Kettle Crew, Millie. Essentially, you are in the hood and a right gangbanger.'

'I most certainly am not,' declares Millicent, pushing back her chair and getting to her feet.

I put my hand on Millicent's shoulder. 'I think Stanley's referring to street gangs in America.'

'But *why*?' asks Millicent plaintively, sinking back onto her seat.

'It's all about staying young,' harrumphs Stanley. 'I'm keeping in with the kids and up with the latest trends.'

'By turning us into some sort of New Jersey gang?' Millicent shakes her head. 'We read books, Stanley. We're a group of people in the Cotswolds who love literature – though I do wonder sometimes with the types of books we end up reading.'

Everyone starts squabbling about the merits of different literary genres while I bitterly regret texting Stanley at all. My head was still throbbing and I obviously wasn't thinking straight.

I pull myself together and sit down beside them. 'It's lovely of you all to come in but I think there's been a misunderstanding. I texted Stanley and asked him to ring me when he was free so I could update him on something that's happened.'

'So no emergency, then?' asks Millicent, giving Stanley another filthy look. 'I was halfway through booking tickets for a performance of *Aida* at the Oxford Playhouse when you summoned me.'

'And I had to leave Callum with Kevin, and he wasn't happy,' moans Mary, pushing her long brown hair over her shoulder. 'Though Callum is as much his son as mine. Not that you'd think so when he's acting like he deserves a medal for changing a nappy. Honestly, he's so…' She stops and draws in a long, loud breath as Phyllis pats her hand and starts murmuring, 'There, there'.

'I'm really sorry you all felt you needed to come in, though I'm touched you responded so quickly. But all I wanted was a quick chat with Stanley.'

'About what?' barks Millicent. 'You might as well tell us now we're all here.'

I lean forward and lower my voice. 'Don't say anything but I wanted to let Stanley know that Logan has asked me out on a date.'

'Whoop, whoop!' yells Stanley, punching the air. 'I knew my methods would do the trick.'

'It was nothing to do with you because Becca is a very attractive young woman,' insists Millicent. 'Or she will be when my hairdresser has sorted out her tragic hairstyle. Are you still on for Tuesday evening? Caroline is primed to give you a cut and colour.'

'That sounds lovely, if you're sure. Thank you. But the reason I wanted to tell Stanley about my date with Logan is because I need him, and all of you, to back off a bit or Logan will go off the idea. And don't, for goodness' sake, mention anything about my wish list to him. Please.'

'Of course not,' says Phyllis. 'We don't want to scare him off. Where's your young man taking you then?'

'We're going to Tuckers, which is a night club, after the Cosy Kettle Christmas party has finished.'

'The party that we're not invited to,' grumps Stanley.

'Get over it, man,' says Dick, shaking his head. 'It's a corporate party and Becca can't get you in.'

'I really can't. You know I would if I could.'

'Oh, I say!' Stanley is staring over my shoulder. 'Where's Auntie Edna? She's not on top of the tree. Has she been stolen?'

'Who would be desperate enough to steal a plastic fairy with a flashing halo?' asks Millicent, craning her neck to look at the tree.

But Stanley isn't listening. He's gesturing wildly across the café. 'And the kettles are gone. All of them. Where are Moira's copper kettles? Becca, you've been ram-raided and everything's been nicked.'

I've never seen Stanley so agitated. Anxiety is surging from him in waves. I wrap my fingers around his bony arm and squeeze. 'They're fine, Stanley. Honestly. Auntie Edna and the kettles are perfectly safe. They're all boxed up and in the attic, upstairs.'

'But why?' he asks, his face crumpled in confusion.

'Please don't get upset, Stanley. It's just until after the party. I didn't think they quite suited the theme of the event so I've packed them away for a few days.'

'But the copper kettles *are* The Cosy Kettle because they gave this café its name. My granddaughter, Callie, set up this place for Flora and called it The Cosy Kettle in honour of her gran, my Moira, and this place isn't the same without them.'

'It's not for long. Really. Please don't get upset.'

'It's long enough for this place to go all fancy-schmancy. Don't think we haven't noticed all the changes that are going on in here.' He glances at the counter and his jaw drops. 'Even Rudy has been banished to the attic. The kids loved that red-nosed reindeer but he's been culled!'

'It's just for a few days.'

'So you say, but who knows if this place will ever go back to normal? And what's wrong with the kettles?'

'Nothing, they're just a bit… shabby.' Oh dear, that is so not the right word to use but my brain is still befuddled. 'What I mean is that the kettles are dented and Auntie Edna is…' How can I say this politely? '… not terribly sophisticated.'

Stanley pulls his lips into a thin line. 'They were sophisticated enough for my Moira and plenty good enough for The Cosy Kettle before you started chopping and changing.'

'He's got a point,' says Millicent. 'You don't want this place to become like every other soulless café. That's not to say I don't like your changes. Auntie Edna is an acquired taste and the new decorations are rather more my style. But you have to think of your clientele, Becca, and changing a much-loved venue is not good for people like Stanley.' To my amazement, she scoots her chair along until she's beside him and puts her arm around his shoulders.

'It's just a bit of a makeover for a few days,' I insist, wincing as my head starts to throb again.

'First, it's a bit of a makeover, and what's next? Banning the book club for being too shabby?' grumps Stanley.

'Obviously not,' I insist, as the mood in the café dips further. Even without Luna on hand, I can identify the negative energies swirling around me as the other customers stop eating and drinking to stare at the hubbub in the corner.

'It's no wonder you don't want to invite us to your posh party with its weirdo singers and lah-di-dah decorations.'

'I *can't* invite you,' I say, but Stanley's so upset he's not listening.

He gets to his feet and the rest of the book club follow. 'We know when we're not wanted,' he sniffs, heading for the door.

'Of course you're wanted,' I call after him but he's either ignoring me or he hasn't got his hearing aid in.

'I don't think anyone could ever accuse me of being shabby,' says Millicent, but she still follows Stanley and Dick to the door.

'It's coming up to the anniversary of Moira's death. So it's bad timing, Becca. That's all,' whispers Phyllis to me, before Mary starts pushing her towards the exit. 'It's a shame, though, about this place.'

A hush falls across the café as the book club disappear into Flora's shop. 'Get back to your cake and coffee, everyone!' I bark, slinging the club's coffee cups onto my tray with no care whatsoever.

I wander back to the counter and sit on my stool with the day's remaining cakes in front of me. They smell sweet and delicious, but I've never been less hungry in my life. I've managed to upset the entire book club and I feel so bad about Stanley. But changing the café was a business decision: a clear-cut business decision that Flora approved of and Jasmine would make in a heartbeat. I can't let my Christmas wish be scuppered by negative emotions, not when I'm getting close.

I ferret in the pocket of my apron and pull out my beer mat wish list which is peeling at the corners.

1. *Be more assertive and confident, particularly as regards café.* That's ongoing, but I've pushed through the current changes in here, and I'm definitely feeling more arsey. Does that count? I reckon it does. I find a coffee-splattered pen next to the fridge and give that wish a half-tick.

2. *Impress Flora with business acumen.* Again, it's a work in progress but she seems impressed with my party planning so far and I'll make sure the actual party knocks her socks off. That warrants another half-tick.

3. *Make parents proud of me.* I suck the end of the pen which tastes of caramel macchiato. I'm pretty sure my parents still view me as an emotionally unstable disappointment, though Mum did call me wise when we were walking through the park. She hasn't made up her mind about the art course yet, and I still haven't spoken to Dad about it. My pen hovers over the beer mat for a moment before I decide that, sadly, one compliment doesn't warrant a tick.

4. *Conquer fear of public speaking.* Heaven knows why I thought putting this wish on the list was a good idea. Public speaking still scares the pants off me, though I did just order the whole café to get back to their beverages. I cringe inside at the memory. Nope, it's no tick for that one.

5. *Secure date with Logan.* Yes! Tick, tick, tick. And it's going to be amazing. I ignore a wave of sorrow as Zac's face pops into my head, and bury it down deep.

6. *Make myself look more like Jasmine.* That's really going to up a gear over the next few days. Or it was until I managed to annoy the book club. Fingers crossed that Mary will still want to take me shopping tomorrow, and Millicent won't cancel her hairdresser in a fit of pique.

I put the list back into my pocket and force a smile. No one ever said that making wishes come true was easy, and I hate upsetting friends, but they'll come round and it'll all be worth it in the end. No gain without pain.

Chapter Sixteen

I've locked the bookshop door and pocketed the key when a voice sounds in my ear. 'I thought that was you.'

When I turn around, Logan is standing so close I can feel the warmth of his breath on my cheek. A grey scarf is tucked into the neck of his black coat and his hair is shining almost white-blond in the warm light from the bookshop's window display. Next to him, looking bored, is Stu, the workmate he came into The Cosy Kettle with a while back.

'What are you doing here?' I ask, immediately feeling wrong-footed and slightly stalked. I need to build up to seeing Logan – calm my breathing, brush my hair, generally get myself in hand.

'Stu and I were in town and I thought you'd be locking up about now. You're a bit later than I expected, to be honest, and my feet are freezing.'

'Our feet,' mutters Stu, stamping his boots in the snow that's lingered all day on the cold pavements.

Logan ignores him. 'I hope it's not my party that's keeping you here after hours.'

'I just had a few things to finish off before I left for the day – a few more decorations to get up.'

'They're looking amazing, by the way. You're doing such a brilliant job.'

'How do you know that?'

'I nipped into the café at lunchtime but didn't spot you. Flora was serving coffees so I assumed you were at lunch.'

'Yeah, I was out shopping.' I'm lying because I don't want to tell him I was crashed out on the old camp bed in the attic. I faced down my fear of spiders lurking in dark attic corners – go, new Becca! – and snatched half an hour of shut-eye which helped to revive me for the afternoon.

'Are you busy this evening?' asks Logan, still standing very close.

'Why?'

'Stu and I are nipping to the pub for a quick pint before hitting the bright lights of Oxford, and we'd like it if you'd join us.'

Stu definitely wouldn't like it. He has the sullen face of a man with too much experience of playing gooseberry to his better-looking friend – an expression I perfected when Jazz and I used to go nightclubbing together during uni holidays.

When I hesitate, Logan laughs. 'It's not a date or some kind of weird threesome. I'm saving our date for after the Christmas party when it's just the two of us.' He gives me a slow, sexy wink. 'This is more a non-date – a quick catch-up about the party and a chat between friends. But don't worry if you've got other plans.'

My plans for the evening consist only of a long hot bath with lots of bubbles, followed by a comatose evening on the sofa with a crap sitcom on the telly. That, and avoiding Zac and Jasmine as much as possible.

'I've nothing planned, it's just that it's been a long day.'

'And a long night by the sound of it when we spoke on the phone. How's your head?'

'A bit delicate.' I look up at him and grin. 'Sorry if I was a bit tipsy on the phone.'

'You were ever so slightly tipsy, and absolutely adorable.'

Wow, that's a first. When we were growing up, Jasmine was the twin always described as 'adorable', with her long blonde curls and pretty smile. I was more often described as 'kind' or 'clever' – or 'sturdy' (thanks, Grandma). But handsome Logan thinks I'm adorable, even when I'm off my head.

Stu gives a long, loud sigh. 'Can you make your mind up 'cos I'm freezing my bits off here?'

'A quick drink would be lovely,' I tell Logan, slipping my arm through his when he crooks his elbow towards me.

'Excellent! The pub it is, then.'

The Pheasant and Fox is packed with people out enjoying the festive season. 'Fairytale of New York' is playing on the jukebox, rainbow lights are blinking on the tree, and the smell of roast turkey is wafting through the pub. Logan and Stu stand at the bar, getting the drinks in, while I find a seat near the door to the garden and scan the crowd. I recognise a few people from the café but there's no sign of Stanley or the CK Crew, thank goodness. They'd either harangue me for daring to change The Cosy Kettle, or earwig while I'm talking to Logan and give feedback on my conversational technique with prospective boyfriends.

'So how are things going with the party preparations?' asks Logan, placing a mulled wine in front of me and sliding into the seat opposite. An overwhelming smell of woody aftershave tickles my nose as Stu drops onto the seat next to me.

'The preparations are going really well. I've ticked off most of my spreadsheet.'

'I love a woman with a spreadsheet,' murmurs Logan, who seems to be smouldering again. 'Are you sure I can't get you anything to eat?'

'Absolutely sure, thanks,' I reply, even though I have a sudden craving for the roasted honey cashews they sell in here. I'm addicted to them but feel anxious at the thought of eating in front of Logan and Stu. Food in the teeth isn't a good look.

Logan slips off his jacket and stretches his legs under the table. 'Go on then, tell me what you've already arranged, party-wise, so I can relax and enjoy my weekend.'

'Well, I've redone the café decorations, the food is on order and the madrigal quartet are booked. Three patio heaters have arrived for the garden and I've ordered the extra strands of white lights we need for outside. I paid a little extra so they'll definitely be here in time for the party.'

'Wonderful. And I noticed you've moved that tacky angel off the top of the tree, and the dented kettles.'

'Yep, they're all packed up and put away,' I say, overwhelmed by a sudden rush of guilt. 'The kettles belonged to Stanley's wife and gave the café its name.'

'Stanley?' Logan wrinkles his perfect nose.

'The elderly man in the skinny jeans who seems to live in The Cosy Kettle.'

'Oh yeah. He's a bit of a strange one.'

'He was rather upset, actually, that the kettles had been moved. And Auntie Edna.'

'Who the hell is Auntie Edna?' demands Stu, who's still wrapped up in his jacket as though it's below freezing in here.

'She's the fairy on top of the tree.'

'Right.' Logan opens his eyes wide and takes a gulp of his beer. 'Well, the café's looking rather lovely after all your hard work – and so are you, Becca. There's something different about you recently. I can't quite put my finger on it.'

His unblinking gaze is rather disconcerting – thrilling and slightly uncomfortable.

'Thank you,' I squeak, rather nonplussed by all this attention. For a non-date, especially one with his grumpy friend in tow, this is getting pretty intense.

Logan starts running his index finger around the rim of his pint glass in a frankly erotic manner and raises an eyebrow. 'So how are things going with your liberal boyfriend… Thor, was it?'

'Thor?' snorts Stu, beside me.

'His name's not really Thor. That's just a nickname. His real name is…' Great; my mind's gone completely blank. There must be hundreds of boys' names out there. Thousands. And I can't think of a single one. I glance around the pub. 'Jeremy,' I blurt out, after spotting a Cosy Kettle customer propping up the bar who always reminds me of Jeremy Clarkson.

'Jeremy?' Logan frowns. 'I guess people call him Thor because of his muscles?'

'That's right. He's got loads of very big muscles 'cos he spends so much of his time at the gym.'

'The same gym that Zac and I go to?'

'Nope, definitely not that gym. It's another one, nearer Oxford. A new one that not a lot of people have heard of, actually.' I trail off.

'Does he live in Oxford?'

'Mmm,' I say, taking such a huge swig of mulled wine, I almost choke.

'So how long have you two been going out then?'

'Not long. We're not really going out. We're more friends, really.'

'Friends with benefits?' The corner of Logan's full mouth flickers upwards.

'Just friends,' I murmur, shifting uncomfortably on my chair.

'Good to know,' says Logan, hugging his pint to his chest. 'I don't mind not being exclusive when it comes to first dates but in the future…' He leaves that thought floating in the ether and sucks his bottom lip between his perfect pearly teeth. 'So what makes you tick, Becca?'

'Um, The Cosy Kettle, I guess.' I launch into explaining all about the café and how involved I was in setting it up, ignoring a stab of guilt at the changes I'm making. Stu eye-rolls beside me to signal his boredom, which makes me nervous and my mouth goes dry. My lips start sticking to my teeth which is so uncool. Jasmine would be keeping everyone's attention by throwing her head back and laughing in a tinkly, sexy way.

I give it a try – a quick flick of the head and my best sexy laugh. Oops, that sounded more like a bark. Logan frowns slightly and Stu gives me a sideways glance before downing half his pint in one.

'What's happening with your family?' asks Logan. 'How's your sister doing?'

Ah, I wondered how long it would take for Jasmine to come into the conversation.

'She's fine and working hard. I saw her yesterday actually just before she went out with' – I swallow hard – 'her new boyfriend.'

'Nice,' is Logan's only comment on Jasmine's love life before Stu starts talking about impressing his boss with his latest ideas for a new order retrieval system. I get a bit lost after a while because I'm still cringing inside at my lies about 'Thor'. And then my phone beeps with a text message while Logan is telling Stu about a new approach to fixing corporate printers, and it throws my concentration completely.

When I glance at the screen I see that the message is from Zac: *Are you in this evening? There's a lager here with your name on it and* Stranger Things *lined up and ready to go. You still at work?*

'Important message?' asks Logan.

'Just Zac wondering where I am.'

'You live with Zac, don't you?'

'That's right.'

'So what's the deal with you and Zac? Is there anything going on between you two?' Blimey. Thor *and* Zac? Sadly, Logan has seriously over-estimated the extent of my love life. 'Any benefits involved, at all?' asks Logan, staring into his almost empty pint glass.

None, unless you count living with a great housemate, a fabulous hugger when I'm upset, and a marvellous mickey-taker.

'No, we're just good friends. No benefits involved – not now, not ever.' My lower lip trembles and I wave my phone at Logan so he won't notice. 'I'd better send him a quick reply, if you don't mind.'

'Fill your boots.' Logan and Stu chat as I text back: *Finishing up in café. Not sure when I'll be home. See you later.*

I press 'send' and immediately feel guilty, even though Jasmine is probably at our cottage right now, keeping Zac company. Why did I bother lying? Zac doesn't approve of my taste in men but he knows Logan has asked me out on a date, and he'll be too busy with my sister to give it much thought.

Sighing quietly, I put my phone away and try to concentrate on Logan and Stu's conversation. I'm laughing in all the right places and everything's going OK until Logan asks what I did after university and I get totally tongue-tied. All I can think about is how everything went horribly wrong in Birmingham and how awkward I feel right now.

Logan grins and puts his hand on top of mine. 'You're miles away, Becca. Come back to me.' He leans forward and, with his other hand, hooks a stray strand of hair behind my ear. 'I do appreciate all the work you're doing to make my party a success,' he says softly. Suddenly, he drops his hand from my face and nods over my shoulder. 'Isn't that Zac?'

Twisting in my chair, I spot Zac at the bar, staring at us. He takes his change from the barman and wanders over.

'Hey, Logan and Becca. Fancy seeing the two of you in here.'

'Hey, Zac,' says Logan, folding his arms. 'This is my mate, Stu. I haven't bumped into you at the gym recently.'

'I've been really busy with a work project. Still, it's good to see you in here, with Becca.'

'Logan and I are having a kind of work meeting to talk about the party,' I gabble, feeling horribly caught out for lying.

'Yeah, Becca is doing a fabulous job. I'm so glad I chose her to organise the party. So how come you're in the pub? I thought you were at home.'

'I just nipped out to buy something,' says Zac. He shoves his purchase into his pocket but not before I've spotted that it's a packet of roasted cashew nuts. He nipped out specially to buy me a treat because he believed my lie and thought I was working late in The Cosy Kettle. I truly am the world's worst best friend without benefits.

'How's Jasmine?' I force myself to ask as a penance for lying.

'Good, when I last saw her. She said she'd see you soon.'

'Not this evening?'

Zac frowns. 'No, she said she's got some Christmas drinks thing with friends. Anyway, I'd better leave you and Logan to talk business. Bye, Logan. I'll see you in the gym this week, maybe?'

'It's mad busy at work with the Christmas break coming up but I'll try to get there.'

'And I'll be home soon,' I add.

'No worries,' he calls over his shoulder as he wanders off. 'Be as long as you like and have a good evening.'

'That felt a little awkward,' says Logan with a frown as Zac ducks under the low beam of the pub doorway and disappears into the darkness outside. 'I got the feeling Zac didn't approve of you being here in the pub with me.'

'No, he's fine. He's probably just miffed because he's cooked me something and it's getting cold.'

'You make him sound terribly domesticated.' When Logan laughs, I get a fleeting urge to push his gorgeous, handsome face into his pint and hurry home to Zac.

'We share the cooking which is only fair when we share the house.'

Logan shrugs. 'I guess so. Anyway, enough about Zac, what about—?'

'Hadn't we better be making a move, mate?' interrupts Stu, tapping his watch. 'The roads to Oxford won't be great in this weather so you won't want to drive fast.'

'He's worse than my mother.' Logan grins. 'OK, I guess we'd better get going so Stu can try out his chat-up lines on the women of Oxford. And you'd better get back to your cold tea before Zac throws a hissy fit.'

I give a weak smile and start slipping my arms into my jacket. Logan gets wrapped up too and he and Stu follow me out of the pub into the cold night air. The temperature has dropped while we've been inside and frost is sparkling on patches of dark, damp pavement that are no longer covered in snow.

'Thank you, both, for letting me join you for a drink.'

Stu grunts but Logan smiles. 'You're welcome. We'll do it again soon, on Friday.'

He bends his head to kiss me on the cheek, but does a mini-swerve at the last moment and his warm lips press briefly against mine. It's only a peck but I can taste the beer he was drinking and feel the heat radiating from my cheeks. He moves back and stares at me, under the pub's flashing fairy lights, with an amused look on his face. 'I'll be seeing you around, lovely Becca.'

Stu drags him off and I watch them disappear into the darkness. Not only did Logan Fairweather describe me as both 'adorable' and 'lovely' within the last half hour, he also kissed me on the lips. That's amazing, and a few days ago I'd have been over the moon. It's funny how things change.

I let myself in quietly to the cottage, hang up my jacket and wander into the kitchen. Zac has left me some shepherd's pie in the oven and I spoon it onto a plate while I heat some peas in the microwave. What a day! While I wait for the oven to ping, I run my finger along my lips and try to make sense of everything that's happened in the last twelve hours.

What should have been a mega-high was Logan going out of his way to invite me to the pub and kissing me goodbye. He's off to Oxford now, probably to try out his chat-up lines alongside Stu, but he'll be all mine after the party. I mentally give Christmas wish number five another enormous tick, without much enthusiasm.

The transformation of The Cosy Kettle is really coming on, but I can't help feeling sad about my spat with the book club. Their favoured corner of the café seemed empty without them this afternoon and I'm not convinced they'll come back after the party. Stanley was very upset.

And then there was the bombshell discovery that my best friend and my sister had spent the night together. That was the lowest point of the past turbulent twelve hours. Jasmine's no longer here but I can still feel her presence and picture her standing next to Zac, wearing only his shirt. *It should have been me,* echoes in the back of my mind, but I wrench open the microwave door and try to ignore it.

I pile my food onto a plate, grab a knife and fork and head into the sitting room. A sudden snore from the sofa makes me jump. Zac is lying there, in jogging bottoms and a T-shirt. He hasn't got round to shaving today – there's a shadow of stubble across his chin – and his dark hair is tousled. I fight an urge to brush a stray curl from his forehead and stand staring down at him.

'Hey, Becca,' says Zac, opening his eyes and holding out his arm to focus on his watch. 'I must have nodded off. I'm knackered today.'

'I expect you're tired, after last night.'

I mentally kick myself for mentioning last night right off the bat. No build up, no gradually getting around to the subject, just wham! And after the day I've had, I really don't feel like discussing his night of passion, let alone my feelings that could kill our friendship stone dead.

I needn't have worried. All Zac says is, 'Yeah,' as he sits up and slips his feet into the plaid 'old man' slippers I bought him last Christmas. They were a joke present and he laughed when he saw them, but he's been wearing them ever since. I wonder if he'll still wear them when Jasmine is around.

Normally I'd tell Zac to budge up and go and sit on the sofa next to him but I remain standing, the food congealing on my plate.

'You came back then.' When Zac stands up and stretches, his T-shirt rides up, revealing his tight, flat abdomen. He really has been working out. I sit down heavily on the chair behind me and balance my plate on my knees.

'Of course I came back. Why wouldn't I?'

'It all seemed a bit hush-hush and I thought you might go home with Logan to do some rather more intense party-planning.'

'It wasn't a date, Zac. That's on Friday, when his miserable mate, Stu, won't be around. I'm sorry I didn't mention I was in the pub with him but he saw me locking up at work and suggested it. I didn't say anything because I know you're not that keen on him.'

'He's all right and I get why you like him. He's your usual type.'

'What do you mean by that?'

Zac sighs. 'Nothing. Forget I said anything.'

'No, tell me.'

'All right. What I mean is that he reminds me of Charlie, who was an ultra-confident man oozing with charm who didn't treat you brilliantly. I sometimes think you're trying to get from them what you feel you're missing in yourself.'

'Logan is nothing like Charlie. And all I'm trying to be is a better person. That's what my Christmas wish is all about,' I retort, stung by his criticism.

'I approve of you trying to be a *happier* person. Anyway, it's none of my concern who you do or don't go out with.'

'Just like it's none of my business who you go out with. Anyway' – I take a deep breath – 'Logan is OK, honestly.'

Zac stares at me for a moment and then his shoulders drop. 'Yeah, he's fine, and I know you really like him.' He smiles but the skin around his eyes doesn't crinkle like it usually does. He looks exhausted.

'Thank you very much for making my tea,' I say, stiffly.

'You're welcome, though it's probably dry because it's been in the oven for ages.'

'No, it's great,' I assure him, gulping down a mouthful of dehydrated mince and mash.

'How was your day at work? You didn't look too well this morning.'

'I had the hangover from hell, but it's eased off now.'

'That's good.'

There's a strained silence as I take another mouthful of food. Usually I'd tell Zac about how I upset the book club and he'd make me laugh and we'd sort everything out. He's always been the one person I can confide in, but our relationship has shifted. Jasmine and Logan are standing between us, along with the secret I can never share – *I'm in love with you.*

'It was stupid of me to drink so much.'

'You were celebrating securing a date with Logan and crossing another wish off your list. You'll have the full set before you know it.'

'Yeah, my Christmas wish will come true and I'll live happily ever after.'

'Which is all I ever want for you. You know that, don't you, Beccs?'

'Yeah. You too.' Tears suddenly prickle the corners of my eyes and I bend my head over my food to hide my face.

'Right then, I'd better go and have a shave. Some friends from work texted a little while ago and invited me out for a drink. Will you be all right here on your own?'

'Of course. I'll watch a bit of telly and I could do with a long hot bath.'

'Sounds good.'

Oh, this is awful. *I could do with a long hot bath* would usually elicit some sarcastic comment about me sparking a water shortage or a joke about my personal hygiene. But there's nothing. Just a polite 'Sounds good,' as though we're nothing but passing acquaintances. Sleeping with your best friend's twin sister is bound to make the friendship a bit awkward but I didn't think it would have such a corrosive effect so quickly.

I prod at the shepherd's pie on my plate as Zac pads upstairs. It's lukewarm when I take a mouthful but I plough on, shovelling in food without tasting it.

Chapter Seventeen

My makeover day is still on! Mary texted me late last night to confirm our arrangement which means that today is the day I'm hoping to put at least a half-tick against wish number six: *Make myself look more like Jasmine.*

At eleven o'clock on the dot, I knock on the front door of Mary's small modern semi. It's on the outskirts of Honeyford and down a nondescript side road, hidden away from tourists. All they see are winding streets and butter-yellow buildings mellowed by centuries of sunshine and rain.

A few moments after knocking, the door is flung open and there's Mary, with a screaming Callum on her hip.

'Thank goodness you're here,' she says, pushing back her long dark hair and ignoring Callum's blood-curdling shrieks. 'Kevin!' she yells. 'Becca's here!' She lowers her voice. 'If I don't get out soon, I'm going to go totally nuts.'

A harassed-looking man in blue jeans and a burgundy sweatshirt comes to the door. He's barefoot and has huge bags under his eyes. He's probably good-looking but it's hard to tell because he looks so haggard.

'How long are you going to be, Mary? You'll be back soon, won't you?'

'I won't be too long,' she tells him, handing over Callum, who starts screaming even more loudly. 'See you later.'

She grabs her coat, steps outside and slams the front door behind her. Callum's screams follow us as we walk along the path and climb into Mary's small car.

'I don't intend to go back for hours and hours,' says Mary, looking over her shoulder as she reverses out of her parking space. 'I might never go back at all.'

She drives us out of Honeyford and over the hills towards Oxford. The sky is overcast with a blanket of white-grey cloud, and the colours around us are muted. Mary doesn't say anything about the bust-up in The Cosy Kettle so I bring it up as we drive past banks of trees, dripping with melted snow.

'Was Stanley all right after you left the café yesterday? I was a bit worried about him.'

She takes her eyes off the road and shoots me a quick glance. 'He didn't like the kettles and Edna being moved but he'll get over it. It's three years next week since his wife died so he's a bit emotional at the moment.'

'I didn't mean for the changes in The Cosy Kettle to upset him. I'm very fond of Stanley – of all of you – but I'm running a business and setting out the café as my client wants.'

'I get that and it looks good, all decked out in silver and white. It's just quite different from what we're used to. That's all. It doesn't feel like The Cosy Kettle any more. Anyway, enough about work stuff, tell me all about your fancy-free life and make me envious.'

Mary relaxes more with every mile we get farther from Honeyford, as we drive through tunnels of trees and past long wide valleys dotted with golden villages huddled around pale stone churches. We chat easily about where we grew up and Flora's dishy boyfriend and what my life is like without children. I think I rather disappoint her with my boring tales of work and watching *Love Island* on the sofa with Zac.

'Your housemate seems nice,' she says, crunching down into third gear as we zoom around a corner. 'He's pretty cute.'

'He's a lovely man. Really kind and caring.'

'And then there's that handsome bloke you're going out with after the party. You're drowning in good-looking men, you lucky cow.'

She glances at me and grins and I have to laugh. 'Logan is rather nice-looking.'

'You think? My knees start knocking whenever I spot his rugged jawline across the café. Let's just say that I definitely would. And he'll be totally smitten when he sees your new look.'

'I'm not changing how I dress just for him.'

'I know. I saw your wish list – more assertive, more confident, yada yada. New, more flattering clothes will help with that. But, as an important side effect, they'll also knock Logan's socks off – and a lot more clothing besides.' She gives a throaty chuckle and slams the car into fourth gear as I wish my new wardrobe would knock Zac's socks off instead. But I'm not daft – it would take more than a new pair of trousers to compete with Jasmine's many attributes.

Before long, we reach the outskirts of Oxford and drive along wide streets lined by large elegant houses. As we get closer to the centre, the roads narrow and the beautiful buildings become older. Oxford is wonderful, especially at this time of year when Christmas lights are strung along the streets. I love visiting but I'm out of sync with city life now and am always happy to get home to more peaceful Honeyford.

Mary eventually finds a parking space and the shopping spree begins. I say 'spree' but my financial situation means it's more of a trip – a low-key budget trip to, as Mary describes it, 'tart you up a bit'.

As the quest to look more like Jasmine begins, I get a sudden attack of nerves. Especially when I wave a few photos of Jasmine under Mary's nose to give her an idea of the style I'm aiming for.

'Is that your sister?' asks Mary, her eyes opening wide in a familiar expression of disbelief. 'She's very… well… she's…'

'Not much like me?'

'She's definitely related,' says Mary, squinting at the pictures. 'I can see a likeness in the shape of your eyes and nose, and the way you both stand, but your colouring is so different. I presume from the colour of your eyebrows that your hair is naturally darker than hers?'

'Yeah, mine's a nondescript shade of mousey brown. Do you reckon I can look like Jasmine?'

Mary thinks for a moment. 'I reckon you can borrow a little of her style and look like a brilliant version of you. Does that sound OK?' She smiles when I nod. 'Good. Now, brace yourself because this is going to be intense.'

She isn't joking. Mary starts dragging me into shop after shop and thrusting clothes at me. With her encouragement, I buy a pair of smart but inexpensive trousers, a couple of thin jumpers (for layering, apparently), a pretty long-sleeved top with cut-out shoulders and tiny hummingbirds on it, and two cotton scarves, one in shades of green and blue, and the other a deep shade of burgundy. I also buy a pair of nude stiletto shoes that I'd never normally wear in a month of Sundays, but Jasmine would.

'Are we done?' I ask, ready to drop after taking my clothes on and off umpteen times in tiny changing cubicles.

'Almost,' says Mary, who seems more alive than I've ever seen her. There's a spring in her step and a fervent zeal in her eyes as she flicks through clothing on the shop rails and chooses suitable items for me to try on. 'There's just one more shop we need to visit.'

I troop out into the cold Oxford air and follow her as she marches along a narrow street and stops outside a shop that has two miniature Christmas trees flanking its doors. Oh dear. As soon as I glance in the window, I can tell this is the kind of shop I usually avoid.

Two female assistants by the till glance at me, unsmiling, as Mary and I go inside. They give my scruffy jeans a once-over and sniff, but cheer up when they spot all the bags that we're carrying.

'Why are we in here?' I hiss at Mary, staring at the rows of dresses hanging on silver rails.

'To get you a couple of dresses that you can wear to work.'

'I don't wear dresses like these to work. I don't wear dresses at all. Well, only my wool dress which is pretty old.'

'Exactly.'

She starts running her fingers across the thick cotton of a blue shift dress, while I sigh inwardly. These tailored dresses aren't me at all. But maybe that's the point when I'm supposed to be changing who I am. Old anxious Becca doesn't wear pretty dresses to work, but new Becca who wants to be a little more like Jasmine does.

'Try these,' says Mary, thrusting four dresses at me. 'They should fit OK and flatter your shape.'

This shop has a better class of changing room. There's a thick velvet curtain rather than a thin wooden door, the floor is free of balled-up tissues, and the lighting is so flattering I don't look in the mirror and wince. Actually, I don't look bad at all in this light. I do a slow twirl and pout as if I'm a model.

I've been letting my hair grow recently and it now reaches my shoulders, with a natural wave near my ears. It's still a vivid shade of blue, but the style is softer than usual.

'How's it going in there?' calls Mary through the heavy curtain. 'I suppose I had better get back to Kevin at some point. And I know it sounds ridiculous but I'm starting to miss Callum. He's quite sweet when he falls asleep on my shoulder.'

'Just coming,' I say, peeling off my jeans and sweatshirt yet again and trying on the first dress which is scratchy on my skin and tight around my waist. It also has frills down the bodice. Frills! There is a limit to how far I'll go to make my wish come true. I peel off the dress and try garment number two. It's so fitted, I can hardly get it over my hips and I quickly decide that I look like a lumpy sack of potatoes in it. *This* is why I don't wear dresses!

But the third dress I try on looks OK. It's a simple short-sleeved 'T' shape with a self-tie belt in the same rich red fabric. The hem rests just above my knees.

'Let's have a look,' declares Mary, sweeping back the curtain, impatiently. 'Oh, my! You look lovely and very elegant in that. Team it with black tights and boots and you'll be a knockout. What about the others?'

'These two don't fit properly but I'll give the last dress a go.'

This one also looks rather nice when I've struggled into it. The black fabric fits tightly across my boobs and then it falls into a swirly full skirt that swishes when I move.

'That one really suits you, too,' says Mary, who's standing watching me get changed with her hands on her hips.

'I'm not sure it's very practical for The Cosy Kettle.'

'Shove an apron on top to protect it from coffee spills and it'll be fine. It's up to you, Becca, but you look great in those dresses. You look really different, which is what you wanted, isn't it? What do you reckon?'

I reckon I don't actually look very much like Jasmine. Our body shape is so different – she's all bony and angular while I'm more round and squidgy. But I quite like the way the dresses make me feel. As though I'm someone else – someone professional, confident… and sophisticated. Someone who's at home in the new-look Cosy Kettle.

'I'll take them!' I declare. 'How much are they, by the way?' Oops, maybe that should have been my first question. I glance at the swinging price tags and swallow hard. 'That's quite a lot.'

'What price can you put on making your wish come true?'

That's a fair point. I fish my credit card out of my purse and try not to look intimidated as one of the snooty assistants wraps my purchases in tissue and puts them into a glossy branded bag.

The sun is starting to set as Mary drives us out of Oxford and slides behind the darkening hills as we get closer to Honeyford.

I twist round in the passenger seat towards her. 'Thank you so much, Mary, for giving up your day to help me with my shopping. I really appreciate it.'

'Ah, it's nothing. It was good to have an excuse to escape domestic bliss for a while. I'm just sorry we didn't get anything suitable for the party itself. That pink top I made you try on in the second shop we went to looked nice.'

'Yeah, it wasn't quite me, though, with all the bows and the ruffles. I looked like one of the raspberry meringues we sell in the café. I can always wear the black dress to the party. That'll be fine.'

'I guess so. And I'll definitely do your make-up on party day to make you look extra special. I'm pretty good with a make-up brush though I hardly wear any these days. There doesn't seem much point when I'm home all the time. I really love Callum and I'm glad I had him but my life's very different these days.' She sighs and glances across the valley at the darkening sky and the deepening shadows. 'Anyway, I can vicariously enjoy your reinvention and your lascivious love life with gorgeous Logan. What more do I need?' She nods as we drive past the sign that bids us *Welcome to the ancient Cotswold market town of Honeyford*. 'Here we are. Home again!'

I step into the cottage and pile my shopping bags on the floor. Good grief, I can't believe I let Mary persuade me to buy so much. I'll still be paying off my credit card next Christmas.

'Zac, are you in?' I shout, but the cottage is cold and empty. Maybe he's out with Jasmine, or perhaps she's given him the brush-off and he's drowning his sorrows with friends somewhere. I don't suppose he'd drown them with me because the whole sleeping with my sister thing is just too awkward.

I haul my shopping bags up the stairs and stop at Zac's open bedroom door. With a quick glance over my shoulder, in case he might magically appear, I drop my bags, go into his room and sit on the bed, just where Jasmine sat when she called in before their date.

She's right. It is very macho in here. There are no frills and flounces and hardly anything on display, apart from a large Bluetooth speaker. Zac loves turning his music up loud and playing air guitar, when he thinks I'm not looking. His dark hair flops over his eyes as he moves in time to the beat, like the bass player in an indie band who all the shy goth girls lust over.

The last time I spotted him air-strumming, I joined in too and we headbanged our way around the sitting room. I smile at the memory. That was the weekend before we walked to the wishing well and I made my Christmas wish. Lots of things have changed since then and I've made a lot of progress – the ticks on my wish list are totting up. But not all of the changes are what I expected. Don't people say, be careful what you wish for?

I gather up my shopping bags, go into my bedroom and hang my new clothes in my wardrobe.

Chapter Eighteen

The Christmas party is in three days' time and it's all systems go in The Cosy Kettle. The tree has been moved into the corner where the book club used to sit, so there's more space for people to mingle, and I've added a few more tasteful decorations to the room. One of them – a large perforated silver star – is lit from behind and casts tiny pinpricks of light onto the wall.

The place looks amazing and yet... it doesn't feel like The Cosy Kettle. Stanley was right when he said the cosiness had gone and several regular customers have grumbled about it over the last couple of days. My café looks like Christmas as imagined by someone who's trying to keep up with the upmarket Joneses – everything is carefully placed and over-thought. But it's what Logan wants, and he's the client.

I switch off the lights and close the café door behind me. I'm definitely feeling less at home here but haven't had a chance to speak to Zac about it. We're like ships that pass in the night at the moment. I've spent the last couple of evenings here, catching up on party paperwork, and Zac has been out at Christmas dos with friends. I miss him and his chats. Even the banter over breakfast has dried up and I miss his insults that used to make me laugh. I guess realising you're in love with your best friend shifts the relationship in subtle ways that can't be prevented.

'Are you off?' calls Flora, who's working late tonight. 'Good. You deserve a break after all your hard work. I hope you've got a lovely relaxing evening planned.'

'Millicent is picking me up in ten minutes and taking me to have my hair done, ahead of the party.'

'Oh gosh. Not terribly relaxing then.' Flora laughs and balances another book on top of her display of novels set in the Cotswolds. 'Good luck, and I look forward to seeing the new you tomorrow.'

Fifteen minutes later and there's still no sign of Millicent. She said she'd pick me up near the Pheasant and Fox, which is kind of her, but she's late, and it's snowing again. Thick fat flakes are drifting down from the dark grey sky. They dance in the street lamp's yellow light, before settling on the pavement. The ground is wet so the snow isn't sticking yet, but the old tiled roofs of Honeyford's shops and cottages are dusted in white.

I check my watch again and wrap my thick woolly scarf more tightly around my neck. It's all very well wearing dresses – I've got the new red one on today – but tights don't keep my legs as warm as my jeans do. I stamp my feet and start walking up and down to ward off the cold.

The town looks chocolate-box pretty tonight, with Christmas lights strung across the narrow street and light spilling from the pub's windows. And it's peaceful. There's a low thrum of traffic from the High Street nearby and snatches of conversation as people walk past. But compared to the city, Honeyford has a laid-back vibe which is good for my mental health. It's been months since I experienced the crushing, *I'm about to die* terror of a panic attack.

I pull out my phone to see if Millicent has cancelled because of the weather. It's very kind of her to help me but I'm kind of dreading spending time alone with her. She's so spikey, she makes me nervous.

I've just started checking my text messages when a gleaming huge black Audi with tinted windows pulls up beside me. The window glides down.

'Don't stand there like a lummock,' barks Millicent, leaning across from the driver's side. 'Get in!'

I slide into the passenger seat and Millicent accelerates towards the High Street. Inside and out, her car looks as though it's just been driven away from the showroom. Zac's car is littered with sweet wrappers and smells like a hospital, thanks to the muscle rub he uses after going to the gym. Millicent's is pristinely clean and there's a strong leather smell overlaid with lemon. A citrus air freshener is swinging back and forth from the rear-view mirror.

'Right,' says Millicent, pulling out in front of a Mini. 'Are you ready to have your hair sorted out? It'll make such a difference to your overall appearance, and your confidence, I dare say.'

'I'm looking forward to it and thank you for arranging things. Um, where exactly are we going?'

'To see my hairdresser,' says Millicent, driving out of Honeyford and into the darkness of the countryside. Snow is still coming down and she puts the windscreen wipers on full speed.

'I thought you went to the hairdresser on the other side of town.'

'The Krafty Kuts salon?' Millicent sniffs. 'I don't think so. I couldn't possibly frequent a business that can't spell its own name correctly. I have a top-notch hairdresser who comes to my house every week.'

'So, is that where we're going now? To your house?'

'We are.' She shakes her head as I grip the sides of my seat when she takes a bend in the road rather quickly. 'This car has four-wheel drive, Becca. You're totally safe with me.'

She's probably right but I'm still relieved when I spot the lights of Little Besbridge and she stamps on her brakes as we drive into the tiny village that attracts tourists like bees to a honeypot. Time has stood still in Little Besbridge. Thatched cottages cluster around a village pond to my right, and a stream, edged with trees, snakes its way along the side of the narrow road.

Millicent drives past the green and turns in to a gravel driveway just before the village ends. I crane my neck for my first look at Millicent's house which I've heard so much about, and I'm not disappointed. Flora says the house is a new-build, but it looks old with its Cotswold stone walls and white pillars flanking the grey front door.

Millicent stops quickly outside the door, sliding gently on the gravel, and waits for me to get out of the car before fishing in her handbag for her front door key.

'No one else is home,' she tells me, fitting the key into the lock. 'So Caroline can work her magic on you in peace.'

She flings open the door and we step into a beautiful square hallway with paintings of Cotswolds landscapes on the walls. Millicent turns off the beeping burglar alarm and leads me up thickly carpeted stairs onto a wide, square landing. So this is how the other half lives! There's a chandelier hanging from the ceiling, suspended over the drop to the hallway below, and a huge potted palm, that's taller than me, in the corner next to an enormous sash window that shows inky darkness outside.

'Here we are. You and Caroline had better use my bathroom.'

She pushes open a bright white door and I walk into what must be Millicent's bedroom. A huge bed, covered in cream silk, takes up only a fraction of the room which is larger than The Cosy Kettle plus its garden. The softly draped cream curtains must be silk too, from the way they ripple when Millicent closes them using a remote control on her bedside table. Millicent is so posh, she doesn't even have to open and close her own curtains!

'Here's the en suite,' she says, opening another white door which leads into a room half the size of her bedroom. A roll-top bath with clawed silver feet is positioned underneath the sash window, and there are twin basins across the back wall. One of the basins has a spray attachment on its mixer tap, and a leather hairdresser chair next to it.

'Caroline comes in every week to give me a trim and blow-dry. How long is it since you went to the hairdresser?'

'Um…'

'I thought as much. Well, don't worry. Caroline will work wonders.'

I certainly hope so. But I can't help worrying as Millicent pats her hair-sprayed ash-blonde perm because it doesn't move. Not one inch. I doubt a force ten gale could budge it. If Caroline does the same to me, Logan will break bones should he ever feel inclined to run his fingers through my hair.

'Do you have a dress for the party?' asks Millicent, suddenly.

'I've got one that I bought when I was out with Mary.'

'Is it a dour colour?'

'It's black.'

'Black? For a festive gathering? Oh no, that won't do at all. What size are you?' She gives me a once-over. 'I might have something in my wardrobe for you to borrow that would suit.'

'Please don't bother,' I say, following Millicent back into her bedroom.

Please, I beg you, don't bother!

Millicent is sturdy and middle-aged and I don't like to be rude about people, but her clothes are boring. I know my jeans and black sweatshirts wouldn't make the heart of a *Vogue* journalist beat any faster, but at least they're age-appropriate. I simply can't turn up to Logan's party wearing a frumpy beige number. Zac would wet himself laughing, but I don't think Logan would find it funny. He'd probably cancel our date there and then. I'm going to have to be assertive and say no to Millicent. My heart starts thumping at the prospect of upsetting her when she's trying to be kind, and it sinks when she opens the floor-to-ceiling wardrobe that spans an entire wall of her bedroom.

In front of me are rows of no doubt expensive but mega-frumpy clothes – knee-length skirts, long-sleeved blouses, V-neck jumpers, slacks with pin-sharp creases. And almost every item of clothing is beige, cream, caramel or camel… Millicent's wardrobe looks like someone has sucked out all colour.

'I'm not sure that—'

'Oh, don't worry. I'm not expecting you to wear any of these,' says Millicent, cutting across me. 'I was young once, you know, and I think I still have…' She pushes the wall of clothing apart and reaches behind the clothes for three large boxes on a shelf. 'Ah yes, here we go.'

She places the boxes on the bed and pulls off the lids.

'Take them out, Becca, and have a look.'

Millicent sits on the edge of the bed while I push apart layers of white tissue paper and pull out the contents. The first box contains a long dress made of scarlet satin with wide shoulder straps and a large butterfly embroidered across the bodice in peacock-blue and cerise threads.

'Wow, Millicent. This is magnificent! When did you wear this?'

'I wore that on my first anniversary when we were on a Caribbean cruise to celebrate. I was rather slimmer then and so happy to be visiting such exotic locations with Phillip. It was a wonderful holiday.' Millicent's lower lip trembles and she tightens her jaw to control herself. I get an urge to comfort her but she folds her arms as though batting off any sympathy. 'Go on, try the next box.'

Beneath the tissue paper lies a long dress made of the most exquisite green silk. It has a high mandarin collar and short sleeves, and the fabric feels feather-light in my hands.

'That one was specially made for me while we were in Hong Kong,' says Millicent. 'We had such a wonderful time there.' She smiles to herself while I carefully fold it back into the box.

Both of the dresses are beautiful and they look as though they might fit me. But I can't wear a full-length dress to the party, however sophisticated it might be. The Cosy Kettle and long dresses just don't go together. Plus, I'd chuck a drink all over me and stain the fragile fabric. It's inevitable.

'Not quite right?' Millicent nods at the third box. 'Then this one might do the trick.'

I feel the fabric before I see it. This dress is heavier, less likely to pull or tear. I unfold it from the box and my mouth drops open as light reflects around the room. The dress seems to be made of diamonds; tiny diamonds glinting in my hands. A closer look reveals hundreds of overlapping silver sequins across the strapless bodice and fitted skirt that ends just above the knee.

'Every single sequin is applied by hand. Philip bought me that after Celeste was born – an incentive to get back to my pre-pregnancy weight. And I managed it.'

'It's absolutely beautiful. Where on earth did you wear it?'

'We used to go to dances, back then, and I'd dance for hours.' She clocks my expression and raises an eyebrow. 'I haven't always been this staid and bossy, Becca.'

'I don't think you're staid and bossy.'

Millicent raises an eyebrow. 'Are you sure?'

'Yes, you're more…' I swallow as Millicent gives me a warning look, but I plough on. '… more sad than anything else.'

'Sad?' Millicent's laugh sounds brittle. 'Sad, when I live in a house like this, my husband is a high-flyer, my children are doing magnificently well in their careers abroad, and my Christmas present to myself is a brand new car? What on earth gives you the idea that I'm sad?'

'I just sensed it. Sorry. I'm obviously wrong.'

'Wrong and rather too assertive when it comes to talking rubbish.'

'Sorry. I didn't mean to upset you.'

Millicent opens her mouth and takes a breath, as though she's about to have another go at me. But then she sighs and her shoulders drop.

'I suppose I am sad sometimes. I see these dresses and remember who I used to be, before Philip and I had lots of money. You might find it hard to believe but we lived in a terraced house on the outskirts of Oxford.' She shudders. 'It was a horrible little house with a back yard instead of a garden and small dark rooms. But, ironically, I sometimes think I was happier there than I am here. I had friends nearby, Philip came home from work on time every night, and the children needed me. Now, well, it's all very different.'

'You have a wonderful home here.'

'I do, and I'd rather live here than in our old house, believe me. But my friends have drifted away over the years, the children have their own lives now, and Philip sometimes doesn't come home at all. Who knows what he's getting up to? Business meetings, he says.' She stops and takes short, shallow breaths. I know anxiety when I see it.

'You have friends at The Cosy Kettle,' I say, gently, suddenly no longer scared of Millicent.

'The book club? Yes, I like to think that they like me, rather than just tolerate me.'

'They do like you. And Flora does, too. And me.' I hug the diamond dress to my chest. 'I'm your friend, Millicent.'

Millicent stands up in one fluid movement, walks over and stands in front of me. 'Bless your heart, Becca. I know you have your wish list, but don't change too much.'

For one weird moment, I think she's about to hug me. But she catches herself and draws herself up tall. 'Anyway, enough of this maudlin talk. One thing you do need to change is your dress sense, so what do you think about wearing this to your party?' She runs her fingers across the silver sequins.

'I think it's beautiful but it's too much for me. It's not right, someone like me wearing a dress like this.'

'Someone like you?'

'Yeah, I'm nothing special.'

'How dare you!' Millicent sounds so fierce, I take a step back. 'Everyone's special, Rebecca.'

'Even Stanley?'

Millicent's mouth twitches in the corner. 'Stanley is *very* special. He's also very sad about the changes in The Cosy Kettle.'

'I know. I didn't mean to upset him.'

Millicent's face softens as she puts her hand on my shoulder and squeezes. 'Just wear the special dress while you can and enjoy it. You'll be in beige elasticated slacks and aubergine gilets before you know it.'

'Do you think the dress will fit me?'

'Try it on at home and see. If not, you've always got your dour dress to fall back on, so you've nothing to lose. Ah, that sounds like Caroline now. Wait in the bathroom and I'll bring her up.' She pauses at the bedroom door and looks back. 'And if you repeat any of what I've said this evening and imply that I have a heart, I'll deny it all.'

I'm sure she winks at me before she goes out onto the landing and I hear her padding down the stairs. I carefully put the party dress back into its box and head into the bathroom to be transformed.

Caroline is younger than I expected, which is a relief, and she assures Millicent that she can banish all traces of blue from my hair.

'What's your natural colour, Becca?' asks Millicent, flicking through the range of colours that Caroline has brought with her.

'It's a rather boring mousey-brown.'

'Hmm. I was thinking that you'd look rather lovely with an overall chestnut shade.'

'I'd quite like to be blonde.'

'Really?' Millicent stares at me in the mirror. 'I can't see you as a blonde, personally. Caroline, what do you think?'

Caroline, whose own hair is so platinum blonde it's almost white, wrinkles her nose. 'Blonde works for me if that's what Becca prefers.'

'I do,' I say, assertively, picturing Jasmine in my mind. Surely one quick and easy way of looking more like my sister is having the same hair colour?

'Whatever you wish,' says Millicent, with a wave of her hand. 'Let the transformation begin!'

In the end, I'm not so much transformed as improved. There's only so much you can do with short hair, but Caroline gives me a good cut that brings out the natural wave, so it curls beneath my ears and at the back of my neck.

The colour is shocking at first. I've had red hair the colour of post boxes, green hair the colour of Cornish sea, and blue hair the colour of twinkling sapphires. I once had a rainbow stripe that cut across my head like a landing strip. But I've never been blonde before, and it rather takes my breath away at first.

'Do you like it?' asks Caroline, holding a mirror behind my head so I can see my new hairstyle from all angles.

'I love the cut and the colour looks very natural. I'm sure I'll soon get used to it. What do you think, Millicent?'

She twirls my seat around until I'm facing her and puts her hands on her hips. 'I still think a rich chestnut would have been better but I prefer it to the ridiculous colour you usually sport. Do you look like you expected? Are you pleased?'

I swing my chair back and stare at myself in the mirror. I expected to look more like Jasmine, to be honest. There are echoes of my sister in my face and the blonde hair brings out those similarities, but I still look rather a lot like me. Maybe the new clothes will help.

'I'm very pleased. Thank you so much, Caroline, and Millicent for organising everything.'

By the time Millicent drives me home, the ground is coated in white and snow is settling on the trees and stone walls that edge the country roads. I watch thick flakes hitting the windscreen and wonder at the transformation taking place around me. Every now and again, as we drive through tiny villages all lit up for Christmas, I sneak a look at myself in the wing mirror and smile. My reflection, all fuzzy in the wet mirror, does look a fair bit like Jasmine. I can definitely tick off wish number six.

Chapter Nineteen

Two days to go until the party and I think nerves are getting to me. I've found it hard to settle all morning, and I'm feeling rather disappointed. I thought being blonde would give me a boost but so far the reaction to my new hairstyle has been rather muted.

Zac's eyes opened wide when he saw me at breakfast, and I braced myself for some mickey-taking, but he didn't call me a cut-price Marilyn Monroe or wannabe Madonna or anything. He just said I looked 'good'. Regular customers have hardly mentioned my new look and Flora said it was 'nice', which is so anodyne it's almost insulting. I have no idea what the book club think about it because they still seem to be boycotting the café.

But at least The Cosy Kettle is looking great. The whole place is understated and sophisticated and Logan will think it's wonderful. The party is going to be a brilliant success and he'll be blown away when he sees me in my fabulous silver dress. My wishes are coming true and I'm happy – that's what I keep telling myself.

I break off a piece of cinnamon bun and nibble the edges. Zac loves cinnamon buns but I think he's eating out again this evening so there's no point in taking any home. He's out with friends all the time at the moment. Or at least that's what he says. Maybe he's seeing Jasmine and not telling me. I haven't heard from her since the morning after their date and I feel ridiculously nervous about contacting her. I suspect she's avoiding me because she feels awkward that she and Zac are an item.

'Is everything all right?' Flora, who's just come into the café, pushes a couple of chairs underneath their table and tweaks the festive red tablecloth straight. The fabric is covered in images of Christmas puddings and won't do for the party. I've got a box of white and silver paper tablecloths under the counter, all ready.

'I'm fine, thanks. Why?'

'No reason. You just looked miles away and a bit sad.'

'No, I'm great. Really great.'

'I hear on the grapevine that you have a date with Logan after the party.'

'Who told you that? Has Stanley been spilling my secrets?'

Flora laughs. 'You can't keep anything secret for long in Honeyford. I learned that very quickly after arriving here. It was actually Phyllis who spilled the beans, when I bumped into her in the post office earlier. She also said that the afternoon book club aren't coming in at the moment.'

'They're not too keen on the changes I've made in here.'

'So she said. I'm afraid some people find change difficult but you've done a good job in here, Becca. You've really transformed the place.' She grins and smooths down her pretty purple dress before tucking her dark hair behind her ears. Quite how she manages to work hard all day and still look fresh and elegant is beyond me.

'The Cosy Kettle is party-ready. I don't think there's much more to organise before the big day.'

'That's great then.' Flora hesitates as though she's about to say something but smiles instead. 'I'd better go and sell a few more books because Caleb's Christmas present cost a fortune.'

She heads back into the bookshop while I think about the happy new life she's made for herself. I really admire the way she's coped with the changes that followed the break-up with her husband. My life seems to be changing too, which is what I wanted when I made my wish list. I just wish I felt happier and more at ease with the changes that are happening. I wish Zac and I were still the best of friends, I wish I didn't care so much what people think of me, and I wish I didn't feel out of place in The Cosy Kettle.

I look around the café and suddenly realise that Stanley is absolutely right; the café has lost its soul. I've been so busy transforming it into what someone else thinks is right, I've lost sight of what Flora, with her business head on, would call its USP – its unique selling proposition. The thing that makes it stand out from other cafés. And, Zac would laugh at me for saying so, but the place feels… sad. Hell, *I* feel sad at the moment.

There's a burst of laughter as two new customers carrying bulging bags of shopping get caught in the doorway, and I slide off my stool, plaster on a smile and get ready to make reviving cups of coffee.

The lunchtime rush is almost over when Logan rushes in, throws off his coat and flings himself into a chair. 'Becca, it's so good to see you,' he puffs.

Aw, that's sweet. I pull out a chair and sit opposite him. 'It's good to see you too.' But my smile fades as I notice the tension in his cheek muscles. I'm a connoisseur of anxiety. I can spot it at fifty paces. 'What on earth's the matter?'

He starts drumming his heels on the floor and shakes his head. He's so upset. Would putting my hand on his seem too forward in the circumstances? Probably not, seeing as he's already asked me out on a date, and kissed me. I move my hand towards his but Logan jerks back and puts his head in his hands.

'I've made a terrible mistake, Becca. A dreadful, stupid mistake.'

Cold resignation hits the pit of my stomach. Of course, it was too good to be true. Women like me don't get asked out by men like Logan. Ah, well. I'm not exactly heart-broken.

'It's all right. It's not like we signed a contract or anything. I won't hold you to it.'

Logan looks up, confusion flitting across his handsome face. 'We did sign a contract – I signed to say that the party would be here. Why, what did you think I—?'

'Doesn't matter,' I say quickly, my mind whirling. Friday's date still seems to be a goer, but I'm not so sure about the party. 'Just tell me what's happened. I'm sure it can't be that bad.'

'That's what I like about you, Becca,' says Logan, settling back in his chair. 'You're optimistic and kind, but I'm afraid it is bad. It's a disaster. I've basically cocked up the party and I can see my promotion disappearing in a puff of smoke. Everything's ruined.'

He starts drumming his heels again as though he can't sit still, and sympathy floods through me. He's wired with anxiety and I recognise that urge to move constantly, as though you're trying to run away from life.

When I reach out and stroke his arm, he calms down and the drumming slowly stops. 'Why don't you start at the beginning and tell me all about it.'

Logan draws in a deep breath. 'My boss wants to impress our select French customers with a Christmas party, to round off the day after they've been Christmas shopping in Oxford.'

'Yes, I know. That's why we're pulling out all the stops.'

'The wrong stops,' wails Logan. 'I thought his French guests would want sophistication and class but it turns out I got the wrong end of the stick and what they most want to experience is authentic

Cotswolds charm. That's what they're expecting in bucketloads on Friday. So I'm screwed.'

'Authentic charm,' I repeat slowly, looking around my poor pimped-out café. I've spent hours switching decorations, ordering fussy finger foods and negotiating a fee with full-of-themselves madrigal singers. There are three shiny new patio heaters ready and waiting in the garden and Millicent's classy dress hanging in my wardrobe. I've fallen out with friends, upped my stress levels and cricked my neck bending over spreadsheets. The Cosy Kettle's authentic charm has been extinguished.

'So are you telling me that you're cancelling the party?'

Logan sighs. 'No, the party will have to go ahead 'cos there's nothing else. But it's going to be a huge disappointment 'cos it's not authentic, my boss will throw a wobbly and he'll give the promotion to Simon, who will make my life a misery. I really hate Simon and the feeling is mutual. Bloody hell.'

He puts his head back in his hands and the light above him glints on his lovely blond hair. I sit back and gaze around me at the swathes of silver and white on the ceiling, the walls and the tree. It looks beautiful and cold and not how The Cosy Kettle should be at all.

This definitely wasn't what I had in mind when I stood at the wishing well in the moonlight. I wanted things to change for the better... and they still can. I sit up tall and pull my shoulders back. It's time to kick my Christmas wish into gear and make it start working for me and my beloved café.

'Listen up, Logan,' I say, as resolve and confidence stir in my soul. 'We're going to fix this.'

'How?' he mumbles into the table. Tall, handsome Logan might exude confidence and savoir faire, but he certainly gives up easily. He could do with a wish list of his own.

'If your guests want authentic charm, that's what they'll get.'

'It's impossible. There's no time to change everything. I'm backed up with urgent work at the office and the party's the day after tomorrow.'

'I'm all too aware of that fact.' My stomach has started churning but I keep going. 'I'll do what I can and I'll salvage your party.'

'I so wish you could.'

'Oh, believe me, I've had a lot of practice at making wishes come true.'

Logan raises his head at that. 'It'll need a miracle to rescue the party.'

'Not a miracle. Just plenty of hard work and I've got a few people in mind who might be able to help out. We need to get The Cosy Kettle back to how it was and involve local people because meeting them is the best way to introduce Cotswolds charm. We'll give your guests an authentic cosy Cotswolds festive experience they'll never forget. Believe me. It'll be all right.'

'I do believe you,' breathes Logan, lacing his fingers through mine. 'I knew there was something special about you, Becca, from the moment we first met.' I have to smile because that's total rubbish. He suddenly reaches out and touches my hair. 'And you've turned into a blonde in time for the party. You look wonderful, just like your sister.'

That's one big fat tick for wish number six, though looking like Jasmine doesn't seem quite such an achievement any more. It's certainly not authentic, which is ironic seeing as authenticity now appears to be Logan's holy grail.

He unlaces his fingers from mine and rubs his hand across his mouth. 'So what's the first step in sorting out this disaster and getting my new-look party underway?'

'The first step is calling in the Cosy Kettle Crew.'

Chapter Twenty

I've convened an emergency after-hours meeting of the book club at my house. I wasn't sure everyone would respond when I texted the SOS, not after the fracas in The Cosy Kettle. But all five members of the club have turned up and Zac, bless him, has cancelled his evening out and is currently busy serving coffees.

'So let me get this right,' says Stanley, who's still rubbing his knees after being folded into Dick's ancient sports car for the journey here. 'Logan insisted on some fancy gathering that involved patio heaters, minimalist decorations and' – he puts the next word in finger quotes – '"nibbles", none of which sounds very Christmassy to me.'

'He was going for an atmosphere of festive fusion – sophistication melding with tradition,' I tell Stanley, feeling faintly ridiculous.

'Festive fusion, my arse.'

I nod because I have to agree with Stanley. Festive fusion in a cosy Cotswolds café? It was never going to be a great fit but I shoehorned it in because that was what Logan wanted and I wasn't confident enough to make my reservations clear. Plus, I was trying to secure a date with Logan. Well, I've managed that but it hasn't made me as happy as I thought it would.

'That's all very well but why are we here talking about a party that we're not even invited to?' butts in Millicent, taking a sip of her coffee and grimacing. 'It's very close to Christmas and we all have things to do.'

'The problem is that Logan's found out that his guests don't want a festive fusion event. They're looking for authentic Cotswolds charm instead.'

'Which is what The Cosy Kettle had in spades. Before it was' – Millicent hesitates – 'fusioned-up.'

'Hey, Millie. I'm loving the lingo,' says Stanley, grinning and patting her leg. 'We'll drag you into the twenty-first century yet.'

Millicent harrumphs but looks quite pleased in spite of herself. She turns to me. 'And I suppose you want our help in some way to dig you out of this hole?'

'I wondered if you might...'

'Typical,' snorts Millicent. 'We're too shabby for The Cosy Kettle one minute and saviours the next.'

'You took down Moira's kettles and ditched Auntie Edna. You even culled Rudy!' says Stanley.

'I know and I'm sorry, Stanley. I didn't mean to upset you.'

'You didn't treat us very well, dear,' adds Phyllis.

Dick starts to add his two pennyworth but I raise my hand. I'm so tired and stressed and my brain is whirling. 'You don't owe me anything, Millicent. None of you do, and I know the recent changes have upset you all and I'm sorry about that. But I thought you might want to help because I like to think that we're friends. And I'm not keeping count but how often do you all sit in The Cosy Kettle for hours over one cup of coffee each? Do I ever make a fuss about it, even though you're hardly adding to the café's profits? Do I ever complain when you're all arguing loudly during your book club get-togethers and startling other customers? No, I don't. And it wasn't my fault you weren't invited to

Logan's festive fusion party – he's a client with a set guest list. You lot treat The Cosy Kettle as if it's your own private club but it's not, it's a business and I'm doing the best I can in difficult circumstances. Now, are you going to help me or not?'

Crikey. I swallow hard and put my hands on my hips, trying to keep hold of the indignation and anger that suddenly bubbled to the surface. I can't believe I just spoke to the book club like that. Zac puts down the cup of coffee he's carrying and looks at me with wide eyes.

There's a pause as though all the air has been sucked out of the room, and then everyone erupts into laughter.

'Well done, Becca,' says Millicent. 'That was magnificently assertive.'

'Top class arseyness!' chuckles Stanley beside her. 'How did it feel?'

'I don't know. Quite good, actually.'

'Liberating, isn't it?' Stanley reaches out and shakes my hand. 'Welcome to the world of having the confidence to speak your mind. It's wonderful.'

Hmm. My anxiety levels have shot up because I've just insulted a group of people I care about, but they don't seem to mind.

I glance at Zac, who's shovelling sugar into Dick's tea. I can't imagine Logan serving drinks as Stanley scratches his backside and Millicent complains that her coffee isn't decaf so she'll be up all night. Zac smiles to tell me that my outburst was OK. I haven't done anything awful. His eyes crinkle in the corners like they always do, and my heart aches.

But I've finally got a date with Logan, who's my dream man, and Zac has spent the night with my sister. He's probably thinking of her every time he looks at me and sees the resemblance that I've been trying so hard to enhance. Everything was fine when Zac and I were just best friends who loved each other in an uncomplicated way. Can't I just go back to that?

'Are you OK, Becca?' asks Mary, flicking long brown hair from her face. 'Are you feeling unwell?'

'No, I'm fine. Sorry. I just, um…' I watch Zac push his hands through his thick curls and sigh.

'So let's work out how we can all help out with Logan's authentic charm offensive,' says Dick, coming to my rescue. 'Before Becca gives us another telling-off.' He winks at me. 'I can feel another of Stanley's plans coming on.'

An hour later, I close the front door behind the last of the book club, lean forward and rest my forehead against the wood and close my eyes. This evening has been unreal.

'Is everything all right?' asks Zac softly behind me.

I spin round so fast I almost overbalance and he grabs my elbow. His fingers close around my skin, sending what feels like little electric shocks up my arm. This is ridiculous. We've both slouched on the sofa together, with my legs across his lap, watching *Line of Duty*. He often gives me a hug when I'm feeling rubbish. That was all easy and uncomplicated, but now it feels like he's plugged into the National Grid when he touches me.

'I'm fine. Just a bit overwhelmed by the evening, really.'

Zac grins and lets go of my arm. 'I'm not surprised. You were pretty assertive back there.'

'Was it too much?'

'Nah, they can take it.' He glances at his watch. 'It's getting late. We'd better start sorting the kitchen out and go to bed.'

'I'll sort all the coffee cups out in the morning. You go on up.'

'Are you sure?'

'Definitely.'

Zac walks to the bottom of the stairs and pauses, with his hand on the bannisters. 'I feel the same way, you know,' he says softly, his face illuminated by the soft glow of the dying fire.

'The same way?' I squeak, my heart hammering.

'Yeah. Logan isn't my favourite person but I know how much he means to you and I want his party to go well for the café's sake. So I'll help to sort things out too. You can count on me.'

Disappointment lodges in my chest. 'I know I can always count on you. Zac,' I say, stepping forward, fighting the anxiety that's threatening to overwhelm me. Keeping my feelings for him a secret is just too hard. 'There's something I need to tell—'

'And Jazz can help too. We were going out for a drink tomorrow night but we can come along and help you instead. You'll get two for the price of one. What do you think?'

I think I'd almost forgotten that Zac and my sister are now an item.

'That would be great,' I tell him. 'I'll be up in a minute.'

Zac goes upstairs and, when I hear him moving about in the bathroom, I go and kneel in front of the fireplace. The dying fire is casting shadows around the gloomy room and I shiver. The book club played a blinder in this room tonight and have promised me their full support but, for the first time ever, the cottage feels full of ghosts and secrets.

Chapter Twenty-One

There are a number of things I'd rather not see. These include Jasmine snogging Zac, Stanley in skin-tight Levi's, and yet another talking heads programme about Brexit. They also include Mum on my doorstep with a suitcase but here she is and it's not even – I check my watch – half past six.

'Mum?' I say blearily, opening the door. I've been awake for half an hour, going over the Cosy Kettle rescue plan I pulled together late last night, but I'm still in my pyjamas. 'What are you doing here? Is Dad all right?'

'I don't know and I don't care,' declares Mum dramatically, pushing past me and hauling her large suitcase inside.

'What do you mean you don't care?' I quickly close the door behind her because it's freezing out there.

Mum turns to me, her eyes red-rimmed, and sighs. 'I've left him, Becca. After all these years, I've left him.'

'You've left Dad? What, properly left him?'

Mum points at her suitcase which is bulging at the seams. 'Lock, stock and barrel. I've been awake all night thinking about it.'

'I can see how upset you are, but making spontaneous decisions after not sleeping isn't always—'

'It's not a spontaneous decision,' interrupts Mum. 'I've had my case packed for a day or two and hidden in the spare room. But I've only just gathered the courage to actually leave, and it's all thanks to you.'

'Thanks to me? Are you sure?'

I start racking my brains about what I said to Mum in the park. *It's never too late to change. Be the person you're meant to be. Fulfil your potential.* But I never said, *throw away three decades of marriage and leave your husband.*

Mum's face suddenly crumples and tears start spilling down her cheeks. 'I hope it's all right to come here,' she sobs, 'but I didn't know where else to go. I don't want to be a burden on my children.'

'Of course you're not a burden.' I put my arm around her shoulders and lead her to the sofa. 'I'm very glad you came to me, though Jasmine's nearer.'

'I didn't want to see your sister,' gulps Mum, pulling a tissue from her handbag and loudly blowing her nose. 'Jasmine's sorted and sure of herself, just like your father. She doesn't understand what I'm going through. I need someone who's kind and caring and empathetic.'

'Thanks, Mum,' I say, genuinely touched by the compliment. But then she ruins it by adding: 'I need someone who's a worrier. I keep it well hidden but I've always suffered with my nerves, like you, and I feel guilty that I might have passed on my dodgy genes to you. I'm so sorry.' She starts sobbing again, loud gulping sobs that break my heart.

'It'll be OK, Mum.' I pat her shoulder, wondering how best to handle this family crisis. I've never seen my mum so upset before and it's destabilising. She's always been a rock – stoical and solid as life events whirl around us. 'Try to calm down and tell me what's happened with you and Dad.'

'Your father is stifling my creativity,' gulps Mum. 'He found the letter offering me a place on the art course and forbade me from accepting it.'

'He forbade you! I didn't realise I had a dad from the Dark Ages.'

'His exact words were, "I forbid you to go off gallivanting, Pauline. Your time is already taken up with your job and the house, and it's selfish of you to think of rocking the boat at our time of life."'

'What does he mean, *our time of life*? You're only in your late fifties. You've got loads of life left.'

'And he said I was selfish. After all I've done for him and you and Jasmine. That really hurt.'

'I can imagine. You're definitely not selfish. You've been a brilliant wife and mother for decades. So what happened next?'

'I thought of you,' says Mum, dabbing at her eyes. 'I thought of what you said about having the courage to change and do something for myself after all these years. And I thought of you running that café and making a new life for yourself after...' She pauses.

'After what happened in Birmingham?' I sigh.

'Yes. And so I told your father that I was going to go to university and study art and we had a terrible row and haven't been speaking for days, and I can't bear to stay in the house.' When her mouth starts wobbling, she pulls her lips tight. 'Maybe it's for the best. Can I stay here for a while? Please. I know you don't have a spare room but I can sleep on the sofa.' She glances at our lumpy sofa and winces. 'Then I'm going to find myself a nice little bedsit somewhere.'

'Of course you can stay, Mum. You're always welcome here, and I think Dad has behaved really unkindly. But are you sure that leaving Dad is the best way to deal with this?'

'I need to put some space between us. I've put everyone else first for such a long time and now that I finally want to do something for myself, he doesn't give me any support. Even though I've supported him over the years with his work and his golf and his daft DIY projects that invariably go wrong. It doesn't seem fair.'

'It's not fair at all,' I tell her, wondering if it would have helped if I'd actually phoned Dad and spoken to him about the art course, as I'd planned. I sigh and squash down a surge of guilt. 'Maybe you and Dad can sit down and talk about it when you're feeling a bit calmer.'

'He won't talk about it. He just keeps saying I'm being selfish. It's so upsetting.'

'What's upsetting?' Zac has appeared at the top of the stairs in his dressing gown. He yawns and pushes a hand through his tousled hair. 'Is everything all right?'

'Can I tell him?'

When I glance at Mum, she gives a tight nod. 'Might as well. He'll find out soon enough when I'm sleeping on your sofa.'

'Mum's had an argument with Dad and has left him for a little while.'

'For good, perhaps,' says Mum, pushing out her bottom lip. 'I rather fear that the man I married is a dinosaur. It's good to see you again, Zac, by the way.'

'You too,' says Zac, giving me a faint smile. 'How have you been, Pauline, apart from the… um, leaving thing?'

'Fine, thank you. Did you enjoy going to the Christmas do with Jasmine?'

'Yes, I did, thanks.'

'She did too. She was full of it on the phone yesterday and said you'd both had a great time. You looked very handsome in your suit. Jasmine texted me a photo of the two of you.'

'He looked brilliant,' I butt in. 'But what about you and Dad, Mum? Won't he be worried about where you are?'

'I doubt he'll even notice I've gone.'

'Of course he'll notice. You've been together for thirty years and it looks as if you've brought half the house with you. The two of you need to sit down and talk and try to resolve this.'

'I don't think I can.'

A sudden pounding on the front door makes me jump. What now? Pulling my dressing gown more tightly around me, I open the door a crack. There on the doorstep is Dad, wild-eyed and wild-haired, in jogging bottoms and a sweatshirt. And next to him is Jasmine with her coat over her pyjamas. I can see the cream silk of her trouser legs poking out underneath.

'Is she here, Beccs?' asks Dad. 'Tell me the daft woman is here.'

'Don't let him in,' shouts Mum.

'Of course I'm coming in, Pauline. Don't be so ridiculous. I'm your husband.' He pushes past me and Jasmine shuffles in behind him. And although I'm upset and tired, my brain still registers that even make-up free and with her hair unbrushed, she looks fabulous.

'Morning,' says Dad, gruffly, giving Zac a brief nod as he stomps through the room and stands in front of Mum with his hands on his hips.

'Morning,' says Zac, walking downstairs, his bare muscular legs showing beneath his short dressing gown.

Jasmine moves to stand beside him. 'What's going on, Mum? I don't appreciate Dad turning up at stupid o'clock on a Thursday morning and demanding to know if you're hiding in my flat. And why weren't you hiding in my flat, anyway? Why did you come straight to Becca's?'

'I came here because Becca is a caring and understanding person.' *Please just leave it there,* I plead silently. 'And she's as emotionally unstable as I feel right now.' *Thanks, Mum.*

When Jasmine nods as though that goes without saying, Zac gives me a sympathetic wink. He looks so strong and kind and steady, standing there in his grey towelling dressing gown with his hair all over the place. All I want is for him to walk over, put his arms around me and tell me that everything will be all right. I gulp and refocus my attention on my parents' crumbling marriage.

'Right, Mum and Dad, I suggest that the two of you sit here and talk things through while I make us all a drink.'

'Talk what things through?' demands Jasmine. 'And what the hell have you done to your hair, Becca?'

'I've coloured it.'

'Blonde?'

'Yeah, it's been blue, red and green in the past and you've never mentioned it. Anyway' – I bring my attention back to the family crisis playing out in my sitting room – 'Mum's upset because Dad has forbidden her' – I give Dad a disapproving glare – 'from taking the art course I told you about.'

'Is that all? I can't believe I got hauled out of bed for a stupid art course. I thought at the very least one of you was playing away.'

'An affair? Never,' says Mum, looking properly shocked at the very idea.

'I'd never cheat on your mother. She has her faults but we love each other. Or at least I thought we did.' The fight suddenly goes out of Dad and he sinks onto the chair opposite her.

'So that's all good then.' Jasmine yawns and rubs her eyes. 'You both love each other so you can go home together, everything will be back to normal and we can all get on with our lives. It's really upsetting to see you both fighting like this.'

'Sounds good to me, Pauline,' says Dad. 'Come home and we can forget all about this. You don't want to cause a fuss and inconvenience everyone.'

Mum's wavering, I can tell. She's biting her lip and her breath is coming in short gasps. And even though it would be better for me if everyone did get the hell out of my house – I've got a fancy-arse party to transform, people – I just can't go along with it.

'No,' I say, so loudly everyone looks at me. 'Mum has every right to take that art course and you both need to talk about it, not sweep the whole thing under the carpet. So Mum and Dad, you're both going to sit here and talk until it's sorted out.'

'When did you get to be so bossy?' mutters Jasmine.

'I'm not being bossy, I'm being assertive. It's Dad who's the bossy one in our family. Mum's the rock. You're the golden girl and I'm…' I don't know what to say. I'm the screw-up, the disappointment, the person who's trying so hard to change? '… I'm not sure who I am. But the point is, people don't always have to do what you want, Dad.'

'I'm not bossy,' he protests.

'Yes, you are,' says Mum, quietly, 'and I'm proud of Becca for having the courage to say so. I've gone along with what you want for years and now I want something for myself so we need to talk properly about it, without you flying off the handle and laying down the law.'

'I didn't lay down—'

'Yes you did, Dad. You said Mum was forbidden to take the art course, which is outrageous. She's allowed to make her own decisions. So will you sit here and properly discuss the options with her?'

'I s'pose so.' He uses the same sullen tone of voice as Jasmine.

'Great,' says Zac. 'Now that's sorted, I'll make some coffee.' He beats a hasty retreat towards the kitchen.

'And I need the loo,' says Jasmine, following him. 'Dad was in such a state I didn't have time to do anything except put a coat on. There's one out the back, isn't there?'

'Yeah, past the kitchen, by the back door,' I tell her, glancing at Mum and Dad. He's moved to sit on the sofa so they're side by side, but they're not touching. Are they going to be all right? I know I'm in my mid-twenties but I'm not sure I can cope with my parents splitting up.

Is that me being a wuss? Zac would know. Suddenly, more than anything, I need to talk about what's just happened with my best friend and have a hug. I need Zac to put his strong arms around me and tell me that everything will be all right. I want to bury my head in his chest and feel his hands in my hair.

'We'll be fine, love,' Mum tells me, with the ghost of a smile. 'You go and get yourself ready for work. I've held you up enough.'

'I'll give Zac a hand with the coffees first.'

I scurry out of the room and burst into the kitchen.

'Zac, are you…?'

I stop dead. Jasmine and Zac are locked in an embrace, illuminated by the light from the open fridge. His strong arms are around her and her head is resting on his chest. It's like a physical blow to my heart. Zac is definitely Jasmine's now.

This has got to be the worst run-up to Christmas ever. There's a party to rescue and a marriage to save, and now I stumble across my sister and my best friend, the man I can't deny I'm head over heels in love with, having *a moment* in the kitchen.

'Oh, Becca, there you are.' Jasmine steps away from Zac. The belt of her coat has come undone and her satin pyjamas are on show. I'm suddenly hideously aware of my cheap cotton PJs and towelling dressing gown that's gone bobbly in the wash. Of course Zac would be interested in Jasmine and see me as nothing more than a good friend.

'Jasmine was upset about your mum and dad,' says Zac.

'So Zac gave me a hug. Anyway, I'm feeling better now and I'd better go and see how the parents are doing. Honestly, what is Mum like with all this empowerment crap?' She eye-rolls me as she leaves the kitchen.

'That was a bit awkward,' says Zac, turning to spoon coffee into the mugs lined up on the counter. 'Jasmine was tearful and kind of…'

'It's all right. It's fine.'

Zac stops with his spoon mid-way between the coffee jar and a mug. Granules of coffee fall onto the work surface. 'You really don't mind if I hang out with your sister, do you?'

'Why would I?' I say, as cheerily as I can muster. 'What you and my sister do is none of my business.'

The spoon moves again and coffee falls into the mug. 'Good to know. I guess you're getting excited about your date with Logan.'

'Yeah, I can hardly wait,' I say, though at this precise moment I honestly don't care whether wish number five comes true or not. 'Do you need any help with the coffees?'

'No thanks, I can bring them in.'

'OK.' I stop at the kitchen door and take a deep breath. 'Look, Jasmine is a lovely person. I know I've bitched about her sometimes but she's vibrant and fun and decent. And so are you, Zac. You're my best friend. Anyway,' I gulp, tears filling my eyes. 'Best get back to the war zone.' And I flee, back into the sitting room.

The summit seems to be going fairly well. Dad is listening, at least, while Mum sets out her case for taking the art course. So Jasmine heads home and I go upstairs to get dressed and ready for a full-on day of crisis management at work. It's been a stressful morning and a year or so ago I'd have crumbled when faced with so many problems. I *did* crumble, as my family are only too quick to point out. But now, though I feel under pressure, I also feel fired up – to take action and make things right, to speak up for myself and stand up to my dad, and to do the best for the people I love, however much it hurts.

My Christmas wish seems to be coming true but not in the ways I expected. I seem to be making myself proud as well as other people, which is wonderful. But when I made my wish under the stars, I thought achieving all those goals would make me happy. Now I'm not so sure.

Chapter Twenty-Two

The Cosy Kettle rescue plan is underway and running like a military operation. This is in part due to the actions spreadsheet I hammered out in the early hours of this morning. But it's mostly down to Dick, an ex-army man, who's stepped up to the plate and is bringing his military training to the fore. He's standing at the back of the café, barking out orders and everyone is doing what they're told. I think they're a bit frightened not to.

'He's like Captain Mainwaring in *Dad's Army*,' mutters Millicent, mutinously. But she collects the empty boxes from the attic to store the fancy decorations all the same – just as she's been ordered to do.

As for me, I've already cancelled the finger food from Logan's posh chef. He didn't seem too bothered when I agreed to pay him a cancellation fee. And I've got John, The Cosy Kettle's usual baker, on board to provide a range of mini Christmas cupcakes tomorrow night.

I've also cancelled the madrigal group – which involved another cancellation payment from Logan's firm to keep them sweet – and I've been in touch with local choir, the Honeyford Warblers.

'They sing at the old people's care home in the village up the road,' says Phyllis, when she hears what I've done. 'They're a bit amateur, to be honest. Slightly tin-pot.'

But tin-pot or not, they're going to sing carols for us in the garden. If Logan's guests want to experience an authentic small-town Cotswolds Christmas, that's what they're going to get – bum notes and all.

Stanley disappears halfway through the morning and reappears after lunch with a large bag under one arm and a beaming smile on his face.

'What have you done?' I ask him, nervously, because when it comes to Stanley, anything's possible.

'Don't look so stressy, babe. I nipped to the fancy-dress shop to pick up some threads for me and the sergeant major over there. What do you reckon?'

From the bag, he pulls a sack-like red tunic edged in what looks like cotton wool. Four big black buttons have been sewn down the middle of the garment and there's a wide black belt with a gold buckle attached to the belt loops.

'There's a hat too for The Cosy Kettle's very own Father Christmas. I didn't bother with the beard because it wasn't as impressive as Dick's own. And here's what I'll be sporting on the night.' He pulls out a lime-green tunic and worn red leggings that bag at the knees. 'I got these too so I'll look right on fleek.' He proudly shows me a battered pair of green shoes that narrow to a point and curl up at the ends. 'Elf shoes!'

'They're… exceedingly elfy.'

'I know, right? What do you think?'

'I think it's totally naff and absolutely magnificent.'

'We'll give Mr Fairweather and his fancy guests more authenticity than they know what to do with,' says Stanley, with a wink.

Mary and Phyllis nip out to buy up loads of cheap, plastic gifts for Santa's lucky dip sack – as per my spreadsheet and Dick's orders – while I continue taking down the silver and white decorations.

It's taking ages because I have to nip up the stepladder when the café's not busy. But Millicent has been helping and plenty of our regular customers have been pitching in too. Amy from the sweetshop, butcher Vernon, unemployed Janine, who calls in every morning for a coffee and a chat, widow Gladys and Paul, who's too unwell to work. They all get involved, and even Luna gives up her lunch break to help after Flora tells her about my predicament.

'You seem better,' she informs me as the last tasteful white bow and frosted bauble come off the Christmas tree. 'Your energies are starting to settle. Your aura too, and you're more like your old self.'

'That definitely wasn't the plan.'

'Don't be so sure. Maybe it was the right plan all along.' Then she gives me one of her enigmatic smiles which always send shivers down my back.

I would challenge what she's saying if I wasn't so busy rescuing a party. But how can it possibly be the right plan – the right Christmas wish – if I've ended up feeling more rotten than I did before? I might be more assertive and look more polished but I know too much now. I know I'm in love with my best friend and I know he's not in love with me. For a moment, my shoulders slump and a wave of sadness sweeps over me. But I don't have the luxury of wallowing in my feelings because there's too much to do if The Cosy Kettle is going to benefit from a successful party.

At last, The Cosy Kettle looks more normal again. It's taken all day, in between serving coffees and making customers feel at home, but the café has been stripped of the carefully chosen decorations that didn't suit it at all. Our old Christmas decorations – the ones Logan initially thought of as too tacky – still need to be put back up, but the café already seems more warm and welcoming.

'She's back,' murmurs Stanley beside me, as the last silver reindeer goes back into his box.

'She?'

'Yeah, The Cosy Kettle is defo a chick.'

And while Stanley's retro slang puts my teeth on edge, I agree with the sentiment. My unpretentious Cosy Kettle, just right for a tiny ancient town in the midst of beautiful rolling hills, is back. Almost…

'Wait right there,' I tell Stanley, before disappearing into the bookshop. I make my way up the rickety steps to the attic room, pick up a large box and manhandle it down the stairs. The contents glint when I open up the box, next to the Christmas tree. 'Stanley, would you care to do the honours?'

'I would be absolutely delighted.' He bends over the box and takes out Moira's precious kettles that glint in winter light from the back window. Carefully, he places them on the shelf where they belong before pulling a handkerchief from the pocket of his jeans. 'They're back, my darling girl,' he whispers to himself, wiping a tear from his eye.

The afternoon book club have gone home after hours of sterling work, and the café is closed, but it's going to be a late night for me. There are still lots of the old decorations to be hung, presents to wrap for the lucky dip, and the tree is bare. I sit on the floor, surrounded by boxes of rainbow tinsel and paper garlands, and start cutting out a square of Christmas paper to wrap a plastic trumpet. How on earth does one wrap a trumpet?

I'm making a pretty bad job of it when there's a rap on the small glass window in the back door.

'Hey, let us in,' shouts Jasmine, when I peer outside. 'It's me and Zac, the cavalry.'

I unlock the door and usher the two of them inside. 'What are you doing here?'

'Didn't Zac tell you we'd come and help, rather than go out for a drink? Oh, blimey!' She bends over and starts rubbing mud from her stiletto ankle boots. 'It seemed a good idea at the time, as did coming through your garden to get in. But it's pitch black out there and I've brought half the garden in with me.' She gives up rubbing, slips her boots off and stands in front of me in her socks. 'Go on then. Put us to work.'

'Are you sure?' I ask, my chest tightening at the sight of the man I love and my sister together.

'Of course,' says Zac, taking off his jacket and cracking his knuckles. 'What are family and friends for if not to spend an evening close to Christmas helping a loved one wrap…' He stares at my half-wrapped parcel and frowns.

'A plastic trumpet.'

He grins and slaps his forehead. 'Of course, I should have known.'

'Obviously. Because no Christmas is complete without an eco-unfriendly facsimile of a brass instrument.'

Jasmine sighs and rolls up the sleeves of her taupe angora jumper. 'Honestly, you two do my head in. Let's get on with it because I'm gasping for a drink.'

'I can turn the coffee machine on again.'

'That wasn't the type of drink I meant but I guess one of your cappuccinos is better than nothing. Go on, then.'

The rich aroma of coffee beans wafts through the café as Jasmine starts wrapping and Zac loops red paper garlands and rainbow tinsel across the ceiling.

'You do know that this place is starting to look like Mum and Dad's house, don't you?' says Jasmine, sitting next to a growing mound of wrapped gifts. She's making a much better job of it than I would have.

'I'm not going that far over the top but Mum and Dad's place is always welcoming, and that's what I'm aiming for here.'

'I don't know how welcoming their place will be if Mum moves out for good. Do you think she will? That was pretty heavy stuff this morning.'

'No, I don't think Mum will move out. She doesn't want to leave him, not really. She's just feeling unfulfilled and ready to start a new chapter in her life, if Dad stops being such an idiot about it. And he needs to take her out more. He's always disappearing down the pub with his mates or playing golf with Sid up the road.'

'You could invite them to the party tomorrow.'

'They wouldn't come. Dad would hate it. Though I guess it would be a chance for him to prove that he's willing to start putting Mum's wishes first, for a change.'

'Wouldn't you mind them coming to your party?'

'Not at all. I can square it with Logan, and it might be good for them.'

And good for me too, because I want Mum and Dad to see that I'm not just panic attacks and abandoned ambition. I want them to see what a fabulous party I can organise in the wonderful café that I've helped to create.

'You should invite them, then.'

'I think I will, and you should come too, and Zac, of course.'

'Are you sure Logan will be OK with family and friends pitching up?' asks Zac.

'I don't think he can complain when I'm sorting all this out for him, and I'll feel more relaxed if you're around to calm the book club down if they start going wildly off piste. I can tell Logan you're all here to help make sure the party runs smoothly. So you're both invited and I'll definitely invite Mum and Dad too. She'll love getting all dressed up.'

Jasmine sits back on her heels and brushes hair from her face with the back of her hand. 'You really "get" Mum, don't you, and her "new chapter"? More than me. But then I guess you're starting a new chapter too, with all that's happening in your life, and all those feelings coming to the surface.'

'What do you mean?' I've gone hot and cold at the thought that Jasmine knows how I feel about Zac and is going to blurt something out when he might overhear.

'Yeah, what do you mean?' asks Zac, who's abandoned the stepladder to grab another sip of his caramel macchiato. He gives Jasmine a look I can't decipher – a secret understanding between people who are close.

'I just mean that you've managed to bag a date with one of Honeyford's most eligible bachelors. Are you looking forward to it?'

'Of course. It's…' I pause. 'Well, it's a real confidence boost, if you must know. I'm not always the most confident of people.'

'No shit, Sherlock!' snorts Jasmine. 'I'm happy for you that you're feeling good about it.' She shoots Zac another look I can't make out, before turning back to her wrapping paper. 'Only another ten bits of old tat to wrap. Are you sure your guests are going to like these, Beccs?'

'They're not supposed to like them, exactly. The gifts are reminiscent of lucky dips at Christmas fairs across the country and what you get when you pull a good old British cracker. Ooh, crackers! I must pick some up tomorrow and scatter them about the place.'

'You're flamin' crackers,' mutters Jasmine. 'Both of you. No wonder you're best friends. And I wasn't being rude about your hair this morning, by the way. I was simply surprised that you've gone blonde. I'd have thought blonde would be far too tame for you.'

'I felt like a change.'

'For Logan?'

'For myself, actually.'

'Are you sure?'

I nod, though I'm not sure really. Everything has become muddled and it's getting harder to tell where one of my mini Christmas wishes begins and another ends.

'What do you really think of my hair?'

Asking Jasmine is risky because she's likely to be brutally honest. She tilts her head to one side and considers for a moment. 'Yeah, it's nice. Good cut and a nice colour.'

Urgh, more 'nice'. I grab my cooling coffee and a handful of red glass baubles. 'I really appreciate both of you helping me. I'd have been here until the early hours otherwise.'

'I thought Flora would be here, giving you a hand,' says Zac from halfway up the ladder as I walk over to the tree.

'She wanted to but Caleb is appearing in a play and then she and Daniel are going out for a meal. It's been arranged for ages. She said she'd cancel but I wouldn't let her.'

'And Logan? I'm surprised he's not here helping you to make good the party that he cocked up in the first place.'

'He wanted to help, too, and was really apologetic that he couldn't, but he was working late and then going straight on to his office's Christmas do. I told him not to worry because I could manage without him.'

I start hanging baubles from the branches and try not to think of Logan having a great time, getting drunk and probably flirty with his female co-workers. I thought he might give his Christmas do a miss to help me, but he took me at my word when I said I could manage on my own.

An hour later, everything's more or less done. The original festive decorations are back in place, Rudy's nose is glowing from the counter, the tree is groaning under myriad glass baubles and strands of tinsel, and there's a mountain of wrapped gifts ready for the lucky dip.

'Just one last thing,' I say, climbing the stepladder to the top of the tree and putting Auntie Edna back in her rightful place. She gazes imperiously across the welcoming café, her halo flashing on and off and reflecting in the gleaming copper kettles that mean so much to Stanley.

I climb down, stand with my hands on my hips, and take a good look at The Cosy Kettle. *My* Cosy Kettle. It's fanciful but it seems to me that I hear the café sigh with relief.

Chapter Twenty-Three

'Mary's here!' shouts Zac up the stairs. 'Are you decent if she comes up?'

'I am,' I shout back from my bedroom. 'Send her up, please. I'm all ready for my makeover.'

'You can do it down here, if you like. I won't get in the way.'

'No, thanks. Up here's fine.'

There's no way I'm letting Zac watch as Mary transforms me with make-up from a pale, *meh* café manager into a glowing, party-ready sex goddess. I snigger at the very thought. Magician Mary would need a turbo-charged wand to carry out *that* transformation.

I hear Mary's footsteps on the stairs before she appears in the doorway, with the biggest make-up bag I've ever seen. She drops it onto the bed. 'This is a nice room, and it's such a lovely cottage with so much history. I've always wanted to see what these houses are like inside.'

'We're happy here.' Or at least we were. I plaster a smile on my face. 'Thank you so much for doing this, Mary. Will you have time to get yourself ready for the party?'

'Yeah, it'll be fine. It won't take long and I see you're all ready for me. So that's good.' She rubs her hands together. 'Let's get started, shall we?'

My make-up routine usually lasts two minutes. I draw black liner under my green eyes, slap on some mascara, add a touch of lipgloss, and that's it. I'm done. But it's going to take rather longer with

Mary in charge. She pulls all manner of stuff from her bulging bag and attacks my face with gusto. She uses primer and concealer and foundation and highlighter and blusher and... so many products, I lose count. She's frowning with concentration, her tongue resting against her upper lip.

As she works, I gaze through the open curtains at the cottages opposite, which have amber lamplight glowing in their windows. Snow-heavy clouds are scudding overhead and purple hills are rolling into the distance. It's a view that needs no tweaking, no work done, no improving. It's perfect just the way it is.

Finally, Mary leans away from me and grins. 'Well, that looks fabulous! Do you want to see?' She picks up the mirror that's propped on my chest of drawers and holds it in front of me. 'Allow me to introduce very gorgeous and very sophisticated Rebecca.'

Wow. Gorgeous and sophisticated Rebecca looks... different. The harsh black lines beneath my eyes have been replaced with soft green liner that flicks up at the edges. My cheeks are rosy and light glints on my cheekbones which are artfully highlighted. My mouth has a cupid's bow in the palest pink, and I'm glowing. Just like Jasmine does. It suddenly strikes me that maybe she's merely better with a make-up bag than I am.

'What do you think?' asks Mary, folding her arms and looking pleased with herself.

'I think it's amazing. I hardly look like me at all.'

'Yes, you do. Just an enhanced version of yourself,' says Mary, pushing products back into her make-up bag. 'You'll knock 'em dead like that. Logan will be panting.'

'Thank you so much. I really appreciate you giving up your time to help me.'

'You're welcome. Your hair looks fabulous, too. That hairdresser gave you a good cut. And where's your dress? I can help you get into it without ruining your make-up.'

I open the wardrobe and Mary gasps when she spots Millicent's silver dress glinting in the overhead light. 'Blimey! When you said you'd borrowed a dress from Millicent, I was fearing the worst. I was going to persuade you to wear the black dress you bought when you were with me, but that is utterly marvellous. Did our Millie wear that?'

'Apparently, a long time ago.'

'I'd never have believed it. It's wonderful. Slip off your dressing gown and step into it and I'll do up the zip.'

As the dress tightens around me, I kick my bedroom door shut and stare at myself in the long mirror attached to the back of it. I already know that the dress fits me, more or less, and I know it's amazing. I gasped when I first tried it on and almost made myself give it back to Millicent straight away. I felt like an imposter in silver sparkles, but her warning that I'd be in beige elasticated slacks before I knew it kept echoing through my mind. And it's the kind of dress that Jasmine would wear.

'You look unbelievably glamorous,' breathes Mary. 'Put your shoes on too for the full effect.'

I slip my feet into the nude stilettos and wobble slightly as I take another look in the mirror. Wow. I don't recognise the woman who's staring back at me, biting her lip. The dress, together with Mary's makeover and high heels, have turned me into a different person completely. I look poised and elegant. I look an awful lot like my sister.

'Come downstairs with me and we'll get Zac's verdict.'

Hanging on to Mary's arm, so I won't go head over heels in my stilettos, I walk stiffly down the stairs. The strapless bra needed to keep everything in the right place is horribly uncomfortable and I can't breathe properly, but that's a small price to pay for looking 'unbelievably glamorous'.

'Zac, what do you think of your housemate?' asks Mary, standing aside as Zac, who's sitting on the sofa with his back to us, turns around. My stomach does a flip because I feel so nervous.

'Wow, Becca! Is that really you?' Zac gets to his feet and walks over, never taking his eyes from my face. 'I hardly recognised you. You look...' he swallows, 'absolutely amazing. And so different.'

'Do you approve of my transformation?'

'I've never seen you in a dress like this before.' He reaches out and gently touches the silver fabric that's shimmering over my body. 'Crikey. How does it feel being this new you?'

'It feels great,' I say, confused by the frown that's furrowing Zac's forehead. 'Don't you like how I look?'

'Yeah, of course I do. It's just a bit of a shock – I guess I'd kind of got used to the old Becca and now you look like someone else. But you look really wonderful. Aren't you going to freeze if you go out in the garden?'

'Probably, seeing as I'm basically wearing a hanky while it's almost snowing. I'll have to hog a patio heater.' I hold on to the back of the sofa and lean forward because my feet are killing me. 'You do like it, don't you?'

'Of course I do. And don't look so worried. Come here and have a hug.' He steps forward and opens his arms as though he's about to pull me into them.

There's nothing I'd like more, right now, than a hug from Zac but I'll only smear the ton of make-up on my face, and leave him dotted with sequins. And we both have to leave for the party soon. Looking like a million dollars is not conducive to receiving hugs from handsome men. Plus, I rather fear that a hug from Zac right now will break my heart.

'Better not,' I say, tightly. 'I'll only get foundation on your shirt.'

Zac drops his arms and shrugs, a look of disappointment in his eyes.

'I'd best get back and sort my own face out,' says Mary, who's picked up on the tension between us. 'I'll let myself out and I'll see you both soon.'

'Thanks, Mary, for everything.'

'You're welcome. Oh, you've got a visitor. See you later.' She steps aside from the open front door to let Jasmine in.

'Holy moly, is that you, Becca?'

Jasmine sashays towards me, her bright red dress clinging to every curve and her golden hair tumbling in waves down her back.

'I can't believe it. You look… well, you look unbelievably hot.' Which is ironic, seeing as I'm going to freeze to death in this dress. 'I honestly can't believe it,' says Jasmine again, unhelpfully. 'And this is all for Logan's benefit, is it?'

'Hardly,' I bristle. 'This is all for me.'

And it is. Being different and more confident and more generally 'hot' will make me feel better about myself, won't it?

Jasmine winks. 'You can't tell me you weren't thinking of Logan when you got all glammed up.'

'I wasn't,' I tell her. And I truly wasn't. I was actually feeling like a bit of a prat as Mary layered on yet more mascara and lip liner. Zac stiffens beside me at the mention of Logan's name.

'Whatever.' Jasmine walks slowly round me and smiles. 'You've transformed yourself, Beccs. Congratulations.'

That's kind of her but it strikes me as slightly bizarre that I'm congratulated for wearing an uncomfortable dress that will probably induce hypothermia before the evening is out, and for sporting so much make-up I hardly recognise myself in the mirror.

Jasmine links her arm through Zac's. 'You're looking rather smart in your shirt and tie. Jeez, why is it always so cold in this spooky old cottage?' She pulls herself close to Zac's side for warmth and a stab of envy ricochets through my cold body. 'Mum rang. She and Dad are on their way and she's looking forward to the party. She sounded quite cheerful. Shall we get going, then? Your VIP French guests will be arriving in half an hour.'

'You two go on and I'll catch you up in a bit,' I tell her. 'Everything's set up and Flora said she'd be there by six thirty so you'll be able to get in.'

Zac disentangles himself from Jasmine and starts putting on his shoes. 'Why don't you come with us? You might need someone to lean on in those stilettos.'

'I'll be fine and I won't be long, honest. I could just do with a few moments on my own before everything gets hectic. You go on.'

Zac allows himself to be led off by Jasmine and I close the door behind them and press my forehead against the wooden frame. What on earth is the matter with me? I'll feel like a million dollars at the party, looking like this. A million confident, assertive dollars. For once in my life, people might not be surprised when I tell them Jasmine is my twin sister, my parents will view me as a grown-up professional, and Logan, the most eligible bachelor in Honeyford, will be proud to have me as his date. It's going to be wonderful – a wish come true – so why do I feel so unutterably sad and out of sorts?

Be careful what you wish for, says the voice in my head.

I grin and kick off my hideously uncomfortable shoes.

Chapter Twenty-Four

I walk through the bookshop towards the light spilling from The Cosy Kettle, take a deep breath and adjust my underwear.

'I thought that was you,' says a stern voice behind me. 'What are you doing out here? Your French guests will be arriving soon.' A fist in the small of my back propels me into the café which smells of freshly baked cake and is glowing with fairy lights.

'Look who I found outside,' says Millicent, resplendent in a long caramel-coloured dress and a gold pendant. She peers at me. 'Oh, I say. What have you done?'

'You look amazing, Becca,' calls Phyllis. Pieces of gold tinsel are looped around the arms of her wheelchair and she's wearing her best dress and gold hoop earrings. 'Is that really Millie's sparkly dress?'

Millicent sniffs beside me. 'It's not Millie, as you well know, and yes it is. But that's not the footwear I was expecting you to wear with my dress, Becca.'

'What, these?' I look down at my red and black Doc Martens and grin. 'To be honest, wearing stilettos was not dissimilar to having my feet in a vice, and these feel more like me.'

'The black tights too?'

'I didn't want to freeze.'

'And what about the hair?' She picks up a strand and rubs her fingers along it. 'Does this colour come off?'

'It's sprayed on, so yes.' I glance at myself in the shiny chrome coffee machine. Most of my hair is still golden blonde, but my fringe is a gorgeous rich shade of beautiful sapphire blue.

'Heavens.' Mary wanders over, looking wonderful in a short green cocktail dress with her dark hair swept up into an elegant chignon. 'You've rather customised your look since I last saw you.'

'Sorry, Mary. Do you mind? I've kept a lot of the make-up on. I just toned it down a little.'

I've kept the eyeliner but wiped off the sparkly eyeshadow and some of the blusher and I've swapped my pretty pink lipstick for my usual dark red lipgloss. I've also taken off the pearls that I inherited from my gran and I'm wearing a chunky silver necklace instead that cost me five pounds in Honeyford market.

Mary puts her arm through mine. 'I don't mind at all and I think you look even better – much more relaxed, and you were walking like Bambi on ice in those stilettos.'

'I know. I'd have broken my neck before the evening was out. I feel better like this. I feel more like me. And you all look fabulous yourselves. Where are Zac and Jasmine?'

'In the garden,' says Phyllis, 'sorting out Father Christmas and his elf.'

'How do they look?'

'Ridiculous,' says Millicent, but she smiles so I'm not sure she means it. 'Why don't you stomp out there in your silly boots and have a look for yourself.'

The garden has been transformed into a fairy grotto. Twinkling fairy lights are pinned to the old walls that edge the garden and are reflecting in the light dusting of snow that tops the Cotswold stone. The heaters are casting an amber glow across the patio and there, in the corner, is Father Christmas, AKA Dick in his red robes with the wide black belt around his middle. His snow-white beard has been specially combed for the occasion and his bald head is covered in a red hat with a white fur trim. Next to him is Stanley, and I have to laugh. I always knew Dick would make a great Santa but Stanley is a magnificent elf. His green tunic swamps his skinny chest, his bright red tights are clinging to his thin legs, and his feet look enormous in his curly shoes.

He grins when he sees me and waves. 'Cool, Beccs. You look pretty damn fly. What d'ya think of me and my festive bro here?'

'You both look brilliant. Thank you so much for doing this for The Cosy Kettle and Logan.'

'We're doing this for you,' says Dick, placing his hands on his padded belly as though he's about to shout *ho ho ho*. 'Plus, it's good fun. Don't you think, Zac?' He steps aside and there, behind him, plugging in more fairy lights, is my housemate.

He straightens up as he sees me, looking rather debonair in his dark cord trousers, crisp white shirt that's open at the neck, and dark jacket. The tie he was wearing when he left the house has been ditched. He's never been much of a tie man.

'And my Becca is back.' He grins. 'You had me a bit worried there for a minute. I love the boots. I hear they're very on trend with sequinned evening dresses this season. All the best fashion houses are recommending them.'

'I do like to keep up with what the supermodels are wearing.' I hold my palms up to the sky and do a twirl. 'So what do you think? Better than before?'

'Much better. Though I'm not sure Jasmine will agree. And she's right behind you.'

When I turn round, Jasmine's face crumples in horror. 'Oh. My. God. What have you done, Becca? You looked fabulous back at your house and now you still look a bit fabulous but mostly like… you.'

'I am me, Jazz. And I like it. I felt a prat all glammed up, to be honest. It suits you but it doesn't really suit me.'

'Come on, you lot,' calls Millicent from the back door. 'Logan will be arriving with his fancy French guests very soon and we need to make sure we're all ready.'

When we all troop indoors, I spot Mum and Dad in the corner. Mum has her hand on Dad's arm, which puts hope in my heart, though she lets go to point at me. His jaw drops as I walk towards them.

'Bloody hell, Becca. Is that you, all glammed up like a film star?'

'You look amazing, love,' says Mum, coming forward and planting a kiss on my forehead. 'And The Cosy Kettle looks wonderful. Is this all your work?'

I'm about to say no and point to my book club team when Phyllis zooms up in her wheelchair and puts her arm around my waist. 'It was all Becca,' she tells my parents. 'You're very fortunate to have such a wonderful, talented daughter. You must be very proud of her.'

Mum beams. 'We are, aren't we, Peter?'

'Of course.' Dad nods, and adjusts the collar of his shirt, looking uncomfortable. Not one for parties, he's way out of his comfort zone.

'Wish number three,' murmurs Phyllis, drawing an imaginary tick in the air.

Mum frowns. 'I beg your pardon?'

'Hey, Dad, why don't you go and taste test a couple of the cakes for me?'

'If that would be helpful.'

'It really would.'

Dad doesn't need asking twice. He's off, like a whippet, to check out the mounds of miniature cakes on the long trestle table that's covered with a red cloth – cubes of iced Christmas cake, bite-size pink and yellow Battenberg, crumbly little mince pies, tiny cranberry cupcakes and chocolate-covered Swiss rolls.

'You really do look wonderful,' says Mum, smoothing down the black dress she only brings out on special occasions. 'And Zac looks very handsome tonight, don't you think?' She nods at Zac, who's standing chatting to Jasmine. They look brilliant together, I realise, as my stomach sinks into my comfy Doc Martens. Mum gives him a little wave – she'll be delighted when she finds out they're an item. Finding a 'nice young man' will push Jasmine's street cred with my family even higher.

'How are things going at home?' I whisper.

'Quite well. I think me leaving home brought your father up short and he's trying hard not to be so bossy.' We both glance at Dad, who's shoving a mince pie, dusted with icing sugar, into his mouth. 'I've accepted my place at university and I start the course in the spring.'

'Wow, Mum. That's brilliant. I'm really proud of you.'

Mum's eyes sparkle with unshed tears. 'You inspired me, Beccs, because you're really turning your life around. You do know that Dad and I really are very proud of you, don't you?'

'Yeah, of course,' I say, though I didn't properly know it until this moment.

'You've sorted yourself out and made a life for yourself in Honeyford, surrounded by all these wonderful people. And you've made such a success of this café. You've done well, love.'

'I thought I'd disappointed you,' I say and then bite down hard on my lip to stop myself from crying.

'You've worried us a good few times. And we wish you found life easier. But disappointed us? Never. You're our Beccs, you're a warrior, and we both love you, though your dad doesn't always show it. He loves me too, though he often has a funny way of showing that. Daft old bugger.'

We both smile at the daft old bugger, who pauses, Christmas cake mid-way to his mouth, and gives us a frown. He'll be wondering what we're saying about him.

'Here comes your sister, and she's drinking already.' Mum's eyebrows meet in the middle as Jasmine hurries up with a glass in her hand.

'It's only fruit punch, Mum, and he's here, Beccs.' I do a swift sidestep in case her drink slops over my dress. 'I can't believe you're going on a date with him. He's smokin' hot.'

Logan is standing in the doorway to the café, looking fabulously handsome in dark trousers and a light blue shirt. His square jaw drops as he looks around at my beautiful cosy café and then he spots me and his face breaks into a huge smile.

Rushing over, he grabs my hands in his. 'Becca, you're a miracle worker. This place looks amazing – really cosy and authentic.' He nods at Father Christmas and his elf, who are working their way through a couple of mini cupcakes. 'Santa and his sidekick look adorable and totally traditional. My guests will love them. And as for you…' He steps back so I'm at arm's length and whistles softly. 'I'm loving the punky elegant look. When did you blossom into such a beautiful swan?'

Does that imply I was an ugly duckling before? Over his shoulder, I spot Zac looking at Jasmine and rolling his eyes. OK, Logan is being a bit cheesy but, when they grin conspiratorially, anger sparks through me.

Without thinking, I step forward and plant a kiss on Logan's full mouth, and I feel his hand on the back of my head as he returns my kiss before we break apart. Zac and Jasmine aren't laughing now. Jasmine has walked off and Zac is staring at me with an unreadable expression on his face.

'I'm very pleased to see you too, Becca.' Logan winks, and grabs my arm. 'Come and meet my VIP guests. They're going to love you.'

The party's in full swing and going amazingly well. Carols have been sung, cakes have been eaten, and Dick and Stanley are doing a roaring trade with the lucky dip. Flora keeps telling me I've done a fabulous job, and Callie, who set up The Cosy Kettle almost a year ago, has called in to join the celebrations. It's everything I could have wished for.

'Have you seen Jasmine?'

Millicent breaks off her conversation with a small man wearing round glasses and shakes her head. 'Not for a while. The last I saw of her she was heading into the bookshop. Have you met Monsieur Fournier, Becca? He runs an IT business near Saumur and is quite delightful company.'

'I haven't. It's lovely to meet you.'

Monsieur Fournier bows slightly and shakes my hand. 'I understand you organised this party for me and my colleagues. You have my sincere thanks. It has been wonderful to see a slice of authentic Cotswolds life at Christmas time.'

'Thank you. I had a lot of help from some very good friends.'

Millicent beams at me before I head into the bookshop for a breather. I find parties overwhelming – I've never been a party person – and although this one is going well, I need five minutes on my own. I could also do with adjusting my uncomfortable underwear.

The shop is in darkness and I stand at the back, between the shelves, and breathe in the smell. In and out, in and out, until I feel calmer.

I'm about to return to the party when I spot a glowing ember near the shop window. It's Jasmine, sitting in the window sill, smoking. She jumps as I get closer. 'Hell's bells, Beccs. Don't loom out of the darkness at me like that. I already reckon this shop's haunted. It must have been a house for hundreds of years and heaven knows how many people have died here.'

'I was looking for you. I didn't know where you were. And I'm not sure you should be smoking amongst all these books.'

'I'm only having a break from the parents for a few minutes. Don't tell them I was smoking or they'll throw a wobbly.'

'They can be a bit overwhelming, can't they?'

'Totally. Especially now Mum's located her inner creativity, and Dad's trying so hard not to be bossy. He keeps asking Mum if she minds if he has another cake. He's gone soft.'

'I think it's quite sweet. And Dad hasn't gone soft,' I say, sitting beside her on the window sill. 'It was about time he joined the twenty-first century and realised that Mum needs to do stuff for herself.'

'She was inspired by you, apparently,' says Jasmine, leaning down to stub out her cigarette on the flagstone floor. She brushes the ash into her hands and places it in a little pile on the window sill. 'I'll clear that up in a minute. Get rid of the evidence, and all that.'

'Yeah, we can't have Mum and Dad seeing their precious golden girl smoking.'

Jasmine frowns and I feel awful. That came out more sarcastically than I meant it to.

'You can be a right cow sometimes, Becca.' She shifts along the sill and is silhouetted in the glow from a street lamp outside.

'I'm sorry. It's just hard sometimes when you're always the golden girl in Mum and Dad's eyes and I'm not, though Mum did say she and Dad were proud of me tonight.'

'Of course they are. You know that.'

'No, I don't. You're pretty and clever and you've got a brilliant job. I'm average in the looks department, I have mental health issues and I run a café.'

'A successful café, and it's not a piece of cake being the golden girl, you know.'

'Yeah, I bet it's really hard coping with a constant barrage of adulation and praise. Not to mention all those handsome men who insist on throwing themselves at your feet. It must be absolute hell.'

That was intentionally sarcastic and Jasmine stares at me for a few seconds in silence. But then she throws back her head and laughs.

'At least I can always count on you to bring me back down to earth, Beccs.'

'What else are twin sisters for?'

'Indeed. Actually, it's not easy having the weight of expectation on your shoulders all the time. And my life isn't so great. We need to tell each other the truth or who else will?'

She stares out of the window as tiny flakes of snow start falling from a leaden sky and fluttering down onto the frozen pavement.

'So, here goes,' she says in a rush. 'This party is really good and it was pulled out of the bag at the last minute. You've got a real talent for bringing people together and turning a potentially bad situation into a good one. I admire you for that. Any corporation would value that talent.'

'Really? I didn't think you admired me for anything to do with work. Not with me working in a rural Cotswolds café while you're striking mega-deals with major players.'

'Not so much.'

'What do you mean?'

Jasmine takes a deep breath and twists round until she's facing me. 'Looks like I'm about to start the new year by being made redundant. I knew there were some redundancies in the offing but I didn't think they'd affect me. However, it seems I'm not as indispensable as I thought I was.' She laughs softly and shakes her head. 'I'll find out for sure after Christmas but I've been warned.'

'That's rotten. I'm so sorry, Jazz. Have you told Mum and Dad?'

'No, of course not. They're always telling people about my fabulous job and my amazing career. That's my whole point. I'm the one who's mega successful and sorted in their eyes. The one who can cope with anything. I couldn't bear to see their disappointment if…'

'If you became a little more like me?' I gently rub my hand along her arm. 'You'll survive and you'll go on to even bigger and better things, I'm sure of it. Just remember that redundancy happens to lots of people through no fault of their own. You're not being fired for fiddling the books or… or taking pics of your arse on the photocopier.'

'Though I might do that before I leave,' mutters Jasmine, wrapping her arms around her waist. 'Mum and Dad will still be disappointed and it'll take off some of my golden girl sheen. They'll think I've failed.'

'Ha. Welcome to my world.' I shuffle along until my arm is tight against Jasmine's. 'How long have you known about the redundancies?'

'A couple of weeks.'

'So before you went to your company's Christmas do?'

'Yeah. Daft, isn't it, having a celebration when some of us face losing our jobs.'

'Does Zac know?'

'No, and no one mentioned it at the event. We all think if we ignore it, it might go away. But it won't.'

'So what will you do if you lose your job?'

Jasmine flicks back her long blonde hair. 'I dare say it'll be fine. I'll get another job and I've already started looking around. But my point is, Mum and Dad are softer with you than with me.'

'Softer? They're always on my case.'

'They're always on your case because they worry and care about you. They know you find life difficult sometimes and they just want you to be happy. I do too.'

'I am happy.'

'Are you? I can see you're happy at work and you do a good job. The Cosy Kettle is at the heart of Honeyford and you're an excellent manager.'

'O-K,' I say, slowly, waiting for Jasmine's snarky follow-up comment, but it doesn't come.

'And I can see that you're making efforts to improve yourself, which is great.' *Efforts to improve myself?* While I'm trying to work out whether that counts as snarky or not, Jasmine continues. 'Plus, you've got a date with Logan which is wonderful, and I know it's what you really want, but...' She grabs my hand. 'Are you sure that Logan is the right person for you?'

Here we go. 'Do you think I'm overstretching myself? Is Logan out of my league?'

'Hardly! You look a knockout in that dress and you're a lovely person. He'd be fortunate to have you as a girlfriend, but...'

I swallow hard, not used to my sister being so nice to me. 'But what?'

'I'm concerned that he isn't kind enough for you. I know super-confident blokes like Logan and they're often only really interested in themselves. You're a sensitive person, Becca, and that's not always a bad thing. Oh, I know it makes you worry too much sometimes but you're empathetic and easy to talk to.' She shrugs. 'Mum went straight to you when she left Dad, didn't she? And you need someone who's kind and who cares and who'll always be there for you.'

'Someone like Zac?'

'Yeah.' Jazz smiles, her eyes lighting up. 'Exactly like Zac. He's a really lovely bloke. He's kind and funny and pretty fit with that thick curly hair and he's got abs to die for. I thought he was a bit of a nerd but he's pretty sexy, actually.'

OK, Jasmine, there's no need to rub it in. He's a lovely boyfriend and you're very fortunate. He'll be good for you, actually.

Jasmine nudges me. 'Don't you think he's a brilliant bloke, Beccs?'

'Of course,' I say, sucking in my lower lip which has started wobbling. 'He's my best friend. Are you and Zac definitely…?' I trail off as Phyllis propels her wheelchair into the middle of the bookshop.

'There you are, Becca. And Jasmine too. Everyone's asking where you are. I think Logan and his boss are about to make a speech and I'm sure they want to thank you publicly for doing such a brilliant job.'

'I couldn't have done it without all of you and the book club crew,' I say, glancing at Jasmine, who's standing in front of the window and using the side of her hand to push the tiny ash pile into an empty tissue.

'Go on,' she says. 'Your public awaits. I'll be right behind you.'

Everyone turns to look at me when I go back into the café and I start to feel a familiar gnawing in the pit of my stomach. Anyone would be anxious in these circumstances, I tell myself as Logan comes forward, takes my hand and leads me to the cake table. His boss Colin – a short barrel-shaped man with black sideburns and a comb-over – is waiting for us. I resist the urge to pull down the hemline of my dress, and clasp my hands together to stop them shaking.

Colin coughs to quieten the crowd and bows slightly to the assembled guests. 'I won't keep you from the magnificent cake, coffee and celebrations, I promise. But I wanted to say a few words to thank our wonderful French guests for joining us here this evening. This traditional Cotswolds Christmas party marks the end of your visit to England and I hope you've had a marvellous time. We very much look forward to continued successful trading with you in the new year and we wish you a *joyeux noël*. Finally, a thank you to Logan Fairweather, our dynamic sales manager, who organised this wonderful party with café manager…' He glances down at the notes he's carrying. '… Rebecca.'

'Speech! Speech!' yells Stanley from the corner where he's been scoffing cake. I am so going to throttle him with his red and green elf hat. A band of anxiety tightens around my chest.

'I'm not sure…' I mutter.

'Wish number four!' shouts Stanley.

Conquer fear of public speaking. Why did I shove that wish on the list?

'Of course,' says Colin, stepping back and beckoning me forward. 'Would you like to talk a little about the venue, Rebecca?'

I want to talk about the venue. I want to encourage people to spread the word about The Cosy Kettle, to boost business. But my nerves are getting the better of me. I glance at Flora, who's looking anxious on my behalf, and then at Zac, who purses his lips and breathes out slowly, his eyes locked on mine. That's it. I just need to breathe and I can do this.

'Thank you, Colin and Logan,' I say in a slightly wobbly voice. It's really hard to breathe when you feel as if an elephant is sitting on your uplifted boobs. 'It's lovely to see you all here, in The Cosy Kettle which' – I pause and swallow – 'is a very special place. A year ago, where we're standing was a dusty old storeroom but Flora and Callie from the bookshop breathed new life into the space. I was fortunate enough to be taken on to run the café and I love it. I really do.' I look at the back of the room where the book club are lined up, all giving me a thumbs-up. 'We welcome Honeyford residents and tourists here every day and I'm delighted to say that many of them have become friends. So it's wonderful to see you all here tonight, enjoying the best that Honeyford can offer. Um, I think that's it so I'll let you get back to the party. Thank you, and have a very happy Christmas, everyone.'

Logan's arm snakes around my waist as people raise their glasses of punch and gingerbread lattes to toast the festive season. 'Lovely,' he whispers in my ear. 'Really lovely.'

Stanley sidles over and slips a piece of paper into my hand. 'Boom!' is all he says before scurrying off to carry out more elf duties.

I glance at the paper. It's my wish list. Stanley has copied it down, and every single wish is crossed out. I did it! I achieved every wish and learned a lot along the way. I'm more assertive, more confident and more heartbroken than ever. I fold up the list and slip it into my clutch bag.

Chapter Twenty-Five

It's almost eleven o'clock, the party has finished and only Logan and I are left behind. Everyone else has disappeared into the night.

'That went absolutely brilliantly,' says Logan, closing the bookshop door behind the last guest. He leans against the wooden frame and gives me his best smouldering smile. Good grief, he's handsome. And he knows it. He pushes his hand through his thick blond hair and winks. 'My promotion is in the bag – Colin as much as told me so – and that's in no small part thanks to you, Becca. The party was amazing – just right, the café looked fabulous and as for you... you look fantastic in those very big boots and that very tiny dress.'

He moves close and puts his hands on my waist. 'Are you up for going clubbing, then? I can't wait to show you off to my friends. It'll be you, me, a few Jack Daniels and then maybe back to mine for a nightcap.'

He raises his eyebrow before bending his head and kissing me. This isn't a peck on the lips or a brief kiss in the café. This is a full-on, passionate snog and he's very good at it. I kiss him back. I'm giving it some welly, and so is he, and it's very, *very* pleasant. But that's all. A month ago I would have expected fireworks and unadulterated lust to tingle from my head to my toes. But although my stomach flutters, especially when he runs his finger down my spine, it feels more like anxiety than anything else. The truth is, I feel more awkward than sexy. I'm all dolled up and was feeling buoyed up with confidence and relief after a successful evening, and Logan is his usual super-sexy self. But we're just not gelling.

Before I made my wish list, if Logan had offered me a nightcap at his place I'd have bitten his hand off, but now… how do I know that I won't end up just another notch on his bedpost? What was it Jasmine said about confident men like him? *They're often only really interested in themselves.* And I really don't know how I feel about him seeing me naked. Take off my posh frock and I go back to being my usual self and I'm not sure that's who Logan wants. I'd have to stick my boobs out and hold my stomach in and present my best side at all times – not the side with the birth mark on my thigh. Zac saw it once, when I was wandering round in a bath towel, and reckoned it looked like a courgette… And here I am, in what should be a distracting clinch with a handsome man, and yet I'm still thinking about Zac.

I realise that I'm not concentrating on the kiss at all. My mouth and Logan's are still jammed together but Logan has opened his eyes and is staring into my face. He drops his arms and steps away from me.

'Is everything all right, Becca?' He wipes the back of his hand across his lips.

'Uh, yeah. Why?'

'I get the feeling you're a bit distracted.'

'Sorry. It's been a busy evening and I'm a bit tired.'

'Too tired to go clubbing? Only my friends are there and I want to show you off in that dress. You look like a Christmas present that's waiting to be unwrapped.'

He licks his lips and runs his finger down my bare arm while I try hard not to giggle. Logan is gorgeous and I'm sure he's a lovely man underneath all the smouldering and cheesiness, but he's definitely not the man for me.

'That's really kind of you but, actually, I'm exhausted after tonight. It was pretty full-on.'

'Are you saying that you're not coming clubbing with me?' Logan cocks his head and grins.

'I'm afraid not.'

Logan's grin starts to fade. 'You're joking, right?'

'No, I'm not up for going out tonight, but thank you for asking me.'

Logan looks confused. I don't suppose women often turn him down. I can't quite believe I'm turning him down myself. He's perfect in so many ways – good-looking, successful, sexy. Maybe he and I would hit it off and could double date with Zac and Jasmine. But the very thought of that is like cold water being thrown over me.

Logan's phone beeps with a text and he pulls his mobile from his trouser pocket. I spot the name *Amelia* before he opens the text and reads it.

'Message from a friend?'

He smiles. 'Yeah. Someone asking if I'm going to the club. Are you sure you don't want to come with me?'

I hesitate for a brief moment before shaking my head. 'I need an early night. But I'm sure you'll still have fun without me.'

'I'm sure I will,' he huffs, feathers ruffled. Then he catches himself and smiles. 'It's a shame you're not coming out with me. But thanks again for saving my bacon tonight. You and your friends did a brilliant job.'

'Thanks. My friends are rather special.'

'Especially the elf bloke. My guests absolutely loved him.'

'Especially him,' I laugh. 'Stanley is one of a kind. Have a lovely night clubbing.'

Logan leans in and kisses me, but this time on the cheek. 'Are you sure I can't twist your arm? I promise you'd have a good time.'

'I'm sure I would, but no thanks. You go and enjoy yourself.'

Well, that was bonkers, I tell myself as Logan lets himself out of the shop door and I lock it behind him. Rather than enjoying a night of passion with a gorgeous hunk I'll be spending it at the cottage, in my sensible PJs, while Zac and Jasmine are probably getting it on in the bedroom next door. *Merry Christmas, Becca!*

I wander back into The Cosy Kettle which is looking rather unloved with dirty cups and crumbs everywhere. I'll come in early tomorrow to clean up and get the place ready again for Christmas. It does look wonderful in its festive finery, but I'll be happy to see it go back to its normal cosy, de-blinged self once the celebrations are over. I'm beginning to think The Cosy Kettle and I have a lot in common.

I've just put a handful of cups on the counter when I hear a noise in the garden. Grabbing the first heavy thing I can find – a very large china platter holding tiny cubes of cake – I walk quietly to the back door which is slightly ajar and peer around it. Someone is leaning over Santa's sack in the gloom. Is he trying to steal presents? Summoning up all my courage, I creep into the garden until I'm within throwing distance, raise the platter with both hands and shout: 'Oi, what do you think you're doing?'

It's only when the figure stands and spins around that I realise it's Zac.

'Hell's teeth!' Adrenaline courses through me as I lower the platter. 'I thought you were a burglar.'

Zac raises his eyebrows. 'And what if I was? You should be locking the door and calling the police, not confronting me on your own in a secluded garden.'

'I'm all right. If you got antsy, I was going to throw this at you.'

Zac grins. 'A big plate covered in cake? Were you going to Battenberg me to death, Rebecca?'

'I'd have been all right. I'm stronger than I look and marzipan can be surprisingly stingy if it hits you in the face.'

'Maybe, but I'm not sure you could wrestle me to the ground in that dress.'

'I agree it's not the best outfit for tackling a burglar.'

'Far too short and tight.'

I look away so my eyes won't betray my thoughts, because I'd so like to wrestle Zac to the ground right now… fling my arms around his neck and push him into the flower bed. It would ruin Millicent's dress and probably give us both hypothermia, but it would be worth it to feel his arms around me.

Oh no. I've really got it bad which means, I realise with a sinking feeling, that I need to move out of our cottage after Christmas. I love living with Zac but, ironically, the fact that I'm actually in love with Zac means we can't live together. I can't be with him if he's with my sister and, even if their fledgling relationship comes to nothing, it's built up a wall between us.

Zac squints at me through the gloom. 'So what's going on then, Beccs?'

'What do you mean?'

'What's going on in that head of yours?'

'Nothing.'

'Really? You're lying to the person who knows you better than just about anyone? You've got that faraway look which always gives you away when you're fighting a battle in your head.'

'No, really. Everything's fine. I'm just a bit tired after this evening.'

'If you say so.' Zac stares at me for a moment before steering me back into the café and locking the back door behind us. 'Hadn't you better be leaving on your date?'

'Talking of dates' – I put the platter down on a nearby table and take a deep breath – 'I want you to know that I'm OK about you and Jasmine. I haven't mentioned it much because it's pretty awkward. But she cares a lot about you and I love you both so it's all right with me that…' I stop, unable to go on.

Zac narrows his eyes. 'Exactly how much have you had to drink, Becca? What on earth are you talking about?'

'You and Jasmine being… you know. And it's absolutely—'

I stop. I want to say *fine*. The word is on the tip of my tongue but I can't say it. I can't say it's fine that Zac and Jazz are together because it's not. I love them both and want them to be happy, but I can't pretend.

I'm supposed to be all new and improved now my big Christmas wish has come true, and perhaps I should be able to pretend that all's right with the world, but screw it. What's the point of looking different and being different if all it does is make me feel even less at ease with myself? Zac and I were happy together before I started trying to be what I'm not. All that hard work and I'm pretty much still the same underneath it all, but one thing has changed. I feel braver – brave enough to tell the truth.

'Actually Zac, I know this is going to mess up our friendship big-time, and I don't suppose it'll do much for my relationship with Jasmine, but I have to tell you something.'

'What *are* you going on about?' He glances at his watch. 'It's getting late. Logan will be waiting for you and I'm tired.'

'He's gone already.'

'Gone where?'

'To the club.'

'Without you?' Zac's jaw drops and anger sparks in his eyes. 'He's left you here after promising to take you out? No wonder you're being weird, Beccs. You must be so disappointed.'

'I don't care.' When I shrug, the light catches my sequinned dress and tiny pinpoints of light scatter across The Cosy Kettle.

'Of course you care. Securing a date with Logan was wish number five. But it's his loss if he's bailed on you. What a total arse.'

'It was rather knackering trying to be the woman he expected.'

'It sounds knackering, and why should you become the sort of woman *he* expected, anyway?'

'*You* don't expect anything of me, do you?'

'I expect lots of you. For example' – he starts ticking off things on his fingers – 'paying your share of the rent on time, not leaving wet towels on the bathroom floor, making me unburned mince pies, never *ever* singing in the shower—'

'I love you, Zac,' I blurt out.

He stops and smiles. 'I love you too, Beccs.'

'No.' I swallow hard. 'What I mean is, I really love you, Zac, but I've been too busy trying to make my stupid wishes come true to properly realise it. And I know my feelings aren't reciprocated and that's all right but I just had to say it. And I'll start looking for a new place to live on Monday. So that's all good. Thank you very much for your time.'

Thank you very much for your time? I declare my unrequited love and then end my heartfelt confession as though I'm closing one of Jasmine's marketing pitches. I'm still an idiot. I grab a cloth, turn my back on Zac and start scrubbing a table furiously, blinking back tears.

I'm suddenly aware of Zac standing so close behind me, his breath is warming the back of my neck. He reaches over my shoulder and gently takes the cloth from my hand.

'What do you mean that you're fine about me and Jasmine?'

I sniff and turn to face him.

'You're involved with Jasmine and that's all right because I love you both and want you both to be happy.'

Zac slowly shakes his head. 'I agreed to be Jasmine's plus-one at her work do. That's not *involved*.'

'You're involved because she stayed over that night and you and she—' I start twitching my head and winking, unable to spell out what happened. I must look ridiculous.

'She did stay over because the taxi driver was creepy and I wasn't happy about her being in his cab on her own after they'd dropped me off. She told you that. But she slept in my bed and I slept on the sofa.'

'The sofa?'

'Yeah, which is pretty uncomfortable. I didn't realise it was so lumpy.'

'But if you and Jasmine weren't together, why have you been so weird with me ever since?'

'I haven't been weird, though I guess I have been avoiding you a bit. To be honest, I was upset because I thought you were trying to set me up with your sister.'

'Would that have been so awful?'

'Yes.'

'But she's gorgeous. Why don't you want to go out with my sister?'

'Because, no offence, it would be off-the-scale odd. Jasmine's lovely and all that but… she's not you.'

'But that's good, isn't it? She's clever and she dresses like a model and she doesn't get nervous about ridiculous things.'

'That's true. I bet she doesn't pace up and down as though she's caged in, or cry at adverts, or leave her shoes in the middle of the floor for people to fall over, or insist that the Jaffa Cake is a biscuit when the clue in clearly in the name.'

'Exactly. What's not to like?'

Zac smiles. 'But I love all that about you.'

'Even the shoe thing?'

'Maybe not the shoe thing so much. But you're real, Becca. You worry and feel things so strongly and it causes you pain sometimes but it makes you more human than anyone I've ever met. When Jazz and I went to her work do, she said I did nothing but talk about you all evening anyway. She guessed how I felt but then you were so excited about your date with Logan...' He shakes his head. 'Anyway, I tried to be a good friend and be happy for you so I—'

'Hang on! Back up a bit. *She guessed how I felt?* What do you mean?'

Zac closes his eyes for a moment and sways gently back and forth on the balls of his feet. 'Now isn't the right time for a heart-to-heart.'

'How can it not be? I've just told you that I love you.'

'But you don't. Not really. Not as anything more than a friend.'

'I do. I'm in love with you, Zac.'

'No, you're not. You're feeling vulnerable and sad and reading more into our relationship because you're upset about Logan. I know you, Becca. And I don't want to ruin our friendship for something that will never last. I couldn't bear it.'

He turns abruptly, walks over to the trestle table and starts piling up plates, with his back to me. I can see the tension across his shoulders.

His muscles are taut beneath the snow-white cotton of his shirt, and I feel as if my heart is about to burst.

I walk over and place my hand on his back, between his shoulder blades. His shoulders slump and he says, without turning round, 'You know I'm right, Becca. I don't want to make a total tit of myself because you'll feel differently in the morning when you're not so upset.'

'No, I won't feel differently. I'm not upset about Logan because it was my decision not to go to the club with him.'

Zac turns, confusion marked across his face. 'Why? Securing a date with Logan was on your wish list, and you got there. Your wish came true.'

'It did, but I knew in my heart of hearts a while ago that Logan isn't the man for me. And Jasmine said as much this evening.'

'What did Jasmine say exactly?'

'She said Logan wasn't kind enough for me and then she talked you up, big-time. I thought it was because you two were going out.'

'She was trying to push you my way without actually breaking her promise to me.'

'What promise?'

'I swore her to silence about how I felt about you, and she could see how excited you were about your date with Logan. She didn't want to burst your bubble and mess up our friendship for nothing. She's a good sort, your sister, and she cares a lot about you.'

'Yeah, I know. And her life isn't as charmed as I thought it was. I got that wrong. I've got a lot wrong, actually. Do you want to know the main reason why I turned Logan down?'

'His remarkably tiny brain?'

'That, but also because when he properly kissed me all I could think was that I'd rather be kissing you instead.'

Pain ricochets across Zac's face. 'Don't make fun of me, Becca.'

I grab Zac's hands and hold on tight. 'You know me better than anyone, Zac. Do you really think I'm making fun of you?'

Zac stares deep into my eyes as my breath catches in my throat. This wonderful, gorgeous man has been in front of me all the time and I was so busy trying to be someone that I'm not, I didn't see it. 'Well, do you?' I ask.

Zac steps forward without a word and places his hands on either side of my face. He stares at my mouth as he bends his head and then he's kissing me. Oh boy, Logan, you have a lot to learn. Little shocks of love and lust ripple through me and I close my eyes.

Zac suddenly breaks off and gazes at me, his breathing shallow. 'Would you rather be kissing Logan Fairweather right now? I need you to be honest with me and with yourself, Becca.'

In answer, I put my arms around Zac's neck, pull myself tight against his body and kiss him back. Tears prickle my eyes and one rolls down my cheek.

'Crikey, Beccs.' Zac pulls away but keeps one arm around my waist as he wipes a finger across my cheek. 'Am I making you cry?'

'Mmm.' I swallow, hardly able to speak. 'But in a good way.'

'I thought crying was for wimps,' he says, softly kissing my cheeks where tears have tracked across my skin.

'That was one of the many things I was wrong about,' I gulp.

'I absolutely love it when I can say I told you so.'

'Ah, you're such a know-all.'

Zac suddenly looks serious. 'But what if you're right about us just being friends? What if this doesn't work out and it ends our friendship? I couldn't bear not having you in my life.'

'And what if I'm totally wrong and you and I are meant to be together? All I know is that seeing you with someone else would break my heart. It did break my heart when I thought you were with Jasmine. I am honestly and truly in love with you, Zac, and what if it's best to let things happen the way they're meant to, rather than trying so hard to push our lives in a different direction? What if this is my wish coming true the way it should?'

Zac sighs. 'Do you ever stop talking?'

'Not really. I can't help it. When I get nervous I—'

I would say more, lots more, but it's hard to talk when your best friend, the man you're hopelessly in love with, pulls you against him, and kisses you until the lights of The Cosy Kettle fade away and you feel perfect peace.

Epilogue

One year later

Zac lounges back on Mum and Dad's sofa and stretches out his long legs. 'That was the best Christmas dinner I've ever had, Pauline. Though make sure you never tell my mum that.'

'We'll be sampling the delights of your mother's cooking tomorrow.' I kick off my Doc Martens, throw myself onto the sofa beside him and link my fingers through his.

'Don't remind me. Tough turkey, roast potatoes like bullets and gravy you can cut with a knife.'

'Your mum's lovely. Don't be mean about her cooking.'

'She says it herself and she'll just be delighted to see us, especially you, seeing as she thinks the sun shines out of your...'

He stops, glances at my mum and grins. Then he leans towards me and kisses my nose. And, even though it's been a year since we first shared a kiss in The Cosy Kettle, the feel of his lips against my skin makes my toes tingle.

'I'm sure your mother's cooking is fine,' says Mum, but she looks pleased as she hands Zac a Tupperware box crammed full of mince pies and slices of Christmas cake. 'A little something to keep you going when you two get home,' she tells him with a wink.

If Zac's mum is fond of me, my mum absolutely adores Zac and shows it in the best way she knows how – by trying to feed him up all the time. He reckons he's put on half a stone since we discovered we were in love, but if he has it doesn't show when he's wandering naked around the cottage.

'And are you definitely sure that you like your painting?' asks Mum, biting her lip. She nods at the canvas propped up beside us: her painting of me and Zac walking along a Honeyford street. Golden-yellow buildings edge the picture and white clouds are bubbling over splashes of green hills in the distance.

'It's brilliant, Mum. We love it. Almost as much as Dad loves his painting.'

Dad lifts his head from the *Radio Times* he's studying and clears his throat. 'It's not bad, I suppose.'

'Which is why you've hung it in pride of place,' I laugh, stealing another glance at the large canvas of Dad that's hanging over the fireplace. There's so much tinsel festooning it, it's hard to see the actual painting but I can make out Dad's jawline and the curves of his mouth. It's one of several paintings done by Mum over the last few months. She's loving her art course and even Dad has come round to his wife disappearing for hours with an easel under one arm and a box of paints in the other hand.

'She seems happier now she's immersed in this painting lark,' he admitted in the kitchen a couple of weeks ago. 'But I could still do with a decent cooked meal every now and again.' At least his domestic skills have increased. I noticed that Mum had him peeling the carrots for lunch today when we arrived.

The front door suddenly slams and Jasmine bowls in. She's in jeans and her hair is hanging loose.

'Hey, fam,' she calls, dropping a bag overflowing with presents onto the floor. 'Happy Christmas Eve! The prodigal daughter has arrived.' She grins at me and I smile back. Jasmine has lost a little of her golden-girl sheen within the family recently, and she's all the better for it – less prickly and uptight.

'What time did you say your interview was again?' asks Mum.

'Blimey, let me get my coat off first. It's at ten o'clock a week on Tuesday.'

'That's a good time,' chips in Dad. 'Before the interviewers get tired. They'll remember you.'

'Then let's hope it's for all the right reasons,' says Jasmine. She survived the first round of redundancies at her company last January, but lost her job in the second round a few weeks ago. I know Mum and Dad are worried about her but she's a survivor and she'll be fine.

'How are things going at The Cosy Teapot then?' asks Jasmine, flopping into a chair and swinging her legs over the arm. 'Seeing as you are the queen of Honeyford activities these days.'

'I have been busy with a few parties in the run-up to Christmas. Logan seems to have recommended me to lots of people. Remember him?'

'He's very hard to forget.' Jasmine fans herself with her hand. 'The one who got away, hey, Beccs?'

She grins at Zac, who puts his arm around my shoulders and pulls me tight. 'Don't leave me, Becca,' he implores me, with an exaggerated pout.

'Never,' I tell him, gazing into his gorgeous brown eyes that are flecked with green.

Jasmine shifts in her seat. 'Ugh, get a room, you two. You've been together for twelve months now so hasn't the glow worn off yet? Talking of getting a room, is lovely Logan hooked up yet?'

'He is. I often see him around town with a very attractive brunette on his arm, and he always smiles and waves.'

'Ah, that's a shame about the girlfriend. I might have had another go myself, though I am rather taken with the new barman at the Pheasant and Fox. Can you get me his number?'

'I'm not going to be your matchmaker, Jazz. But we're going to the pub on New Year's Eve and loads of people will be there – Flora, the book club, loads of café customers. Why don't you come too and you can hook up with the barman yourself?'

'I might just take you up on that. Will the old bloke who wears skinny jeans be there?'

'Stanley? I expect so. Why?'

'I just like him. He makes me laugh. Has his granddaughter sprogged yet?'

'Give the poor girl a chance. She's only seven months pregnant but she and her boyfriend are over the moon about it. Stanley is beside himself at the thought of being a great-granddad. He's reading every baby book he can get his hands on and he's even got the book club reading baby manuals.'

'I bet that's gone down well with the scary lady,' chuckles Jasmine.

'Millicent? Yeah, you should have seen her face. Though she's chuffed for Stanley, I can tell. And Flora's happy for him, too.'

'Is Flora still with that older man? The handsome one.'

'Yeah, she and Daniel make a good couple. They seem really happy together.'

'Though they haven't moved yet.'

'Nah, they keep saying they're going to move out of Starlight Cottage and get their own place, but I don't think they ever will. They're settled there, and Caleb loves living with Luna.'

'Is she the weird witchy woman with the long silver hair?'

'Yeah, but she's not weird. Not really. She's just different from you.'

'Thank goodness. I'd rather be stressy like you than different like her.' She smiles to soften the blow and I smile back. She seems more relaxed these days but I can't really say the same for me – and that's OK.

I'm more confident and assertive than I've ever been before, which is wonderful. But I'm never going to be laid-back and zen, however many wishes I make. That realisation has hit home over the last year. But I've come to terms with being an anxious person and have decided, with Zac's wise counsel, that it's better to embrace it and make the most of the benefits it confers – the sensitivity and empathy and kindness – rather than trying to shoehorn my personality into a whole other one that doesn't fit.

Anyway, Zac loves me the way I am, and I'm learning to love me the way I am too. How could I not when all my angst has brought me to where I am now – running The Cosy Kettle in beautiful Honeyford and living with a man I adore.

A Letter from Liz

Thank you so much for reading *A Christmas Wish and a Cranberry Kiss at the Cosy Kettle*. As a rather 'stressy' person myself, I've loved writing about Becca's struggle with anxiety and giving her a happy-ever-after ending with gorgeous Zac. I do hope you enjoyed her story.

This is the final novel in my Cosy Kettle series and I feel sad to be moving on from Flora's bookshop and café, and the beautiful Cotswolds. But my next novel is set in an equally awesome part of the UK, and I'm excited to be writing a whole new story with a host of brand new characters. You can find out when that book will be published by signing up at the following link. Your email address will never be shared and you can unsubscribe at any time.

www.bookouture.com/liz-eeles

You can also keep up to date with my latest writing news via Twitter, Facebook, Instagram and my website. I spend rather a lot of time on social media! My links are below, and I hope you'll stop by.

Before I go, can I ask a favour? If you did enjoy *A Christmas Wish and a Cranberry Kiss at the Cosy Kettle*, I'd be grateful if you could spend a few minutes posting a review. Your opinion might encourage new readers to spend time in Honeyford with Becca, Flora – whose story is told in my second Cosy Kettle book, *A Summer Escape and Strawberry Cake at the Cosy Kettle* – and Stanley's granddaughter, Callie, who features in the first book, *New Starts and Cherry Tarts at the Cosy Kettle*. Many thanks in advance.

Liz x

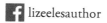 lizeelesauthor

 @lizeelesauthor

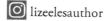 lizeelesauthor

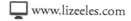 www.lizeeles.com

Acknowledgements

Love and thanks to my friends and family, in particular Tim (who's my Zac), Sam, Ellie, Harry and Freddie. And a huge thank you, as always, to my wonderful publisher Bookouture, and my talented editor, Ellen Gleeson. I love working with you, Ellen, and value your wise advice, your fab ideas, your enthusiasm for my stories, and your unflagging support.

Printed in Great Britain
by Amazon